MERMAID OF
ARCH CREEK

DAVID
RAYMOND

To Mia Rose, who always believed in Mermaids, and to Captain Abie, who caught one.

You amaze me. Love Always, Dad

pproaching the modest, barn-red home on Enchanted Place in North Miami evoked the feeling that you were looking at an oversized box of matches with a flat white roof. You see, there really is a street named Enchanted Place in North Miami, Florida. Google maps it if you are already bored, curious, have trust issues, or all of the above. And, it really is a magical place, rich in history and folklore. Seminole, Tequesta, and debatably, Calusa Indians, lived, hunted, fished, made love, and raised their families on this sacred land dating back to 2,500 B.C.

The few homes on the east end of the street are fortuitously situated along Arch Creek, whose waters originate in the Everglades. Century-old Spanish moss draped Oaks create a regal, transcendent atmosphere, providing a microclimate that is notably cooler than the surrounding area. In addition to providing a cool respite for humans, creatures, and critters of all kinds, while walking the area, you can feel its Supernatural energy radiate through your feet as you look around to fully absorb everything the surroundings have to offer. Despite all the debate ranging from sabotage, to train track vibrations, to erosion, to aggressive tree roots— nobody really knew how the famous Arch Creek Natural Bridge collapsed in 1973, until now.

The red house on Arch Creek was fronted by a chain-link fence, with an ever-open gate, meant to contain the roaming Doberman Pinscher. The dog's ears and tail were uncropped, resulting in a whimsical look, which was quite disarming to passersby thinking it was a friendly hound dog. That is, until he routinely charged with bared teeth, only to turn away at the last moment with a satisfied smile rivaling one of a circus clown. This was typically accompanied by a sneak attack from the Beagle, who due to her low stature, could stealthily rush up barking, only to turn away in unison with the Doberman, its black and white tail wagging in delight. Once past the gauntlet of dogs, there were four steps up to the front door littered with an endless supply of kittens, produced by the clowder of unneutered cats roaming the grounds. As one entered the house, the scuffed, but clean, red oak wood floors hinted to the age of the home built in 1921. At first glance, the home's interior was welcoming, and well-decorated. Upon closer inspection, it presented with a beautiful Bohemian, unmade bed feeling, like an old movie star used to live there.

The living room had a tall, sloped, Dade County Pine beamed ceiling, which gave the impression of a room that was much larger than it actually was. What really drew one's attention was the large picture window at the back of the house, in the huge open kitchen, presenting an almost mystical view of Arch Creek.

The left side of the kitchen ended at a window-paned, white-framed door, leading to the cluttered garage, containing a shiny red Thunderbird. On the other side of the kitchen, glass doors led to a large, screened in patio. Next to the refrigerator, there was a deep bench with seat cushions and a long dining table. Past the table, following a tiny section of wall, there was a walk-in pantry filled with shelves, nooks, and crannies, all bulging with pastas, canned goods, and mason jars. Their contents were a mix of ancient and new, full of beets, peaches, jams, chutneys, and flour.

There was a rolling, stainless-steel table that resembled the kind used for hotel room service with a shelf underneath. The tabletop was custom-built as a sort of rolling spice rack, overflowing with a multitude of exotic spices and seasonings from around the World, along with an assortment of garlic, shallots, and onions.

Above the white farmhouse double sink, the picture window provided an unobstructed view of the huge Oaks and the Creek in the backyard. Surrounding the window, hung a vast assortment of bright copper pots and pans, handles sticking out in every direction, small hooks securing them fiercely to grates.

At first glance, there appeared no order to them; however, upon closer examination, the cookware was hung in order from smallest to largest, with the larger pots toward the outer sections of the grates. Dozens of cookware lids bulged out of the umber Formica cabinet doors under the sink. The gas stove was a high-end stainless-steel model, with large burners, a grill, and a copper fume hood.

The kitchen appeared to belong to an expert, albeit sloppy chef, or at least someone who delighted in cooking— or at the very least, someone who had an appreciation for fine cookware. The kitchen was professional in every regard, with the exception of the cheap white ceiling fan, with food-stained blades, and four struggling candelabra light bulbs, providing poor evening, or rainy-day illumination for such a large space.

Thankfully, the picture window had an easterly exposure providing wonderful natural light on bright South Florida days. In the evening, the lighting set a tone resembling a small Bistro kitchen on some quiet side street in Venice or Paris.

2

*W*ekiwa Sawgrass was born on January 1st in the year 1901 at 12:01 AM. She was the first baby of the New Year *and* the 20th Century. Since she was born on the Reservation, there was no fanfare, unless you counted the slap on the butt every baby got to 'test their lungs' as they used to say.

There were no reporters taking pictures of the first baby of the year back then, but if there had been, you could count on them not coming to an Indian Reservation in the middle of the Everglades. Wekiwa grew up in a humble tourist camp just west of where the Miami River connected with the Everglades. Her Father died before her birth. Wekiwa's Mother made crafts to sell to tourists, took care of their dirt floor home, cooked, and had a small garden that Wekiwa loved to play in as a child. That's where it all started. *The Garden.*

Wekiwa's Grandfather, Holata, was the medicine chief and had no sons. The Great Spirits visited Holata in his garden the day his child, Wekiwa's Mother, was born and told him to name her Catori, meaning *spirit*. They also told him to teach her the healing magic of the plants, that she would have an excellent disposition, would be blessed to help others, and would bear a child bound to change the destiny of their people.

Catori was a delight in every way. She helped all of the Village Elders as if they were her own parents. She took care of the Village children as if they were all her own children, and in all ways, lived up to her end of the prophecy.

Catori gave birth to a flawless infant, with bright turquoise eyes, and a bottomless, bewitching smile. She named her Wekiwa, meaning *spring*. As Holata spoke a blessing over Wekiwa on the day of her birth, a great bolt of lightning hit the Cypress Tree just outside Catori's house.

The Bald Cypress is given its name because it sheds its leaves in the fall. It has beautiful light green leaves the rest of the year and is also highly resistant to fire. So, while the lighting hit the top of the tree, it did not fully ignite, but rather left its bark scarred. Holata went outside and spoke a blessing over the marks in hopes of healing. As he walked around the trunk chanting, he saw what looked like a carving in the trunk. He stopped chanting and looked closer. At first, he thought he was imagining it. He went in the house and called for Catori. She walked outside while nonchalantly holding Wekiwa, like a football tucked in the arms of a running back. Catori followed her Father to the Cypress Tree, and with Wekiwa attached to her breast, slowly sat on the ground, staring in amazement.

"What does it mean, Father?"

"The Great Spirits have spoken. This is clear. What they are telling us is muddy, unlike the clear Creek in the etching."

"Oh, Father, you are always joking. Did you carve us on the Cypress Tree?" Catori said, laughing.

"No, my child. I swear this to you."

"Is it a great blessing you haven't taught me yet, Father?" Catori asked.

"No, my child. The Great Spirits did this. We must honor them by learning to understand this."

"Yes, Father."

They both continued to stare at the carefully crafted images on the tree. The six images were all framed with square borders that looked like picture frames. They seemed like the work of a great artist forced to do cave drawings. Catori viewed them over and over again.

The first image was of her Father holding her as an infant. She just knew it was her.

The second image was of Catori holding Wekiwa. The resemblance was astonishing. There was no artist in the Village capable of such detail, but here they stood, figures carved deep into the centuries-old tree.

The third image was of a tall, stunning Seminole woman, with long black hair, an hourglass figure, and a beguiling smile. Even at a few hours old, Holata and Catori knew the carved woman was Wekiwa, as her eyes shined turquoise on the bark of the tree. Wekiwa was in a kitchen standing over a stove, holding a mortar and pestle, grinding a mixture of herbs and flowers. She had an odd look on her face that was neither happy, nor sad, but rather conveyed great mystery, with just a hint of both good and evil.

The fourth image was of Wekiwa transforming into a large creature with a gorgeous tail. The fifth image was of the creature in a clear blue Creek, its giant tail flapping wildly with a pained look on its deep-set turquoise eyes. The sixth and final image was a blank square frame. Its borders were clearly outlined, but the contents were bare.

"What are the Great Spirits trying to tell us, Father?"

"I do not know, my child. As the images show, even the Great Spirits don't know the future."

"Maybe they do, Father? Maybe they just aren't telling us? Or maybe the future is still undecided?"

"You are very wise, Catori. You must pass on all of your wisdom and my teachings to Wekiwa. She must have all the tools and knowledge of her ancestors. Teach her the healing power of the trees, plants, and herbs. Teach her the magic of the Everglades. The Great Spirits told me on the day of your birth that your child would shape the future of our people. As strong as my beliefs are, my child, I always thought it would be a lot more subtle, like maybe my grandchild would be a Senator and represent our people in the Great Halls of Congress. Now, the jokes on me. Looks more like she may be the hero or villain in a comic book. Geez! Some days it's tough being the spiritual leader of your tribe. I think I need a night in the sweat lodge. Maybe a nice massage. That Jumping Deer, she gives a good neck rub."

"Oh, Father, you always did make me laugh."

"That's part of a Father's job, my child. That baby hasn't stopped eating since she was born. You must be exhausted. Give me that little one for a while, and go get some sleep." Holata took Wekiwa and walked into the woods. He summoned the Great Spirits and chanted blessings over her. He went into the garden, made a medicine bag to guide her path and protect her from evil, and tucked it into her blanket. Wekiwa reached up and wrapped her tiny hand around Holata's index finger as he spoke to her.

"Hey there, little one. I know this is a lot to dump on you, but it looks like you have our fate in your tiny hands. I'll pass on the wisdom of the Great Spirits that my Father shared with me. Basically, it goes like this— Life is pretty damn good. Try not to fuck it up too bad, and if you do, don't blame it all on your ancestors. Capisce?" Wekiwa looked her Grandfather straight in the eye and burped. "Good! Now we are communicating," Hatori said, chuckling.

While Hatori had welcomed and blessed every baby in the camp, he'd never seen eyes the color of this child's. Sure, some babies had blue eyes, which almost always faded in time, but this child had eyes the color of shining bright turquoise stones. The corners of Wekiwa's little mouth curved into a smile. Even at a few hours old, he saw it again, that smile. The same beguiling smile carved in the tree.

"You are definitely going to be trouble, little one. Fun, but trouble. I will pray to the Great Spirits to guide and protect you."

Wekiwa smiled again and expelled a velvety baby giggle that liquefied Hatori's heart.

"Oh, yes, you will be trouble indeed, little one. I guess it couldn't hurt to pray a little for me, and your Mother, too. I think we're going to need all the protection we can get."

3

*O*n this particular Tuesday evening, two teenage girls in jeans and t-shirts sat in the kitchen of the house on Enchanted Place, with open books and coffee mugs. The books were college chemistry textbooks and the coffee mugs contained straight vodka. Three children, ages five, nine, and eleven, sat in the living room, where a Beatles album was blaring from the four stereo speakers suspended from the ceiling.

She strolled into the kitchen on bare feet, wearing nothing but a long, white tank top, shamelessly exposing the tanned sides of her nineteen-year-old breasts. She looked past the girls and sleepily made her way to the counter, looking out the picture window at the kittens playing in the yard.

Noisily, she lifted a large wooden spoon from a copper bowl containing spatulas, tongs, a meat thermometer, serving spoons, and a myriad of other assorted kitchen utensils. She passed the girls again on her way to the cupboard, opened it to get a jar of peanut butter, and filled the spoon.

The girls caught each other staring at her with an embarrassed acknowledgement and then looked away—from each other at least. They both looked back at the girl now standing on her tiptoes reaching to get down a copper pot from above the window.

"Can one of you science geeks help me get a pot down? I can't seem to reach it."

The brunette immediately jumped to her feet. The blonde still sitting said, "I thought you were still up at college. That's why your mom had us here watching your brothers and sister."

"I got in early this afternoon and wanted to surprise everyone."

"What are you cooking?"

"Just boiling water for tea. Do you young ladies want anything?" With a smirk, she filled a pot from the water spigot above the stove, then lit a burner and put the pot on the stove with the girls watching her every move. She knew they were watching. She could feel their eyes on her, and she enjoyed the audience. With a little extra curve to her step, she walked over to the counter, reached up into a cabinet containing coffee mugs, teacups, saucers, and glasses, and grabbed a cup, exposing her buttocks to the girls.

The blonde asked, "So how's college, Jemma?"

Without turning around, she answered, "All the drugs, alcohol, and sex you could ever want. It's just like high school, except no parents." Jemma said, laughing, "You're both eighteen now, you know how the world works."

The girls coyly looked at each other and returned to their studies. The water reached a boil, and Jemma poured it into her cup, turned back around, looked at the girls and said, "Are you sure you don't want anything?"

The girls shared a quick glance, grimacing to hold back any crude remarks they were thinking, and in unison, slowly shook their heads no. Jemma turned around to face them, walked to the kitchen entrance, and pulled out the handle of the pocket door. "You kids be good out there. We are talking grown up stuff."

She slid the door closed, came over and sat down on a chair across from the girls. Jemma picked up the book that was open in front of them and asked, "So, college chemistry? Impressive for high schoolers. You geeks ready to create a new life form or something like that?"

"Yeah, something like that," said the brunette.

"I bet that chemistry stuff gets you all the boys."

"No, just the smart ones," the blonde retorted with a lift of her brow.

"Touché. I deserved that. So, do either of you have boyfriends? Or, sorry, no judgment, girlfriends?"

"I don't," the blonde responded.

"And how about you?"

"Me? No. Well, there is someone special, but I just know they don't feel the same way," said the brunette as she played with the edges of the chemistry book.

"I'm intrigued. Tell me."

"They have long sandy brown hair and the dreamiest eyes…" The girl drifted off, lost in her own imagery.

"Sounds like you got it bad. Oh, come on, give us the dirt, huh?"

The brunette struggled to evade responding, shifting in her seat before she finally gave in and answered, "It's complicated. They're older."

"You wouldn't be the first girl to have a crush on an older person. Are they in college?"

"Does it matter?" the brunette asked, looking up at Jemma from her fidgeting fingers.

"I guess, not really," said Jemma lifting her feet off the floor, under the table, and placing them into the brunette's lap.

"You know I'm a psych major. Tell me about your childhood," Jemma said, laughing.

"Hah. No need to analyze me, Doc."

"Fine, then how about a foot massage?" she said with a sly grin while wiggling her toes in the brunette's lap. The brunette never looked down from gazing into Jemma's eyes and started softly rubbing her feet.

Jemma thought to herself, *'This won't take long. I'll have her going crazy soon.'*

"Why don't you tell us about your great love. Have you two hooked up yet?" Jemma asked.

"I've said too much already. Let's drop it."

"Oh no, I'm not letting you off this easy."

"That's okay. We have a chemistry test tomorrow, and we really need to get back to studying."

"Too bad. I could have used a good love story," said Jemma as she slowly slid her feet off the brunette's lap, got up from the chair, and turned to leave, her butt cheeks poking out from under her tank top as she walked away.

Jemma went into her room, the Doberman silently following behind. She lay down in bed, lit a joint, took a couple of hits, and fell asleep with the Doberman's head resting on her leg. If Jemma had been awake, she would have seen the look on the dog's face, which could only be described as rascally.

4

The nine-year-old woke up in the darkness. He was thirsty and headed to the kitchen in his pajama bottoms with bare feet. It was November, and the temperature was just bearably cool enough to sleep with the windows open without a fan. The boy got a glass of water and made his way to the hotel cart in the pantry.

He would play on the bottom tray of that cart ever since he could remember. It was always cold on the stainless steel, and although he just barely fit under there anymore, he enjoyed the coolness of the steel on warm Miami nights. Sometimes, he would imagine he was a secret agent being wheeled into the hotel room of his foe.

He sat sipping his water as the Doberman lay silently by his side. He was just about to get up and walk back to his room, when he heard his Mother and Father enter the kitchen. They were yelling at each other, in that don't wake the kids, but I hate you tone, that he had never heard before.

"You really want to do this now, Gina?"

"I can't live like this anymore, Ben. I want out."

"That's great. I haven't loved you for years. I can barely look at you."

"My Sister was right about you. I never should have married you."

"Your Sister is an ignorant slut."

The nine-year-old dared not move but wanted to with all of his might. He wanted to run out of the pantry and yell for them to stop, but it was too late. He heard it, the sound of someone's flesh being hit. He couldn't tell from the pantry whose hand did the hitting and who received the blow.

A moment later he heard his Mother sobbing, and the front door slam. He sat on the cart rocking, with tears streaming down his face. He tried his best not to be heard. A few minutes passed, then he heard his Mother talking on the phone from her bedroom. He crept down onto the pantry floor and slowly crawled to his room, looking only forward. He got in his bed, pulled the covers over his face and lay there in the fitful silence of his nine-year-old brain.

5

The sound of the door slamming woke Jemma up that night. She thought she heard her Father drive off. Pot always made her sleep well. She traipsed toward the kitchen hungry and thirsty, having no idea that her parents just had the fight of the century. As she approached, she heard small, muffled sounds coming from the kitchen. The pocket door was closed. She attempted to open it, but it was locked.

The sounds grew a bit louder as she stood there. Music was faintly playing in the background. It was Cher- Gypsies, Tramps and Thieves. Jemma loved Cher. She went out the back door and around to the garage, which was musty and filthy; not a place that she wanted to be, especially at this time of night.

The Red Thunderbird, the only clean thing in there, took up all of the floor space that wasn't already crowded in disarray with assorted power tools, two surfboards, a pressure cleaner, a folded dog kennel, three bicycles, two skateboards, roller blades, a hydraulic car jack, a multi-shelved Sears Craftsman Toolbox, various cans of paint, mineral spirits, paint rollers and brushes, a rusty lawnmower, and a wide variety of garden tools.

Jemma felt grimy, and when she looked down, her feet were covered with black, powdery dirt. She made her way to the window-paned door looking into the kitchen. A woman in a clown mask was on her back on the kitchen table; her legs wide open with someone on top of her. The woman was making little whining noises as her legs flailed back and forth in the air. Jemma smiled and turned to leave.

For a moment, she thought, this is kind of sick, watching my parents like this, and a clown mask—yuck! Whatever floats your boat, I guess. But then Jemma looked back. Who the hell was the woman in the mask, and who was that on top of her? It wasn't her Father. This person was too small. Then, she saw a reflection in the fridge. It wasn't a man. It was Margo, the brunette high school student. She looked even more blissed out than the woman in the clown mask sounded, and was grinding away with her hips, like she was trying to win a race, as only a teenager would.

The garage was hot and smelled of oil and auto parts. Jemma started to feel sick to her stomach, so she sat on the Red Thunderbird to catch her breath. It was like watching a terrible train wreck, and she couldn't turn away. The woman in the mask rubbed Margo's back as she softly nuzzled her ear, then she slowed her pace, as if this were a signal. Perhaps the clown was training her? Who the hell was this clown, anyway? Maybe Aunt Tina? She was a slut, after all. Margo stopped and rose off the clown a moment later, and Jemma thought to herself, '*Thank God that's over with,*' then turned again to leave. But she had to get one more look before she did.

Jemma glanced back and saw the clown sit upright on the table as Margo walked around to the other side. Margo was so close to the garage door, that Jemma held her breath and closed her eyes in an attempt to make herself invisible, like a small child trying to hide from a make-believe monster.

Jemma opened her eyes again and was surprised to see the Clown and Margo in a sensual embrace on the table, their arms and legs entwined like two old trees whose branches had grown together and were swaying in the breeze. The Clown was moaning softly, with a rapidly gaining pace, as was Margo. Jemma had never witnessed lesbian sex. And a clown mask? What the hell was that about? Sure, Jemma had kissed a few girls at drunken parties, and she liked it, but she had never witnessed anything the likes of this.

After what seemed like hours of pleasured sounds, Jemma thought one of them would have come already. Then the Clown started squealing, "Now! Now!" Margo grabbed the Clown's long hair and playfully bit her neck as they both shuddered together. Jemma wanted to close her eyes, but instead, helplessly watched the Clown open her arms and invite Margo in for a tender embrace. Jemma heard the muffled cry of both women as they held each other.

Jemma thought, *'That was actually a beautiful act of love. It was delicate. It was tender. It was sensuous. It was...'* The mask fell to the ground. Jemma continued watching in disbelief but remained frozen in place. She was too scared to move for fear of both being discovered, and of *her* discovery. Nausea started to overtake her.

She tore her gaze away and crept toward the back of the garage as fast as her dirty, bare feet would carry her. Jemma thought about running into the house to face them. She thought about screaming at them, 'What. The. Fuck?!' Instead, she ran, and ran, and ran, and watched as she vomited on her own feet. Jemma scampered down Enchanted Place. Hard, bumpy pavement wounded her puke-covered feet, until she found herself unconsciously stopped at her childhood friend's house. Frantically knocking on the door, she yelled in a sobbing voice, "Gretchen, it's me! Let me in! Please, please, please!"

The Doberman exited the house after Jemma ran away, stealthily following her down the street. He stopped to sniff the vomit, almost ate it, and thought, "*this really is disgusting, even for a dog,*' then trotted off into the backyard to sit by the Creek. He turned his head and cocked his ear to listen to the sounds of the night. His position resembled the dog staring into the RCA phonograph on those old posters; like he was expecting someone to speak to him. He listened very carefully, almost forcing something to occur. The dog felt free and powerful out here at night. He never enjoyed swimming, but he felt compelled to jump into the Creek. The water was colder than he remembered it.

His tongue fell from his long snout, lapping the cool water as he swam to the center of the Creek and sank like a stone. He stood fast on the bottom of the Creek, anchored there without the need for oxygen. The Doberman cocked his head again. In the distance, his supersensitive dog hearing detected sounds dimly traveling through the Creek bed. It was primal. It was haunting. His paws were vibrating though the sandy Creek bottom. It was the rhythm of ancient drumming and chanting.

Ommapapo! Ommapapo!

6

*H*is gaze was lost in the mirror. The eyes looking back at him belonged to his Father. Ben's fleeting, gentle smile was the genetic basis for the Buddha-like expression he aspired to bear in permanence, while it was perpetually engraved on the quietly Zen face of his eleven-year-old son. Ben never experienced such darkness and loneliness. His insides were squished into a mass of pulsing fibers. It felt as though he swallowed a jellyfish that was methodically making its way from his tightening throat, through every one of his constricted internal organs, to the tip of his bowels and then back up again, in pulsating waves of pain.

Ben hadn't been without her since they were young. They met one night, years ago on Miami Beach. That evening, Ben happened to park at the Haulover Pier. It was not his typical habit; however, that night, the moon was nearly full, and he wanted to see if any mackerel were biting—they weren't. He tied his sneakers tight, and stretched his legs, before he hit the beach. Ben loved running along the calming shoreline, water lapping at his feet.

As luck would have it, when he hit his stride, a girl in a black, sleeveless Buddy Holly t-shirt, red shorts, and black sneakers was running at his pace just fifty yards ahead. He quickly made his way through a group of children dressed in Orthodox clothing, playing in the waves.

A young boy, who looked to be all of six, tripped him. Ben regained his stride and caught up with the girl in the red shorts. Now that he got there, he didn't quite know what to do next. Ben was always nervous trying to meet girls. As Ben was thinking of his best opening line, she turned around, looked him straight in the eye, and asked if he wanted to race to the Newport Pier.

He was a bit taken aback as she was all of five feet tall, and he had a foot on her easy. Ben was 6'1, with brown curly hair, green eyes, broad shoulders, a muscular chest, thin waist, long legs, and big feet. From a distance, he was almost gangly looking. Up close, he was as the girls used to say, *dreamy*. Ben had a very odd feeling about this girl right away. He felt his heart go pitter patter.

His stride alone would overtake her in a few blocks, Ben thought, but he could always take it easy on her if he had to. Besides, it was Saturday night, and he was all alone. He nodded his head yes. She smiled and took off like a rabbit ahead of him.

Ben was watching her in awe and barely remembered they were racing, as his brain directed his feet to move faster. It took everything he had just to stay a block behind her. He enjoyed the moonlit view of her small, athletic body, her perky little breasts, and just-right ass. Her body looked as though it was flying toward its goal, her ponytail flipping side to side like a rudder, as she ran.

When she got to the Newport Pier, she turned around and as she passed him running back in the other direction, yelled, "Now I'm done taking it easy on you! See you back at Haulover, if you can keep up?"

"Sure. First one at Haulover Pier wins," a very-winded Ben replied.

Ben almost quit halfway. He couldn't even comprehend how she ran so quickly. He didn't think he could make it back at that pace but was determined. She was so far in front of him; he could barely see her ponytail bobbing along three blocks ahead. By the time Ben got to the Haulover Pier, he could barely breathe, and his feet felt like molten lead. There she was.

The moonlight danced off the waves, in and out of the Pier's pilings, framing her form. She was barely out of breath and looking so sexy. She thrust her hand out. When she did, her persona struck Ben as Katharine Hepburn-ish, like in one of those old movies where she played a reporter taking on the world. Not that she looked like Hepburn, but she had that air of confidence that was very businesslike and quick-witted, yet friendly and engaging. Like the kind of person you wish you knew, or could be.

"Gina Phylaxis, nice to beat you," Gina laughed. "Nice try there, hotshot. For a minute, I didn't think you would make it back."

Ben sat down on the sand, still trying to refill his lungs with much-needed air. "I'm Ben." He took a deep breath before continuing, "Ben Fox. Where did you learn to run that fast?"

"Heck, I was taking it easy on you because you looked like a nice guy."

"Yeah? What's a nice guy look like?"

Gina looked him up and down and stared for a moment. "Oh sorry, on second thought, I was wrong about you. I don't really think you're a nice guy. Just slow."

Ben was still barely able to catch his breath, but laughed nonetheless.

"Did you leave your asthma inhaler in the car, hotshot?" Gina teased with a big smile.

"Hey, I was the captain of my track team at Beach High."

"They must have really sucked."

"Come to think of it, we were pretty bad," Ben said, laughing and gasping for air.

Gina sat there in silence, watching him breathe. She asked him to walk her to her car, and he followed her through the parking lot, like a stray cat following a can of sardines. They got to her red Ford Thunderbird convertible, and Gina opened the trunk, took two bottles of Pepsi out of a cooler, then tossed him one. She opened her glovebox and took out a business card, handing it to Ben.

"If you ever catch your breath, give me a call. Maybe I can give you some running tips," she said as she got into her car and drove off before he had a chance to respond.

He read the card. *Gina Phylaxis, Goldfish & More.* He called her as soon as he got home to discover that it was the Pet Store's answering machine. "Hey, this is Ben. Ben Fox, your running buddy. Give me a call when you are ready for a rematch." Ben left his phone number and hung up. Weeks went by and no call. He thought he would never see her again. He even jogged the same Beach Path nine more times looking for her.

Three weeks later, when Ben was feeling particularly alone and fragile, as only an empty Saturday night could do to a single person, his phone rang.

"Rematch?"

It took him a moment and then Ben responded, "Only if you give me a head start?"

"No way, track star. See you at Haulover Pier in an hour?"

"Absolutely. I got new sneakers, though, so you better watch out."

After another solid thrashing, Ben once again found himself breathless, sprawled out under the Pier's pilings, looking at Gina with admiration.

"Hungry?" Gina asked.

"Always."

"Follow me. I'll make us some pasta."

"So, that's your secret. Lots of Carbs! You're so little. It doesn't look like you eat any pasta."

"I'm Italian, with a Greek grandfather. Just wait until you see the damage I can do to a bowl of linguini with feta cheese, spinach, and pine nuts!"

Ben still didn't remember driving to her house that first time, or much of anything else, until they walked into the kitchen. He'd never seen so many copper pots. Gina took down a large one, filled it with water from the spigot above the white farmhouse sink, set it on the stove, and lit a burner. He sat on the long bench next to the fridge as he took in his surroundings.

He was impressed with the kitchen, and that a girl who couldn't have been more than twenty had a house at all. Gina walked over to the bench seat and sat across from him. She appeared like a work of art that was painted into the kitchen, with a glowing white complexion, and a heart shaped face. Ben looked into her eyes and was mesmerized. He wasn't sure how he missed this before. Perhaps because he only saw Gina in the moonlight in their prior encounters. Her left eye was copper colored, and the right was blue; no, it was more of a light turquoise. Ben read that Native Americans attributed the quality of two different colored eyes as giving the possessor sight into both Heaven and Earth.

Ben never felt this way about a girl and saw something from the reflection in her unusual eyes that she may have felt the same. Neither had Ben ever kissed a girl before without asking. He was so respectful that even in his sexual fantasies, he always wore a condom. He leaned across the table and pressed his lips to hers. His bold action was rewarded with a passionate kiss that seemed like it lasted forever. They both felt transported in time and place before they simultaneously opened their eyes. Gina said, "Wow! I didn't think you had that in you!"

"Well, speaking of having it in you," Ben said giggling, and kissed her again, as they began to make love on the kitchen table. When they were climaxing, Ben could have sworn the kitchen walls were moving in and out, in rhythm to their heavy breaths. He attributed it to love. Ben started hanging around Gina's house the next day and never really left.

That was long ago. Every night since, Ben slept next to Gina. Every night, as he drifted off to slumber, he reached over in bed and tenderly held Gina's thigh. Just the touch of her flesh excited and comforted him every single time he held her. It was as if he had never touched her before, and like he had never let go, as if they were affixed for eternity. Ben never slept well without his hand on her thigh.

During their first few years, this habit annoyed Gina to no end. She told Ben his hands were too hot and heavy, and not in a good way. Gina felt as if Ben was zapping her energy molecules through his grasp on her thigh, like he was trying to possess her. But, after a few years of Gina's failed attempts at shoeing Ben's hand away, she realized it comforted him, and perhaps even transferred some of Ben's loving energy to her, so she surrendered to it. After a while, it comforted Gina as well. Last night was the first that Ben fought sleep without Gina's thigh in his grasp.

Ben leaned against the wall of the bathroom in the Marina where his boat was docked. His body felt as though it was dismembered from his brain, and he could no longer command it. After a deep breath, he mustered the energy and looked into the mirror again, his Father's eyes gazing back at him. The right eye was black and blue. Ben never felt so empty.

7

The next morning, Mother did her usual walk by the kids' room, cheerfully yelling, "Get the hell out of bed, you delinquents; time for school. It's delightfully cold outside, so bring your jackets." He tickled his younger sister awake and told her to get up. Walking into the bathroom, he splashed water on his sleepy face, brushed his teeth for all of five seconds, spit, and walked into the kitchen.

Mother was looking out the window, watching the dogs torment a neighbor—Mrs. Goldbloom. She was a mean-spirited old widow, and every Halloween she hung up a 'Deadly Poison Fumigation' sign on her front door so the neighborhood kids wouldn't trick-or-treat there. This only prompted them to leave little souvenirs on her lawn, like a dead snake or rat. The nine-year-old especially liked it when the dogs chased after her. Even though he knew they would do her no harm, she always jumped back in fear when the Doberman approached. Mother got a kick out of it as well.

"They are after Mrs. Goldbloom again," Mother said.

The nine-year-old chuckled. In that moment, he had forgotten again about the night before. Then Mother turned to face him. The realization crushed his small chest all at once, the arguing from last night, the terrible feeling of doom he had. Maybe Dad wasn't coming home?

He was looking for proof in front of his small, tired eyes. Did Mother have a black eye? He wondered to himself why they called it a black eye, anyway. He had one last year from bumping into an open stall door at the pony ranch, but his eye hadn't been black. His eyelid turned purple and brown, with yellowish swollen skin all around it. He wondered to himself how sickening that black eye would look against the contrast of Mother's white skin and her glorious, mysterious eyes.

The boy wanted to run over and hug her. He longed to tell her that he heard the whole thing. That he hated his Father for being such an angry shmuck, but instead when he looked up, he saw that Mother's face was as perfect as ever.

"Are you okay, Marsh? You look like you lost something?" The boy got up, ran over, and hugged her tightly. Mother hugged him back. Neither saying another word.

8

Wekiwa grew up a free spirit. Like most of the children, she ran around the camp half-naked until she was four years old. However, Wekiwa was different from the others. The bugs didn't seem to bite her, and she never got cuts or bruises. She had a naturally positive and curious nature, always wanting to explore and experience what the world had to offer. The Everglades was a wonderous place for such a child. Wekiwa could spend hours watching an apple snail crawl along a water hyacinth, a bass fanning it's underwater nest, a blue heron fishing for breakfast, an alligator resting on the water's edge, or the green and gold fields of sawgrass shimmering in the sunlight.

As a small child, she loved everyone and everything. Everyone was happy to see her, and she charmed them all. She had many friends, especially the boys, who started following her around camp from the time she could walk. It was as if she had cast a spell on them. Sometimes there were five or six boys following her around all at once. They would bring gifts, food, ask to hold her hand, and help her tend her Mother's garden. Her mother found it quite humorous, but Holata, not so much. All of this attention made the other girls jealous. Some teased her because of it. Wekiwa didn't like that, but she had a certain magic about her, and when she smiled that beguiling smile, the girls ran off laughing. Over time, some of the girls ended up not liking her at all.

Wekiwa's family was poor. She only had one real toy; a cloth, stuffed panther her Mother made for her. It was embroidered in colorful, dyed thread, and had turquoise stones for eyes—almost the same color as Wekiwa's. She named it Rainbow.

One day when Wekiwa was ten, she was bathing in the river that ran near their camp. A group of girls picked up Rainbow, who was sitting neatly on top of Wekiwa's folded dress on the shoreline. The girls waved and laughed at Wekiwa, as they threw Rainbow deep into the sawgrass. Upon seeing this, Wekiwa seemed unphased. She quietly exited the canal, threw her hair over her head with a twist of her waist, shook off like a dog, and walked uncovered into the sharp-edged sawgrass.

She was gone all day, all night, and most of the next day until she reappeared, still unclothed, without a scratch on her, and with a Florida panther cub at her side. The whole camp gathered around as she passed them, the panther cub growling at anyone who came close. Wekiwa stopped when they passed Holata and bowed, as did the cub. Holata looked the cub over with wonder. When she got to the group of girls, Wekiwa smiled her enchanting smile as the cub lashed out its sharp claws and hissed loudly. The girls squealed and dispersed, then Wekiwa walked slowly to Catori who welcomed her with open arms and wrapped her in a colorful blanket.

"My child. I prayed to the Great Spirits for your safe return. Where did go, and who is this?"

Catoria asked as she picked up the panther cub and rubbed its head. The cub purred.

"I was walking with the Great Spirits. Don't you recognize her, Mother? This is Rainbow."

Catori looked deep into Wekiwa's eyes, and then panther cubs. The mesmeric effects of Wekiwa's smile were useless on her Mother. It always had been. "You must take care to walk in concert with the Spirits, little ones," said Catori, looking at both her daughter and the cub. "You are here to do great things for our people, my child, but you must stay on the right path. Your enchantments are great, indeed, as must be the pureness of your heart."

"Yes, Mother," Wekiwa answered as she bowed, never making eye contact. If she had, Catori would have seen the pain, love, and conflict in Wekiwa's eyes.

The next day, Wekiwa awoke early and walked outside, the panther cub matching her every step. Wekiwa fetched firewood, lit the morning campfire, and made breakfast for the camp. It was Sofke, a porridge made from the Coontie plant. The Native American's processing of the Coontie root was simple. A mashed root pulp was soaked in water and strained through skins. This separated the starch, which was then fermented, removing the hydrocyanic acid—a form of cyanide. If prepared improperly, the Coontie's cyanide was deadly. When prepared as it should be, which Seminole children learned to do as soon as they could speak, the Coontie flour provided much of the carbohydrates that sustained the Seminoles, along with protein from deer, alligators, turkey, fish, shellfish, and other animals. It was the custom of the camp that whoever arose earliest prepared breakfast for the others, so no one questioned Wekiwa's cooking, except her grandfather.

When Holata saw Wekiwa preparing breakfast, he thought to himself, *'What is that character up to? She has never been up before the sun in all of her days. And why is that panther cub still hanging around? It should be with its Mother.'* Holata approached his granddaughter. "Wekiwa!" he called out respectfully, but sternly.

Wekiwa gazed up at her grandfather, shot him her most captivating smile, and winked. "Greetings to you, Grandfather. May I offer you breakfast?"

"I have to go visit the woods first, Wekiwa. I think I ate too much of Running Bear's rabbit stew last night. Come to think of it, talk about Running Bear. I could hardly keep my pants on! Must have been to the woods six times last night," said Holata while patting his stomach, laughing and winking back.

"Would you like me to make you a gut calming potion, Grandfather? I have the herbs in the garden."

"No, thank you, my child. I think it's all behind me now."

Wekiwa and Holata both held their stomachs, laughing. Since Wekiwa could remember, she and her grandfather had a special relationship that could go from reverent to ridiculous as fast as a blue heron could snatch a frog from the water's edge.

"You know, I think I will have some Sofke, child."

"Yes, Grandfather," said Wekiwa, handing him a bowl and bowing. "May the Great Spirits sustain you."

Holata took a bite. "This is better than your Mother's, but don't tell her. You should make breakfast more often. Come to think of it, why are you awake at this hour, my child? And why is this cub away from its Mother? Wekiwa gave her Grandfather a mystical smile, as the cub expelled a surprisingly loud *Gggrrrarrrrr*.

"Oh, Grandfather, today is a glorious day and the Great Spirits woke me to revel in all of it."

"And your roaring little friend here?"

"Oh, Grandfather, this is Rainbow. Don't you recognize her?"

Holata picked up the panther cub by the scruff of its neck and held the cub's face to his. Holata looked deep into the cub's face and saw its turquoise eyes—the same color as the stones in Wekiwa's doll, and of Wekiwa's eyes. Holata dropped the cub to the ground. "What have you done, my child? May the Great Spirits protect us."

"Oh, Grandfather, they already have. They caused Rainbow to come to life," said a smiling Wekiwa.

"Yes, Wekiwa. Yes," said Holata slowly while backing away, shaking his head toward the Heavens.

The rest of the camp thoroughly enjoyed Wekiwa's Sofke. Some said it was the best they ever ate. Wekiwa's Mother gave her a hug and told her it was better than hers, but not to tell anyone. By midday, almost everyone in the camp gathered around the fire for lunch. Several Mothers called to their girls to come eat. Three girls did not come and missed a splendid lunch as consequence.

Standing Tree made his special grilled turtle on the half shell. The three girls who threw the stuffed Rainbow doll into the sawgrass were later found together in the woods, holding their bellies and moaning. When the news was shared at the fire circle that evening, Holata looked quizzically at Wekiwa, who for the first time since she was born, was smileless. The panther cub let out his loudest *Gggrrrarrrrr* yet, walked a circle around Wekiwa, and lay down at her feet.

The other girls recovered from their belly aches, but they, and the rest of the girls, steered clear of Wekiwa after that. The boys on the other hand... Oh, the boys!

9

The Doberman walked through the house, leaving muddy pawprints on the wood floors starting at the front door, meandering through the living room, and trailing off toward the kitchen. He was starving after his late-night swim. He learned as a puppy that the most likely place to find food was in the kitchen. He pushed his damp nose into the blue-printed cushions on one of the dining room benches, smelling the remainder of food underneath.

As he pushed his muzzle under to retrieve a tasty morsel of chicken, he saw a flash of four paws below him. The Beagle. Somehow, she always found a way to insert her small self between the Doberman and unearthed food. Not today, though.

The Doberman quickly gobbled down the chicken and uttered a low warning growl to the unphased Beagle, who was already pushing her nose into the cushions on the other bench. The Beagle was fearless. She was the elder dog in the home, and even though the Doberman could render her to bits, he was respectful of this dog who had helped rear him.

One of the Doberman's earliest memories was coming into this kitchen as a shivering puppy, newly separated from his Mother at the Pet Store. He remembered his Mother, her smell mostly, and his littermates. There were nine of them. He arrived in this kitchen to a rush of feet and hands. Human feet and hands. There were many of them, running to greet him while he looked up with apprehension from the kitchen floor.

A hand reached down to scoop him up, and he looked into a pair of friendly eyes. They were the same mismatched eyes that locked into his at the Pet Store, which did little to resolve his terror. He peed. The human being attached to the hands didn't stop smiling. Squealing laughter came from the other small humans as the big human placed him back on the floor and wiped up the pee.

A smaller human placed a round object on the floor, and he slowly approached, investigating it with his nose before looking down into the shiny thing. He had never seen a stainless-steel bowl, and upon seeing his reflection through the water, he jumped straight up. His big, clumsy front paws landed in the dish upon his return to the floor, sending everything, pup included, sliding under the kitchen table. The humans laughed. The pup looked around. It was dark and quiet under the table, and sniffing around, he found some bits of food. He forgot about all of the commotion and began slurping down as much food off the floor as possible. Coming from a litter of nine, he learned quickly to eat whatever he found, as quickly as possible.

He found himself being lifted once again, this time by a medium-sized human with happy copper eyes that reminded him of his Mother's. His tongue frantically released from his mouth as he licked the face of this human. She laughed, kissed him all over, and held him close so he could feel her heartbeat. He immediately sighed and felt his little body go limp against hers. The other smaller humans made a fuss over him, trying to snatch him away from her comfortable grasp. The puppy tensed up, which made the copper-eyed human hold him closer and chase off the others with her loud voice. He was startled when he first heard it, but then realized the human was defending him as his Mother would have. He licked her again, and she patted his head.

"Don't you worry, little guy. I'll take care of you. I think I'll call you, Vlad. Is that okay, Mother?" Jemma asked.

"Come to think of it, Jemma, he does look like a little conqueror. Vlad, it is," Gina replied, laughing.

The larger human brought some rags with a box and set them down against the wall, next to the kitchen table. The copper-eyed human held him until he felt sleepy. When he awoke, he was in the box, with those rags all around him.

Although all alone, Vlad felt strangely at ease in the kitchen. It wasn't just the smells, which were delicious! It was as if he had lived in this place his entire life. Even before that; like the kitchen was part of him, and he it. The kitchen seemed alive. He could sense it through the floorboards and into the dirt beneath them. Like most puppies, he was hungry and headed back under the kitchen table. As his little brown nose smelled a particularly tasty morsel, which he would later learn was called bacon, he looked up to see another canine—a Beagle.

Vlad felt a tang of relief that there was another one of his species in the house, but then he heard a guttural growl, and before he could back away, big teeth were digging into his puppy snout. He yelped as loudly as he could, which always prompted his littermates to let go. This canine apparently was not raised with the manners as Vlad's family since the Beagle would not release its grip no matter how loud he yelped. The pain was unbearable. Just as Vlad was about to surrender to his own demise, the Beagle let go. The Beagle seemed unphased and returned to eat the untouched bacon morsel. Vlad whimpered and peed in submission.

Within weeks, the puppy was twice the Beagle's size. He followed the Beagle around, like, well, like a puppy dog. The humans called her Princess, but to Vlad, she was his Queen. Princess looked gray and ancient, but moved with surprising agility, especially when food was involved. She seemed annoyed by Vlad's attention at first, but later enjoyed having a sidekick.

The Beagle was the first one to take Vlad on a jaunt around the neighborhood, to point out the mean cats, the cats that enjoyed being chased, and the ones who climbed trees in panic. Those were the Beagle's favorite kind of cats to chase. Princess loved watching them frantically claw their way up the trees, with little regard for how they would be getting down. Vlad learned where the tasty bowls of cat food were left out, and later, as he matured, where the female dogs lived. Vlad soon grew to be the biggest dog in the neighborhood. While he could have easily challenged the Beagle, the memory of that one and only bite on the nose never escaped him.

Vlad loved to watch her cook. Gina, the large, mismatched-eyed human, spent a lot of time in the kitchen, and made quite the mess. One day, she was preparing a large wooden board full of cheese and fruit. Oh, how he loved cheese. Vlad learned that Gina loved cheese too. She loved to bring home a variety of delicious cheeses from Laurenzo's Italian Market. Some days, she would sit in the kitchen with a glass of red liquid in her hand. Gina called it *whine*. Vlad didn't like how it smelled; it reminded him of rotting mangos, and they gave him a stomachache. No wonder Gina called it whine. He whined all night after he ate that last bad mango.

On what Vlad liked to call, Cheese Days, Gina would close the kitchen door, and it was only the two of them in there. Well, the two of them and the radio. Gina loved music, especially 50's Rock and Roll. She always turned the radio on when she drank her whine.

Then came the best part of Cheese Days. Gina would take cheese from the refrigerator and let it sit out. How can anything smell better than cheese? Leaving it out made it even better by enhancing the delicious smells that made Vlad salivate.

Gina poured more whine into her glass, then she would hold a small bit of cheese in her closed hand and let Vlad sniff it until he barked. Before she gave him the cheese, she would tell him the names. Some had strange names; Blue, Roquefort, Jarlsberg, Stilton. Those were the smelliest, and as far as the Doberman was concerned, the smellier the better. Sometimes the cheese wasn't as smelly; like Swiss, Cheddar, and Gouda, but he loved them all the same. As he grew, Vlad only got cheese if when Gina identified that particular cheese by name, Vlad barked at its name in response, then she would open her hand and let him eat it. It soon became his favorite game.

Before Vlad was six months old, he could identify over fifty varieties of cheese. At first, it was difficult, as some smelled almost the same, or left a strong scent on Gina's hand. He would soon learn there were many varieties of Blue cheese, and he knew them all. He was particularly fond of Cashel Blue, and for a more moderate, balanced cheese, provolone.

It became very easy for Vlad over time, and he was highly motivated, as if he didn't bark for the correct name of the cheese, he wouldn't get even a nibble. The Beagle would often howl incessantly from the house or yard when the cheese was left out for more than an hour, the fragrances driving her sensitive nose into fits of ecstasy. Despite this, Princess wasn't allowed to play the cheese game. Vlad didn't comprehend why the Beagle wasn't allowed to play the game, but Princess was always cold to him after he exited the kitchen, satiated with cheese.

A few days ago, after playing the cheese game with Gina for a long time, four glasses of whine long, Vlad sensed something under the kitchen floorboards. He started to scratch at the floor and bark. Gina told him to hush. He lay down on the floor and let out a whimper, then he saw it—a mist coming through the boards.

He turned his head sideways and opened his mouth to let out a little warning bark when he saw the mist jump from the floor in his direction. He snapped at it and thought he missed, but the mist went straight into his mouth. He felt a tickle in his throat, and then down in his belly. Vlad started hearing sounds in his head. They were human voices—a man and a woman. The man's voice sounded strange, like Mr. Bucci down the block. The woman's voice was soft, and somehow reminded him of how Ben spoke. Then other voices came; many of them. Vlad thought he must have eaten something like those weird cow pasture mushrooms Jemma was talking to her friends about. Vlad thought, *'I'm definitely laying off the truffle cheese from now on.'*

10

en wanted to pick up the phone and call her. At this moment in time, he missed everything about Gina. He even missed the kitchen, the same room he used to be overwhelmed by when he first started living there. It seemed to be a living, breathing entity. He fondly remembered the day he moved in, going through all of the kitchen gadgetry, naming them off to Gina, one by one. She was greatly impressed. The truth was, at the time, Ben didn't know a thing about cooking. He could barely make mac n' cheese from the box.

He still couldn't figure out what happened. Sure, they had some petty fights over the years, but none turned violent. Ben couldn't recall Gina even touching him last night, but she was too fast for him; always, and in many ways. She'd never hit him, though. Maybe as the soldiers say in those old black and white movies, *I never heard the bullet coming.* Gina was quick to anger, but only with her tongue, and only to unleash a quick barb, then it was like nothing ever happened. Ben envied this quality. Gina has never hit the kids either; not even raising a hand in jest.

And when Ben walked out last night, why was Vlad grinning at him? Damn dog! He had been creeping Ben out lately. To make it worse, the night before, Vlad followed him out to his car, and peed on his front tire. Ben's mind turned to tires, and how he knew so much about kitchen utensils.

When he was young and needed money for new car tires, he was too proud to ask his Father, so Ben got a job doing inventory at Burdines in the 163 Street Shopping Center. He remembered the pre-employment test they gave to see if he was a thief before placing him in the stockroom areas of the store. Question 1. Is it okay to take a pencil home from work? Question 2. Is it okay to take a pen home from work? There were another fifty similar questions. Would anyone looking for a stockroom job be dumb enough to answer *yes*? Then, to further mitigate the potential for thievery, they placed people in stockrooms with things they didn't think they would steal. Ben was sentenced to a week of night inventory, 8 PM to 6 AM, in kitchenware. Burdine's management figured a twenty-year-old guy wasn't likely to steal a ladle. Times had changed. After all this time with Gina, Ben could whip up a quiche in five minutes and would love a new whisk.

Ben mindlessly stumbled down the dock to his boat. When he had to explain to someone how he wound up here, selling bait to fishermen, he still couldn't come up with a reasonable explanation. Ben's Father, Herman, was an investment banker on Wall Street, made a bundle, retired at forty-two, and moved to a Bayfront house on Miami Beach. Herman married Ben's young mother, Betty, late in life, and they expected to live a long, happy life in the fun and sun capital of the world.

When Ben was thirteen, his parents took him on a European cruise. At first, he wasn't crazy about the idea of a cruise with his parents, but this changed as soon as Ben experienced the entertainment and freedom a cruise ship provided to a young boy.

Ben spent his days at Cruiser Camp, playing video games, swimming, and eating as much of any kind food or drinks his growing teenage stomach desired. Ben also found his first real crush; Cruise Counselor, Sandy. In Sandy, not only did young Ben find a woman who thought it was reasonable to eat three hot fudge sundaes with sprinkles for lunch, but when she smiled at him, his heart went pitter patter for the first time.

To be fair, Sandy smiled at everyone, all the time. She was tall and tan, had long blonde hair, green eyes, and wore a red one-piece swimsuit in and around the pool. Ben followed her around like a lost pup. One day, after he finally beat Sandy at ping pong, one of the ship's officers came down to Cruiser Camp and whisked her away. Ben went to get another ice cream. After ordering two scoops, one chocolate and one pistachio, he looked up to see his Father, two uniformed staff members, and Sandy.

"Ben, it's Mom."

11

The five-year-old opened the refrigerator door, reached in, and took out the milk. She went to the pantry and got the box of Cheerios. Taking a bowl and spoon from the dishwasher, not noticing they were dirty, she placed them on the table. She poured too many cheerios into the bowl, and they went spilling all over the table, some even tumbling to the floor.

The Beagle, hearing the sound of food hitting the wood boards, was under her feet in no time, followed by the Doberman, both slurping up the runaway cereal while she laughed. The girl pushed the remainder of the spilled cereal off the table and onto the floor, watching as the dogs quickly gobbled it up. She reached down and pat the Beagle on the head. "Good girl, Princess!" She then poured the milk into the bowl, sat down and turned on the TV.

She was always the first kid in the kitchen, as she postponed washing up and brushing her teeth until after breakfast. She wasn't slovenly, rather highly pragmatic for a five-year-old. There was only one bathroom for all of the kids, and it was very crowded first thing in the morning. She learned that she would have the bathroom to herself if she ate first and then washed up while the others were eating their breakfast.

She didn't mind eating alone, in fact, she preferred it. It was the only time she could watch whatever TV show she wanted. She found Roadrunner, her favorite cartoon, and plunked her spoon into the bowl with her left hand. Her right hand went probing under the seat cushions, as she usually found something of value under there. Last week, she found a quarter that went into her piggybank. She ate some cereal then made a more concerted effort to check between and under the cushions. She found some cereal, likely hers or her siblings' from yesterday's breakfast, a dime, and a baggie with a small brownie in it. Score! She ate the brownie, put the cereal bowl on the floor for the dogs to finish, got washed up and dressed, then headed back to the kitchen to join the rest of the brood. Pretty soon, they were off to school.

She loved kindergarten. She had two best friends: Billy and Diane. They sat at the same table for snacks and lunch and played together every day. Right before lunch, she started to feel funny. She could feel her hands and feet, but they didn't seem to be attached to her. She felt like a floating birthday balloon as she watched Billy color a parrot purple.

"A purple parrot," she said through a chuckle. "A parrot, and it's *purple*." She started laughing uncontrollably, prompting her teacher to come over and ask if she was okay. She guffawed as her teacher bent down to look at her. She hadn't noticed before how big teacher's head was. It was big; really, *really* big. This just made her laugh more. Her teacher held her face and looked into her eyes.

"Gracie. I think we better call your mother."

"Mother?" Gracie said, giggling.

The girl walked out of class with her teacher and into the school office. Her teacher told her to sit down on the bench to wait. The girl looked around the room and saw the other staff members and Mrs. Feldman, the principal, who was coming over to see her.

"How are you doing today, Gracie?"

"I'm very, very happy," the girl said, still laughing.

"I can see that. Did you eat or drink anything before school today?"

Gracie thought about the Beagle eating the spilled cereal and started to giggle again.

"I think we better call your mother."

"Mama. You're calling my Mother? Tell her the dogs ate the Cheerios," she barely breathed out, she was laughing so hard.

"Call Gina Fox," said Mrs. Feldman as she walked back to her office, shaking her head while grinning.

12

Ben could never forget that day on the Cruise Ship. He looked into his customarily composed Father's eyes and saw tears welling up. Ben didn't need to ask. His Father's eyes told it all, but he had to know. "What happened, Dad?"

The night before, Herman and Betty attended the comedy show of none other than the legendary, Murray Ferrari. Murray was born and raised in Venice, Italy; the son of a chef and the nice Jewish girl he fell in love with. Murray's mother wanted him to be a doctor, but his Father wanted him to follow in his footsteps and take over Geppetto's Basement, the family Trattoria.

As a teenage busboy, Murray loved entertaining the restaurant's customers. Murray's Father always thought his boy was amusing and nurtured his wit by installing a small stage and a stool, right next to the Restaurant's woodburning stove. In between busing tables, Murray honed his comedic skills in what he would affectionately call *the piccante seat*. At the ripe age of nineteen, knowing he didn't want to spend his days making pasta for tourists or being responsible for saving human lives as a doctor, Murray did the only thing he could think of at the time—he became a stand-up comic. Most of Murray's material was either about food or being raised by a Jewish Mother in Venice.

Murray had a natural ability with people, perfect timing, and he always ended his show sharing a secret family recipe. He was a good-looking kid; six feet tall, trim, olive skinned, with shiny black hair, and playful blue eyes. When he winked, which he did frequently, the signorinas went crazy.

Venice is one of the busiest cruise ports in Europe, and Murray found a following on the tourist-laden cruise ships. He often did a few shows while the ships were in port or jumped on for a cruise to travel to other parts of the world. Murray had a keen business sense, as he used to joke; it was the only good thing he got from his Mother's side of the family. By twenty-five, he found a niche by creating the one and only Cruise Ship Kitchen Comedy Tour. It was a delightful way for cruisers who didn't want to go ashore for lunch, to tour the ship's vast kitchen, hear food-related jokes, and for the grand finale, learn a secret family recipe from Murray Ferrari himself. Murray loved doing these tours, plus at $500 a passenger, with a minimum of ten, it was a great way to make a quick five grand. Herman and Betty signed up for the tour as soon as they boarded the ship.

The ship's kitchen was magnificent. Its cleanliness sparkled; with white floors, stainless prep surfaces, large cooking vats, and giant cookware as well as utensils that provided the oversized, comical impression that Wilma Flintstone was about to enter with a giant platter of Brontosaurus burgers. Murray effortlessly made his way around the kitchen, joking, stirring pots of sauce, giving out food samples, and as he would often say, having the crowd literally eating out of his hands.

Betty was captivated and stayed by Murray's side for every moment. As they concluded their tour, Murray put on an apron, went to the refrigerator, retrieved a selection of ingredients; mostly seafood, and addressed his audience. "Today we are making my family's take on Frutti di Mare. I need a beautiful assistant. Any volunteers?"

Betty's hand shot up as quickly as her heart was beating from being near the charming, young chef.

"You, Signorina! Perfecto!" Murray tied an apron around Betty, who almost swooned at that simple gesture. Murray picked up a pair of tongs and reached into a pot of boiling pasta, removing several strands of linguine and holding them next to Betty's eager mouth, gently blowing on it to cool off the pasta.

"Now, Signorina, taste this pasta."

Betty bit into the overly al dente pasta.

"How is it?" Murray asked.

"It wasn't in long enough." Betty replied.

"Hey! That's what she said!" The audience laughed, while the silent, smirking crew thought, *'Not this joke again!'* "You see, everyone, this Frutti de Mare is an old family recipe I shared with the ship's chef. He already has it cooking over there. As my Jewish Mother says, this dish is to die for."

At that moment, Murray and Betty were standing behind the stove, heating tomatoes for the sauce, when the unthinkable occurred. A drunken gondolier accidentally crashed into the cruise ship's dock lines, causing the huge ship to lurch sideways. Murray and Betty went flying into the enormous boiling vat of Frutti di Mare sauce. When the ship immediately righted itself, the vat's lid closed. Betty and Murray were instantaneously poached.

Herman helplessly watched the love of his life die before his eyes. In the fifteen amazing years they were married, they never expressed a bad word to each other. It was all so blissful. Fear and despair rose in the bottom of Herman's gut.

He ran to the sauce vat and tried opening the scalding lid with his bare hands, only to be tackled to the deck by a mindful crewman. Herman began shouting her name, "Betty! Betty! Betty! Help! Someone help!"

Within seconds, a hoard of crew members surrounded them, opened the lid, and bowed in respect for the dead once they saw what lay inside. The bodies, drenched with tomatoes, clams, shrimp, and baby octopus, were gingerly removed with giant wooden ladles. The ship's doctor pronounced Betty and Murray dead at 12:55 PM, just five minutes short of when the tour was to end.

Shaking with sore, blistered palms, and with tears flowing like a river down Herman's face, he simply told his son, "Mom drowned." Herman held Ben in his injured hands, and they both wept.

The rest of the cruise was a blur. Not even Sandy rubbing his shoulders helped to diminish the pain Ben's entire being was experiencing. The crew was overly nice to them, but with a guarded sadness in their eyes. Herman realized they were just being kind, but Ben couldn't stand it. They stopped going to dinner in the dining room, and Ben found himself sneaking into the cafeteria for meals at off hours or ordering room service and asking the steward to leave the food outside his stateroom door.

All the while, his Mother's and Murray's lifeless bodies sat in the ship's freezer. Ben couldn't bear the pain of it. In life, Betty doted over Ben like he was the last lion cub in the pride. She lived to serve him. Ever since he could remember, Betty did everything to care for Ben, keeping him entertained, happy, and feeling loved. She even cut his toast in little animal shapes and made mashed potato houses at dinner.

To Ben, his Mother was the most flawless person he knew. She made him feel joyful and loved just by smiling in his direction, which she did incessantly. Betty radiated beauty and grace, and Ben loved her more than anything in his life. He couldn't imagine his life without her. As he sat at the ship's railing, he carefully considered jumping into the sea. He didn't.

13

By the time Wekiwa was sixteen, she looked exactly like the woman portrayed in the lightning carving on the Cypress Tree. She was a tall, beautiful Seminole woman, with a beguiling demeanor, diamond-shaped face, long black hair, an hourglass figure, and those eyes—those turquoise eyes. She carried herself, like a sun-tanned, slightly taller version of Morticia Adams, from the Adams Family.

The boys. Oh, the boys. They were drawn to her like a mosquito to the tail of a deer on a hot summer night in the Everglades. Wekiwa loved the attention of the boys, her Grandfather and Mother on the other hand, not so much. They both reminded Wekiwa of her role in the future of their people, and to not fritter her life away, swept up in the attention of amorous young men.

"Mother, nobody is doing anything to me that I don't want done. Besides, they know to get to this pussy," said Wekiwa as she pointed at her crotch and continued, "they need to get through this pussy first." Wekiwa playfully swatted at the tail of the purring and fully-grown Rainbow.

"You always could make me laugh, child, but you never could fool me. I know what the Great Spirits have blessed and cursed you with. Holding your own future in your hands is a lot when you are a young squaw, but holding the future of the tribe, that's, well, *a lot*. You will see more when you come of age, my child."

"Oh, Mother. The Great Spirits have spoken to me. They have made me young, soft, and supple, and promised them that I would never be old, stiff, and saggy. They provided Rainbow to guide and protect me. There is no stronger totem than a panther. You worry too much."

"That's a Mother's job, my not so little one."

Wekiwa gently kissed her Mother on the cheek, and left. Rainbow licked Catori across the face and followed Wekiwa into the camp.

As usual, there were a half a dozen boys waiting for her. While Wekiwa was young, she learned how to gain any favor she wanted from the boys. She learned that the promise of sex was much stronger than sex itself. Having a grown panther as a full-time chaperone didn't hurt either.

Wekiwa also learned something about herself beginning the morning when she made Sofke for the camp. She loved cooking. And growing boys loved eating. She went out of her way to make interesting dishes, always utilizing the magic of the plants her Mother taught her. Once she made a dish for the boys using morning glory flowers, which had a hallucinogenic effect on them. She took them all in the woods and danced for them. They all pledged their undying love for her and wrestled each other for the right to kiss her.

Wekiwa came to understand the great power she held and used it to her advantage. She would send the boys off with her Everglades shopping list for dinner ingredients, and they would compete to be the first to bring back the most frog legs, largemouth bass, ibis, and just about anything else Wekiwa requested.

By the time she was seventeen, her roadside stand in the heart of the Everglades had gained such fame that sometimes horses were lined up a half a mile down the road, and boats traveled all the way from the mouth of the Mayaimi River, just hoping for a plate of Wekiwa's cooking. Also, it wasn't every day that people saw a tame Florida panther, uncaged and up close. She made so much money, she was able to build a new home for her, and her very proud, Mother. She even built a new schoolhouse for the camp's children.

"You see, Father, maybe this is what the Great Spirits meant. Wekiwa is changing our future," Catori said.

"All this money is great, but something is not right, Catori. We have to keep a close eye on that girl."

14

When Ben and Herman returned home from the Cruise and walked inside, it felt vacant; like all of the air had been sucked out of the house, the neighborhood, the entire galaxy. Ben looked up at Herman, and he looked like he couldn't breathe. What was left of Ben's broken heart shattered for his Dad, but he was grateful to know he wasn't alone in his misery.

Ben went back to school a week after the funeral, still engulfed in an abyss of sorrow. His sadness was so cavernous it felt as though there was nothing before to compare it to. Like the first thirteen years of his life had been wiped clean of the heaven on earth it had been before. Before he lost the person that lived to love him. Ben withdrew. He went to school, came home, and retreated into the Banyan Treehouse in his backyard. The treehouse he built with his best friend, Mike Lawrence, who came over to visit him in that same treehouse every single day for a year after his Mother died.

Herman, previously the most gregarious person you could meet, sat alone in the house for six months. When he finally went out, his first trip was to Haulover docks on Miami Beach. He and Betty used to love to go there at sunset and buy fresh fish from the charter boat captains. Betty, trained as a chef before falling in love with Herman, loved to cook, especially fresh seafood. Her snapper in parchment paper with fresh vegetables was Herman's favorite.

As Herman walked along the dock, he saw a for sale sign on a boat. It was a 21-footer with a 90 horsepower Evinrude engine. On the side of the boat, the words, LIVE BAIT, were stenciled in large, black letters. Herman saw a bearded man loading buckets into a cooler in the bow and spontaneously asked, "How much you want for her?"

"The first $2,000 takes her, but you have to leave my name on the ownership papers, and I get a cut of your bait sales, that's if you want to keep her docked here. County rules."

"How does she run?"

"Good. You can take her out with me if you want."

"I'll take your word for it. Cash okay?" Herman said, pulling out a wad of hundreds.

"Cash is my favorite four-letter word."

"I'm Herman."

"Mitch. Can I ask you something, Herman?"

"Have you ever thrown a cast net?"

"No, but how hard could it be?"

"Oh, you'll find out after a couple dozen throws."

Herman needed a distraction and thought nothing could be any worse than the pain he was walking around with. Serious fishermen in Miami didn't want to waste valuable fishing time trying to catch bait and paid a premium for someone else to do their, as Mitch kidded him, *grunt work*.

Two days later, Herman was throwing a cast net off of Beer Can Island in North Biscayne Bay, not far from his waterfront mansion. The irony of this did not escape him. In fact, he got a real kick out of it. On his first throw, the net released into the water in an almost perfect circle, just like Mitch had shown him. Herman was feeling very proud of himself, until he realized he hadn't secured the end of the cast net rope to his arm, or the boat. He watched his net sink into the bay and cursed, as Mitch looked on, laughing.

After a few weeks, and two more lost nets, Herman found his groove. He hadn't slept well since he lost Betty and was up well before dawn every day anyway. Herman found he enjoyed being on the water before sunrise, watching schools of bait fish being chased by tarpons, snook, and bottlenose dolphins in the water, while the seagulls, frigate birds, and pelicans performed an aerial attack. He soon learned all of the best spots to catch bait. Since he didn't need the money, Herman only charged $2 a dozen, which was a bargain compared to the other boats back then. He soon had a large following of fishermen who loved him, brought him coffee and donuts, and exchanged fish tales. Some fishermen would even hook him up with fresh cobia or grouper, his favorite eating fish.

Herman also made a few enemies who had to cut their bait prices from $5 a dozen to $4 just to get Herman's overflow. One of the bait fishermen who hated Herman the most was LaCroix. Gus LaCroix came from a family of strawberry farmers in Ponchatoula, Louisiana. Gus fancied himself a Cajun chef and moved to Miami Beach to find fame and fortune. He could make a few decent dishes the way his Mama taught him, but his repertoire was limited as he drank too much and was unreliable. Plus, to be fair, Cajun food didn't exactly go over big on Miami Beach in those days either.

Gus was fired from five different jobs. He found solace in Pabst Blue Ribbon beer and the occasional down-and-out lady who was charmed by his Cajun accent and strawberry blonde hair. Gus used to joke that everything in his hometown reminded people of strawberries, even his hair. He soon found day work at the Haulover docks cleaning boats.

One day, while cleaning Buddy the Baitman's boat, Buddy told him how his Mother came from the Tanipahoa Parish, just a hop, skip, and pollywog jump from Gus's Louisiana home. As it turned out, Buddy and Gus were cousins, twice removed on his Mother's side. The other thing Buddy and Gus had in common was their love of cheap women and cheaper whiskey.

After a night of drinking and carousing, the boys invited their evening companions, Laverne and Beverly, out for a boat ride in the Bay. When the girls saw the bait boat, they threw an empty bottle of Gin in Buddy's general direction and turned to go.

"You girls sure you don't want a ride? It's a beautiful night."

"Look up in the sky, you old fool. It's about to storm."

"And that boat is a piece of shit!"

The girls walked off and found a ride with a guy in a black truck with a Confederate flag sticker on the rear window.

"We don't need you whores anyway. Come on, Gus, let's go for a ride."

"I don't think that's such a good idea, cousin. Look at those thunderclouds."

"I didn't think your Mama raised such a wuss. Screw you, coward. I'm going for a ride."

"Be careful out there, cuz."

Buddy's boat was later found floating off Biscayne Point, about three miles south of Haulover docks. His body was found the next day washed into the mangroves between Biscayne Point and Stillwater Island. Gus inherited the boat and dockage, cleaned up his act just enough to stay reasonably sober and catch bait from 6 AM-10 AM on Saturdays, Sundays, and holidays.

The job made him enough money to rent a cheap apartment in North Miami, keep his fridge stocked with PBR, and to afford his other vice; Woody's steak sandwiches. Woody's was an institution in North Miami, and steak sandwiches were their specialty. Underneath it all, Gus was still a chef and he appreciated good food, and being a Cajun Boy from Louisiana, he truly loved to find himself a good Samwich! Woody's steak sandwich combined just the right balance of greasy onions, melted, but not overly gooey cheese, and the perfect cut of nearly grizzle-less steak, all perfectly congealed on a hot-buttered roll. For Gus, eating it was like being home, enjoying a Po Boy. Besides drinking and eating, Gus also tried befriending Herman to explain how he was hurting the other bait fishermen.

"Bonjour, Herman, got a minute?"

"I have nothing but time, Gus."

"You know, Herman, us bait fishermen we gots to stick together, no mon ami? When you charge $2 a dozen, we can't sell them for $5, or even hardly for $4."

"I understand, Gus, but these guys are my friends. I don't really need the money. I just want to make enough to pay for my dockage, gas, and the kickback I have to give to Mitch every month."

"I hear you, brah, but to be honest, you're killing me here. I can barely afford my PBR and steak sandwiches."

"Well, Gus, I'm here six days a week, working from 4:30 AM to noon. You're out here what, two days a week for four hours? Maybe if you worked more, you could earn more money. And, if you don't mind my saying, all those greasy steak sandwiches will kill you."

Gus had very few good qualities, and controlling his vile tongue was not on that list. "Well, I heard your wife died in a pot full of fancy food on some cruise ship, so I wouldn't be so quick to slam what I eat."

Herman had many good qualities, amongst them controlling his tongue while plotting revenge. "Thank you for reminding me of that painful memory, Gus. I think we are done here."

"Hey, I didn't mean nothing by that. I'm sorry about your wife, but can you lay off the $2 a dozen, mon ami?"

"Sure, Gus. Anything for you."

The next Saturday, at 6 AM, a very hungover Gus rode his bike to the docks and climbed into his boat. He looked out at the only other bait boat out there. It was Herman's. There was a shiny new sign on the boat that read, LIVE BAIT $1. Gus cursed, headed for Herman's boat at full throttle and drove circles around him yelling, "This ain't over, Herman, you Somofabitch!" and muttering, "Gris-gris," the Cajun word for a voodoo curse on you.

Herman smiled and waved. "Enjoy those steak sandwiches, you backwoods bastard."

At first, Ben was embarrassed by his Father's new occupation and jealous of the time it took away from their relationship. However, he soon came to see that this was healing his Father's pain. In fact, after a bit, Ben would look forward to getting up early on weekends, and helping his Father catch bait. By the time he was sixteen, Ben could locate and catch bait better than the most seasoned bait master.

While this caused him grief at school, with his friends calling him 'The Masterbaiter', Ben enjoyed being on the boat with his Father. He especially liked talking fishing with the customers, who every week or so, would take Ben out fishing. Ben's heart swirled in bliss as he caught sailfish from the edge of the Gulfstream, and big groupers, snappers, and cobias from the offshore reefs. There was nothing like the feel of a fishing reel whirring out line as fish dove, darted, and jumped when hooked in the glistening, blue waters of the Atlantic Ocean.

After witnessing the confrontation between Gus and Herman, Ben asked, "What was that about, Dad?"

"Just a joke between Gus and me, Ben. Nothing to worry about."

But Ben could see by the look in Gus' eyes, that there was indeed something to worry about.

15

The eleven-year-old left school after second period and walked home. He was a good kid and never skipped school, but something about the day called him home at 9:30 AM. He went straight to the kitchen, turned on Gilligan's Island reruns, took down a medium-sized copper pan, put it on the stove and lit a burner. "Hot pan, cold oil," he said to himself.

He walked to the refrigerator and took out the rye bread and Swiss cheese, then got a cheese slicer out of the rolling cart in the pantry. Mother never bought store-sliced cheese. She said it lost its flavor once it was sliced and exposed to air for a while.

He poured olive oil into the pan and watched it sizzle, spinning the oil around the pan so the entire surface was coated. He enjoyed watching Mother cook and carefully observed everything she did in the kitchen.

As the eldest boy, he thought he should know how to take care of himself, and on occasions when he was feeling generous of spirit, his siblings too. He liked being able to make the kind of food that he wanted to eat.

He put two slices of rye bread into the pan, and it sizzled again. Turning the burner down to medium low, he then sliced several pieces of Swiss cheese and placed them onto each slice of bread. He decided to spice things up a bit and got some gorgonzola out of the fridge, sliced off a thick hunk, then put it on top of the melting cheese. It already smelled delicious.

The Doberman and Beagle appeared in the kitchen, sniffing the floor for any cheese that might have fallen; there was none. The Doberman nuzzled the boy's hand. The boy pet him, and said, "Oh no, Vlad, this is my sandwich." He seemed to comprehend and walked out, leaving the Beagle stuck around hoping for a handout, or a misstep.

Once the cheese got gooey, the boy flipped one piece of bread onto the other and pushed it down with a spatula. Some of the cheese oozed out and melted in the pan, causing the boy's mouth to water at the sight. So did the Beagle's. He flipped the sandwich and saw it was the proper shade of light-yellow brown.

Turning off the burner, he got a plate and placed the sandwich down before cutting it into two triangles. Cheese oozed out the middle and onto the plate as the knife sliced through the crisp bread. He got some corn chips from the pantry and poured a few all around the sandwich so they filled the plate.

Reaching into the fridge, he got a small dill pickle from a jar and placed it on his plate as well. He sat down at the kitchen table, feeling very satisfied with his culinary creation, putting his feet up on the bench across from him and took a bite. The cheese was so hot, it almost burned the roof of his mouth, so he bit into the cold pickle for relief.

The Beagle came over sniffing and howling. The boy shooed her away.

The blonde babysitter walked in the front door without knocking. "Hey Nick, Is your Mom around?"

"Haven't seen her," he replied without looking up from his sandwich.

"How's your sandwich?"

"Great. I used Swiss and Gorgonzola cheese this time."

"You are getting very creative. Can I have a bite?"

"Not a chance!"

"I just came by to see if your Mom had any work for me to do around here."

"Will you do my homework for me if I make you a sandwich, Jeannie?"

"Not a chance. Why are you home from school anyway?"

"Just wasn't feeling it today, you know."

Jeannie knew it was a bad idea to have favorites when she babysat, but Nick was funny, cute, and an old soul. She sat down on the bench across from Nick, reached across the table, and stole three chips from the boy's plate.

"Hey! Get your own!"

"Nah. They taste better this way."

"Why are you hanging around here all the time? Don't you have stuff to do at your own house?"

"I need to make some money."

"Don't you get an allowance?"

"Nah. My Mom lost her job."

"Again?"

"Yeah."

Jeannie stole more chips from Nick's plate, sighed, put her head into her hands, and slumped down on the bench.

"Why does she keep losing her job?"

"It's..."

"Hey, I'm eleven now. You can tell me. I won't tell anyone."

"Well..."

Nick slid his plate to Jeannie with half of the uneaten grilled cheese sandwich. "Go ahead," he offered in a truly empathetic tone.

"You sure?"

"Yeah, looks like you need it."

"Thank you, Nick. Thanks a lot," said Jeannie as she bit into the grilled cheese, choking back tears. "Damn! That's really good, Nick."

"Thanks," he responded, bowing his head. "So, what's up with your Mom?"

"She was doing really well, then she started using again?"

"Using what?"

"Drugs."

"Shit!"

"Yeah. Shit. She seemed fine and then something set her off yesterday. I don't know what it was. She had just caught up on our rent, and now we may have to move."

"That sucks." Nick abruptly left the table, went to his room and came back with a large green, ceramic pig.

"I've been saving my allowance for a TV for my room, but if you move, Mom might get some dipshit babysitter. Take it." Nick used an authoritative tone that was meant for someone well beyond his years. A tearful Jeannie pushed the piggybank back across the table.

"Thanks, really, but I have to earn it."

"You could do my homework," Nick said and let out a laugh.

"Nice try. Thank you. Really. That was a very nice thing of you to do, but I can't take your bank."

"So, what are you going to do?"

"I'm walking over to Woody's to see if I can get a real job."

"Great. Bring me back a medium fry."

"Ha. Ha. Please don't tell anyone about this."

"Don't tell Mom I skipped school and make it a large fry, *then* you have a deal," said Nick with a wink.

"Deal. And, thanks, really," said Jeannie as she got up to leave.

"Hey!"

"Yes?"

"Don't forget my fries."

16

The kids were off to school and instead of her usual start of the day at the Pet Store, Gina mindlessly drove down 135th Street and found herself in the Enchanted Forest Park. She got out of her car and walked to the Pony Stables. Like ice cream, puppies, kittens, and babies, ponies always made Gina smile.

Last night felt like a nightmare, and she needed a smile this morning. She walked to the Arch Creek Bridge because even though she never knew why, standing on this Bridge always brought Gina peace. More than that, it was akin to being transported to another dimension. The Bridge always felt wonderous, with the duck and turtle speckled, gray-brown Creek running under it, and the ancient Grandfather Oaks framing the scene. It all felt timeless.

Gina looked down the bend in the Creek toward her house. Ever since she was a little girl, Gina would stand on this bridge and imagine an Indian Village downstream where her house was located. Her house! Maybe Ben was there? Gina ran back to the Firebird, jumped in, and drove home.

Nick heard Gina pulling up to the house. He poured what was left of his chips into his mouth, went out the sliding doors and quietly slid their red canoe into the Creek. Nick slithered into the canoe's wet bottom where he couldn't be seen, and gingerly paddled away, not leaving a ripple.

Ben's car wasn't there. Gina headed right into the kitchen and approached the stove to start cooking something. She saw her reflection in the bottom of the copper pot and thought to herself, '*God I look old.*' She wondered why the dirty pan was on the stove and called out, "Ben, Ben! Are you home? Please, honey. Please, let's talk." There was no response. As she walked through the house, she hoped Ben was there, just giving her the silent treatment. When Ben was young, Gina used to call him *a quiet storm.* When they were first married, Ben would shut Gina out when he was hurt, brooding. Then he'd finally unleash a verbal outburst that was never commensurate with the initial infraction Gina might have inflicted upon him. If Ben unleashed on her today however, she would have a well-deserved category five hurricane coming her way. Gina opened the sliding doors and looked for Ben outside, hoping he was snoozing in one of the hammocks. He wasn't, so Gina went back inside.

Oh, why did I do that last night? Gina felt rudderless, and she needed to feel better. She'd just have to make something delicious and eat it. That would change her mood. Vlad and Princess ran toward the street, tails wagging, and Gina looked out the front window to see her sister Tina in her red Jeep. Tina was always *dropping in.*

"Hey, Sis! Why aren't you at the Pet Store? I just stopped by to see you. Well, really, I needed some fish food. Why are you home on a weekday? Everything cool?"

"Want some wine?"

"Wine? This time of day? Oh, this is going to be good, or bad! Did you finally throw Ben out? Did he do something to you? I knew it. Tell me everything. I'll beat that jerk to a pulp. Where is he?"

"We had a fight, a big one. Your name came up, by the way."

"What happened? More importantly, who said what about me?"

"I wish I knew. It all happened so fast. Sometimes I think this kitchen has a mind of its own."

"You're blaming the kitchen now? I definitely need some wine. Large glass, please. Since you don't know what happened, do you want to hear about my shift last night? The hospital has been crayyyyzyyy lately."

"Sure, I could use a distraction. White or red?"

"When will that mac n' cheese be ready?"

"An hour or so."

"White it is. So, there's this patient on my floor who's been in a body cast for a month. He's covered from head to toe, except for a few openings. He looks like a Mummy, except for the eye, mouth, and butt holes," Tina stated, laughing, "but he hasn't said more than a couple of words the whole time I've been his nurse. It's kind of spooky when you look at him, you know?"

"I can imagine."

"Every day a woman comes to visit, spends the day, talks to him and cries the entire time. She kisses his cast, cries some more, and leaves. He never says a word back. Not a word. Everyday."

"So, what's the deal?" Gina asked as she handed Tina a large glass of wine.

Tina sips the wine. "This is good. Pinot?"

"Yes, Italian. So, what gives?"

"Well, this morning, I'm tired, finishing my shift, my feet hurt, and I have to ask the guy what's up? He tells me that's his wife, who's visiting every day. So, I ask him why he doesn't talk to her. He tells me her name is Gladys, they've been married forty-two years, live in Miami Shores, and since he retired, she's been bombarding him daily with chores around the house. For about a month, Gladys has been bugging him to pressure clean the barrel tiles on the roof. He finally decides to shut her the hell up and clean the roof. He goes up there with rubber boots, and the pressure cleaner hose. Gladys is so happy she could just burst. Gladys yells up to him that he needs to be careful, and to please tie a rope around himself, so he won't fall off the roof. He's just happy to shut Gladys up, so he heads down the ladder, ties one end of a rope around his waist, and ties the other end to the bumper of their brand new 1973 Ford Country Squire station wagon."

Gina took five types of cheese out of the fridge: camembert, gruyere, swiss, white sharp cheddar, and provolone, along with a red onion, butter, garlic, salt, and truffle oil. "Go ahead, I'm listening."

"So, my patient, Juan, tells me he climbed back up the ladder and walked to the opposite side of the roof to start cleaning, as Gladys sat in her kitchen thinking about what a pain in the ass she's been to him since he retired. She decided to do something nice for him and bake him a cake. Gladys took out her stained recipe cards, her most important inheritance from her Aunt Sarah. She took out the marble cake recipe; Juan's favorite. Gladys gathered the necessary ingredients and discovered she was out of eggs. She grabbed her purse and keys, and ran out the door, shouting up to Juan that she was heading to the store. Juan couldn't hear a thing over the thudding noise of the pressure cleaner and didn't see Gladys leave."

"She didn't???!!"

"Oh, she did! Gladys was so excited about making that marble cake for Juan, that she didn't realize he was tied to the bumper of her car."

"No!"

"Yes! Gladys pulled out of the driveway, felt the car yank, only to look into her rearview mirror to see Juan hurtling off the roof, toward the station wagon's back window. Gladys hit the brakes, but that only served to stop Juan's momentum and he came crashing to the ground in the driveway."

Gina didn't know why, but she broke out laughing hysterically, which only set Tina off laughing in mid-sip, wine snorting through her nose. They both looked up to see Vlad, who was lying on his back, with his feet up in the air, muzzle open, making what could only be described as laughing sounds. They all sat there laughing for the longest time.

Looking down at her ingredients, Gina realized she forgot the sour cream, which she retrieved from the fridge. She took down a large pot and filled it with water from the pot filler over the stove. When she installed the pot filler, Ben laughed at her saying that it was a luxury she would never use, but now they both viewed it as an absolute necessity. She lit a burner and went into the pantry. Gina returned with a box of Italian farfalle pasta, and a colander. She preferred farfelle to elbow macaroni, or penne, as it held an even layer of cheese and stayed al dente longer than the others.

It was 9:45 in the morning, but she poured herself, and Tina another glass of wine. Gina sipped the wine, watching the water come to a boil. She took down a large saucepan, placed it on the stove, and lit the burner, waiting a few seconds while the gas burner heated the pan. She poured some truffle oil into the pan, swirled it, added the onions she diced, and then all five cheeses, and asked, "So, is he going to speak with her again?"

"He's not sure, but I know one thing?"

"What's that?"

"She's never going to give that man a honey-do list again."

Vlad fell back on the floor again, feet dancing in the air, with his mouth opening and shutting like he was trying to grab a slow flying bee.

"What's up with Vlad, Sis?"

"I have no idea, Tina. If I didn't know any better, I would swear he was laughing."

"You know, he is laughing! And, he's had the weirdest expression on his face lately. You might want to take Vlad to see Ms. Alice, the animal psychic."

"Oh, sure. Right after I get my horoscope done."

"I'm serious, Sis. Ms. Alice is the real deal, and that dog seems possessed."

"What are you talking about, Tina? He's..." Gina's words stopped short in her mouth as Vlad came out from under the kitchen table. He was wearing a clown's mask. Gina turned white. Cold chills ran up her body.

"Everything okay, Gina? You look even more ghostly white than usual."

"I think you're right, Tina. After we eat, we better go see Ms. Alice."

17

*G*ina and Tina's Father, Frank Phylaxis, worked as a bus driver in Orange, New Jersey, and because of this, he dreaded getting out of bed every day. He fantasized about moving out of the snow, slush, and muck of Jersey since his second day on the job, when a drunk man, fumbling for bus fare, threw up all over Frank's new uniform.

Two years later, while reading the Sunday paper Frank found a Real Estate ad for Sun Ray homes in North Miami Beach, Florida. It was a quiet place back in the 40's. Safe, close to the beach, good schools, and what really called to Frank and his wife Anna, two Italian Markets: Rippy's and Laurenzo's. Although Anna was an amazing cook, it wasn't just about the food, it meant their people had a foothold in the community.

Frank's time in the Army took an emotional toll on him, but like most of the members of the greatest generation, he never talked about it. On the bright side, being a Veteran qualified Frank for a GI Loan. Back then, $500 down, and $50 a month, would buy a family a decent three bedroom, two bath home. Frank and Anna packed their belongings, and their young daughters, Tina and Gina, into their Chevy Fleetline and headed south.

Ever since Frank was eight years old, he had a dream. It all started with a goldfish he'd won at a carnival. He brought it home and was captivated. He loved watching the orange fins glisten in the sunbeams from the window in his dimly lit room. He loved the way the fish undulated in the water when it gulped down food. He loved how the fish pressed its lips to the side of the bowl and frantically swam up and down following Frank's finger. Frank knew it was probably just hungry, looking for food, but the magic inside of the eight-year-old imagined the fish talking to him.

Frank rushed home from school just to see what the fish had to say that day. He spent hours in his parent's basement, growing his fish collection and learning all he could about fish behavior, breeding, and nutritional requirements. Frank had fresh water and saltwater fish tanks, which were very uncommon back then.

He took such wonderful care of his pets, that they started breeding prolifically. Frank sold their offspring to his friends and a neighborhood Pet Store. While Frank was an excellent fish hobbyist, his business skills were not so great. He sunk all of his profits back into his pets, and over the years, Frank's fish collection grew from a goldfish bowl to twenty-six fish tanks. He knew then what he wanted to be when he grew up: a Pet Store Owner.

When they moved south, Frank needed three things: a job that would only last long enough for him to qualify for a mortgage, a nice house, and the perfect location for a Pet Shop. Until then, Frank and Anna rented two adjoining hotel rooms in a quaint hotel on Biscayne Boulevard. Soon after arriving, a neighbor in Jersey had a nephew in Miami, who gave Frank a job at his bakery.

Anna was a stunning, but reserved, intelligent beauty. She was quick-witted, even-tempered, well-read, and polite to a fault. She could have gone to college, but instead like most women in the 40's, she fell in love, got married, and had a couple of kids.

She had long sandy blonde hair, and just like the trait she passed onto Gina, two different colored eyes—one copper, and one turquoise, but in Anna's case, the left eye was turquoise. Anna dressed like she lived in the 1,800s. She wore long, brightly colored skirts, flowing long sleeve blouses, and carried a parasol in her white lace gloves whenever she ventured outdoors. She looked and behaved like she just floated out of the English Countryside, only with a Jersey accent.

While Frank worked, Anna spent her days searching for houses in North Miami Beach. Three days later, Anna left the girls in the hotel pool, and with a folded newspaper ad on the front seat of the Chevy, she found it by accident: the perfect house.

Anna was driving down Biscayne Boulevard and something made her turn onto 135 Street in North Miami. She was impressed with the Giant Oaks and peaceful vibe. She didn't know why, but she found herself purposefully driving north on 16 Avenue. On the first street in, past some giant Oaks there was a for sale sign with an arrow pointing east on 137 Place.

It wasn't until years later that the street was renamed Enchanted Place, but Anna knew this place was enchanted before she arrived. Anna slowly drove down the Oak lined Street and found herself transported to an ageless era. While she was never one to brag, she knew deep down that there was something special about her. Something magical. And she felt this is where her creativity would bloom, where Tina and Gina could let their spirits soar, and where Frank would feel at peace.

At the very end of the street, there it was: a charming, barn-red, three-bedroom, two-bath, wood frame home nestled in the woods. The house was built on a lot directly on Arch Creek. Anna loved the idea of being right on the water, but worried about flooding. George Washington, the realtor, assured her it was fine.

"I just love it, but of course, I have to come back with my husband. The only thing I am concerned about is flooding. I mean, the house is right on a canal, and this is South Florida."

"Mrs. Phylaxis, please step into the backyard with me for a moment, and I'll show you something that should put your mind at ease."

"Thank you, and please call me Anna, Mr. Washington."

"Only if you call me George, please."

"May I inquire, did your parents give you that name on purpose? It certainly gets one's attention."

"That is does. And when people meet me, and discover I'm a black man, well, let's just say it leads to some interesting facial expressions I have learned to overlook."

"Some people have no class, Mr. Wash... I mean, George."

"That's a nice way of putting it, Anna."

"Maybe one day in the future, people will learn that we are all spun from the same cloth, George."

"That would be a most welcome future, Anna. In fact, people of all colors and races have lived in this very place. This Creek was sacred to the Native Americans who lived here. If you look toward the south, past the bend, the

Creek winds under a stone bridge on 135 Street. For many years, the Native Americans used that area as a mill to grind Coontie into flour. In fact, not long ago there were big companies with Coontie mills in Miami. One was located right here. They used the flour to make animal crackers. Coontie is a native plant that attracts Atala butterflies. Have you ever seen one, Anna?"

"An Atala butterfly, or the Coontie plant? We don't get that lucky in New Jersey, George," Anna said, laughing. She didn't know why, but she felt an instant kinship with George. Like she had known him before or was to know him again.

"Well then, this must be your lucky day, Anna, because there are dozens of Coonties right along the Creek bank, and I see an Atala butterfly on one of them now."

"Ohhhh. It's so beautiful. I've never seen a butterfly with iridescent blue spots, and that big orange spot is stunning."

"The Native Americans say butterflies are the reincarnated souls of their ancestors. They are supposed to bring good luck, as long as you don't cross them."

"Cross them?"

"You know, like polluting the Creek. This Creek's waters flow all the way from the Everglades to Biscayne Bay. The Tequesta, and then the Seminole Indians, all roamed this land. I would even argue that evidence suggests, even Calusa Indians lived here. Some of the larger Oaks on this property, and in the surrounding area, provided the Native Americans with shade, shelter, and dry hunting ground for deer."

"Why, George, you sound like a scholar."

"Yes, why actually, I do teach a bit."

"A teacher! How wonderful. Can you please tell me more about the area? Frank, my husband, had his heart set on North Miami Beach, so I'm going to need to convince him otherwise." Anna knew that Frank adored her and would do anything to make her happy, but she wanted to paint as attractive a picture as she could for him, so he would think it was his decision. Dime-store psychology applied to their husbands, was yet another gift women of Anna's generation excelled in.

"Oh, I would be pleased to, Anna. Arch Creek has a very rich history. It was settled in the 1800's while a few Native Americans still roamed these woods."

"I notice you refer to them as Native Americans?"

"Why, yes. They were here long before us, and hopefully one day, all people will refer to them as such. There is a push to do so in the world of academia I live in; however, I think we are several generations out before people stop calling them Indians. You know how they got that name?"

"Why, yes. I read that Columbus mistakenly thought he had landed in the Indies, when he made it to North America, and called the inhabitants Indians."

"Why, I see I'm not the only scholar here," George replied.

"Well, I do love reading, and history."

George's eyes lit up when he discovered he had met a kindred spirit. "Well, then this might interest you. In the 1850's, the US Army built a military trail connecting Fort Dallas, at the mouth of the Miami River to Fort Lauderdale. Down there, where The Arch Creek Bridge stands, was part of that first roadway built in Dade County. It was quite the battle cutting an eight-foot-wide road through the dense, mosquito filled vegetation. A big portion of this area became farmland, producing, tomatoes, sugar cane, Coontie, bananas, pineapples, and a virtual feast of fresh produce. At one point there was a Stagecoach stop here. The Arch Creek Bridge was the last stop on the sightseeing boat that started its tour at the mouth of the Miami River. People would picnic here next to the Bridge. The Arch Creek Railroad Depot was just up the road on 125 Street, straight down those tracks. The 1940 census records show our population is now almost at 2,000. Experts predict there could be as many as 10,000 people living here by 1950. So, in terms of your husband, you could honestly say North Miami is a great investment, and one of the fastest growing Towns in the Nation."

"That's very impressive, George. I didn't realize realtors were so knowledgeable on local history."

"You might say, I enjoy educating people, Anna. For instance, those oysters I was telling you about. You see, the oysters and clams provided food, and are also this house's strongest selling point."

"What's that? Besides the kitchen, which is fabulous, right?"

"The kitchen is a chef's dream. The original owner was Wekiwa Sawgrass, the first woman chef to open a restaurant in Miami. That was back in 1919."

"She really, really, must have loved to cook. The kitchen layout is amazing, and all of those copper pots, and the stocked pantry. Do they come with the house?"

"As a matter of fact, they do. It's in the deed. And when you sell it, you must pass on the kitchenware as well."

"I'm not planning on moving out anytime soon. I, I mean we, must have you for dinner when we move in."

"Looks like I may have made a sale?"

"I still have to come back with my husband, but I do love this place. It's so tranquil, and those Oaks. They must be a hundred years old."

"Hundreds!"

"So, what was that again about the house's strongest selling point?"

"Sorry, we were having such a pleasant conversation, I forgot I was trying to sell you a house. It's the oysters and clams in the Creek."

"They do make an excellent Frutti De Mar sauce, you know. Now I know what to make when we have you for dinner. If we buy the house, that is."

"Sounds delicious. The Native Americans loved eating those shellfish too, and do you know what they did with all of the shells from their dinner?"

"Made castanets?" Anna said, laughing.

"Ha. After they ate their fill, the shells were discarded, and there were lots and lots of shells. The more shells, the higher the ground. This house is built on the highest shell mound in the area, so no need to worry about flooding. And, one other thing to consider; to the Native Americans this was sacred ground."

"So, butterflies with ancient Indian souls, and sacred shell mounds. You certainly paint quite a romantic picture of ancient South Florida, and this house."

"I'm not sure about romantic, but the Native Americans had a sense of symbiosis with the land, that most races lack."

"Why, George, you are a poet at heart."

"Well, I wouldn't go that far, but I do appreciate the land here and the people who want to live on it. That's one reason I became a realtor. I want to make sure each property gets the right owner. I also have a somewhat vested interest in this property that I must disclose."

"Oh? What's that?"

"You see the house next door?"

"There's so many Oaks here, I barely noticed there was a house there. Now I see it."

"It looks beautiful. Very natural. Who lives there?"

"I do."

18

It didn't take long to get the mortgage approved by the bank. Shortly after, Frank found a 2,000 square foot space for lease on Biscayne Boulevard literally across the Creek from their home. He could walk to work. As a bonus, the property backed up to the Creek, which would provide an endless supply of brackish water for that crossbreeding experiment between fresh and saltwater fish that Frank thought of when he was twelve. Frank borrowed $1,000 from his parents, signed a lease, and opened Goldfish & More. At the time, it was only one of two Pet Stores for miles around.

As a child, Gina loved coming to the Pet Store. Like her Father, she was mesmerized by the colorful tropical fish and loved listening to the customers talk about them. Some people liked the small, live bearing fish, like Swordtails and Guppies, others liked the larger, and more ferocious Cichlids from Africa and the Amazon. Gina loved all of them, but her favorites were the saltwater fish and the outer space looking invertebrates, especially the red and white striped coral shrimp that resembled a spider mixed with a candy cane.

In the 1940s, Biscayne Bay was abundant with many species of tropical fish. Frank was able to net the saltwater fish, shrimp, and crabs, simply by snorkeling in the Bay, or the coral reefs right off the shore of Miami Beach, Key Biscayne, and Hollywood. Not only did this save him the expense of having to purchase the fish, but he loved the peacefulness of snorkeling and simply watching the fish in their native environment. It was as if Frank discovered the world's largest aquarium. Gina loved snorkeling as well and would often accompany her Father in his hunt for fish.

Tina on the other hand, could care less about fish. Thankfully for Frank, Anna had a keen business sense and did the ordering and bookkeeping. Goldfish & More actually turned a healthy profit over the years, and attracted a loyal customer base. Ten years later, Frank suffered a widow-maker heart attack and died. Anna held Frank's hand as he took his last breath in their backyard, in a hammock, right beside the Creek. She took over the Pet Store with help from her girls, who came every day before and after school to help clean tanks, feed the fish, and serve customers. Gina loved this work, while Tina would usually slip out the back door to make out with her boyfriend du jour.

Tina was the oldest, the best student, and the prettiest. Everyone knew it, but nobody in the family said it out loud. She was 5'7 with two sparkling green eyes. She had big, 1970's Farrah Faucet hair, even before Farrah Faucet had it, and a curvaceous body to match. While she always had a brilliant, witty, utilitarian mind, she enjoyed utilizing her body even more. Simply put, Tina loved sex. She loved the feeling of another body next to hers, in the act of pleasure. It was in fact, her favorite pastime, and as a child of the 50's, she wasn't shy about it. Tina was like a Country Song personified, with a slight New Jersey accent, especially when she said *chawcolate* or *Jerzee*. She graduated nursing school three years after her Father's death, knowing that she'd wanted to be a nurse since the first time she heard it was the best way to get a hot doctor.

Gina knew she wanted to run the Pet Store from the first time she netted a black and silver Angelfish into a bag for a customer. After high school, Gina started running Goldfish & More. She loved everything about it. To Gina, the Pet Store was magical. She even lost her virginity there to Sam. God, he was sexy. The sex, like most first times for women, was fast, furious, and forgettable. In fact, her only fleeting memory of the experience, was looking up through the glass bottom of a tank full of Fancy Tailed Guppies. The fish seemed to be watching her. At one point, she could swear the fish schooled and spelled out the words, 'Beware the Creature in the Creek!', but she knew this was just her guilty mind playing tricks on her.

Gina had lots of ideas for expansion and decided to add a puppy section. She only worked with small family breeders from South Florida and kept just one litter of pups on hand at a time. The first night Gina tried to lock up the store with a litter of five crying German Shepherd puppies, she just couldn't leave them. She scooped them into a box and brought them home to sleep in her room. This was to be the way with all puppies from the shop. One night, she came home with a litter of four beagle puppies and found the front door ajar.

"Mom! Come here. You have to see these Beagle puppies. They are the cutest things. I'm keeping one."

"It's me, Sis."

"Hey, Tina. What are you doing here? I thought you had a hot date tonight with that dreamy doctor?" Gina looked deep into her sister's eyes and just knew. "Mom?"

Tina grabbed Gina and held her close as she whispered in her ear, "I'm sorry, Sis. So sorry." Gina burst into tears and heaved against her sister's chest. After what seemed liked forever, she let go of Tina's waist. It was the first time she could ever recall that she let go before Tina did. Gina reached into the laundry basket full of beagle pups, took out the toughest looking one, and held it to her chest, like she would never let it go. Gina looked at her sister, her pleading eyes asking for an explanation that she wasn't sure her shattering heart could handle.

"We were in a car accident. It was bad. Very bad," Tina said, choking on the words, "Mom's in the ICU. They don't expect her to recover."

The next morning, the girls went to the hospital to sign the papers to take Anna off life support. To their surprise, Anna kept breathing.

19

Herman Fox learned to make brisket watching his grandmother in her Brooklyn kitchen at the turn of the 20th Century. His grandmother told him it was a secret family recipe and got its sweetness from the prunes she baked with the meat. When Herman was twelve, he caught his grandmother in the kitchen, sipping from a bottle of bourbon. He watched from the hallway as she poured a large mouthful, then made several pours onto the uncooked brisket.

Herman walked into the kitchen laughing. "I knew it wasn't the prunes, Nanny."

"You caught me! Don't tell anyone. About the brisket, I mean. The rest of the family knows I drink like a Gefilte Fish." Nanny gave him a big wink. "Don't worry, Herman. I'll have a toast with you on your Bar Mitzvah."

The next night, Herman snuck into the counter over the sink, took a big swig of bourbon, choked, and spit it on the floor. It was the most awful thing he ever tasted, but Nanny's brisket was the best. Herman's family was lower middle class. All ten of them, his parents, grandparents, Aunt Lynn and Uncle Warren, their kids, and his sister, lived in a three-bedroom apartment in Sheepshead Bay, Brooklyn.

Even at twelve, Herman knew he didn't belong here. He felt a greatness inside of him. He believed in himself. One day, he didn't know why, he took the subway to the Financial District. He was energized watching the quick-paced, well-dressed, men and women walking in and out of doors held open by doormen. Herman looked up at the tall, dirty buildings, and thought to himself, *'This is where I belong.'* He walked and walked, up and down Wall Street. It was only 8 AM, but the food vendors were setting up their shiny aluminum food carts for lunch. Hot dogs, hot nuts, bagels, chicken shawarma, ice cream, snow cones, gyros, bagels, pizza, everything you could dream of to fill your belly.

Right before noon, Herman watched in fascination as hundreds and hundreds of men and women, anxious to get back to work, practically threw money at the vendors. Herman thought, *'Now I know why they call this the Financial District.'* Over three hours, Herman walked purposely, checking out each food cart. He had $1.50 on him, money he saved from all of his birthdays, so he walked down the street and ate every kind of food there was. There was one thing obviously missing: Nanny's Brisket. Herman was convinced he could make a fortune here selling brisket, but not just brisket, because he also observed how much of a rush these people were in. Herman had an epiphany. He was going to make brisket sandwiches! Fast food for fast moving people. Herman would sell hundreds of them. Thousands! He was going to make a fortune! He was going to be sick! After Herman threw up, he realized something else very important. You can't mix hot dogs, French fries, hot nuts, bagels, chicken shawarma, ice cream, snow cones, gyros, bagels, and pizza, with three cherry cokes.

Undeterred, Herman headed home, burst into the kitchen, and shouted to his grandmother, "We're going to be rich!!!"

2 0

ina finished baking the mac n' cheese, then put it on the top rack of the oven and turned on the broiler. She poured another glass of wine for Tina, and a glass filled to the top for herself.

"That smells amazing."

"Thanks. It will be ready in a minute, as soon as the breadcrumbs crisp and the cheese bubbles brown."

"Yum."

Gina carefully watched the baking dish through the oven door. It was easy to burn a great dish under the broiler. It was like the broiler was just waiting for you to look away for a second or two, and then, nothing but char on a perfectly good dish. Gina put on her Betty Boop oven mitts, opened the oven door, and reached in.

"I've got you, my pretty!" Gina said, as she plucked the red Le Creuset baking dish from the oven. Tina danced over to the kitchen cabinet and retrieved two forks.

"I don't have your patience," Tina said, as she handed Gina a fork and dug hers into the baking dish. As she did, steam floated gently toward her face, and a non-yielding, thick trail of cheese followed her fork, from the dish to her lips.

"This is delicious, and ouch! So, damn hot! It's burning the roof of my mouth, but in a good way. God, this is like rough sex. It sort of hurts, but it's sooooo good, you don't want it to stop. Know what I mean?"

"Mom always said you had a kinky mind, Tina," Gina said, laughing as she dug her fork into the baking dish and lifted a small forkful of deliciousness into her mouth. She got down two large pasta bowls, filling them halfway, and set them on the table.

"Let's eat. I have to get to the Pet Store. Those creatures get very cranky when they miss breakfast."

"Aren't you going to tell me where Ben is? What happened last night? Come on, I'm dying here."

"The whole point of comfort food, is comfort. They don't call it upsetting food, do they? I'm still not ready to talk about last night, Tina. Distract me with something good. Tell me about your love life. "

"Okay, Let's eat. I'll tell you about my night, and boy, was that comforting. So, I stop in to check on Juan. You know, the guy in the body cast?"

"How could I forget? Did he ever get that marble cake?"

"Funny you should ask. Gladys brought two marble cakes yesterday; one for Juan, and one for the nursing staff. Juan wouldn't give Gladys the satisfaction of her watching him eat it, but I fed him two pieces after she left. Juan was tired and fell asleep before he finished the second piece of cake, and in walks the cutest guy I ever saw. I mean he was beautiful. So, I look at him and put my finger to my mouth and make a *shsshh* motion, point to Juan, tilt my head, put my hands under my head, and close my eyes."

"Mom always said you could have been an actress."

"Very funny. So, this guy, he's so hot. He likes my little pantomime and laughs without any noise coming out. I figure, let's take this to the next level. I walk over to the empty bed on the other side of Juan's room, sit on the bed, cross my legs, and make a come-hither motion with my index finger."

"Keep talking, this is getting good."

"This guy is gorgeous, and charming. He points at himself, like *who me?* Then he winks."

"I point at him again, shake my head up and down. He walks over very, very slowly, and sits next to me on the bed. I have never been so excited in my life."

"You didn't. Right there in a patient's room?"

"Keep your skirt on, Sis!"

"I'll bet you didn't!" Gina replied, laughing.

"Actually, I did. He sat next to me, and we just looked at each other for the longest time. Then he took me in his arms and lay me down."

"I knew you wouldn't let me down."

"Hey, I'm not a total slut. Well, yes I am," said Tina with a wink. "Then he lies down next to me, and I think, finally."

"There's the Tina we all know and love."

"Normally, I would agree, but all he did was lie next to me and hold my hand. We are both very quiet. I can feel him breathing. At the same precise moment, we turn to face each. Realize we haven't spoken a word this entire time."

"Got it, so then you jumped his bones?"

"That's the thing, Sis, all we did was gaze into each other's eyes, smiling. It was the strangest connection I ever felt to another human. We didn't move until the sun came through the window. Then we both got up, hugged each other like we were an old married couple, smiled and he started to walk away."

"Wait, that's it?"

"You don't understand, Gina. I'm in love."

"Love. You didn't even kiss him."

"This is the first time I ever felt real love in my life, and it has nothing to do with sex. Can you imagine that?"

"Not in my wildest dreams. Tina, not sleeping with a guy. Go figure. So, what's his name, and when are you going to see him again?"

"That's the thing. When he was leaving, I asked him for his name and phone number, or if he wanted mine. He just looked at me, smiled and said, "Don't worry. I'll find you!"

"So, you don't even know his name?"

"Not even his name. I asked the morning shift nurse, and she said she thought the guy was Juan's nephew, but she wasn't sure."

"I'm very happy for you two, or at least you. Do you think he was messing with you? Maybe someone you jilted wants to get even?"

"No, Gina, this was the real thing."

"Do you think you will see him again."

"The funny thing is, I just know I will."

"I hope it works out for you, Tina. Even sluts deserve true love," Gina said as she playfully patted Tina's butt. "Come on. I have critters to feed at the Store. Are you coming?"

"That's what she said. Hah, but yeah, I'll meet you there. I need some fish food."

Gina took Vlad's leash off the hook by the door and called him over, "Vlad, Vlad, come here." Vlad pranced over and licked Gina's hand. Princess followed close behind, wagging her tail. Gina snapped the leash onto Vlad's collar as Princess licked her hand. "Sorry girl, you don't need a dog psychic." As Princess sulked away, Tina held her pasta bowl to the Beagle's face and let her lick the cheese off.

"Tina, stop! You are teaching her it's okay to eat from the table."

"So, it's not true then?"

"What?"

"You can't teach an old dog a new trick?"

Gina, Tina, and Vlad headed out the front door and toward the car. Vlad turned back to face the disappointed Princess, looked up at the sisters, and peed all over the car door.

"Vlad! Bad boy. What has gotten into you?" Gina said admonishingly.

"I don't know, Sis, but we're about to find out."

21

By the time Wekiwa was seventeen, people traveled near and far to eat her food and see Rainbow. Some came to the Everglades by boat down the Miami River, on horseback, or covered wagon through the Glades.

When Wekiwa was eighteen, she was fully a woman, and a striking one at that. A man who trekked from Miami ate her food every night for a month, ordering one of each dish Wekiwa made, and talking to her as she prepared his food. His name was Ernest Thirst, and he soon became a fixture at the camp.

Ernest was a burly man, with a rugged handsome face, and piercing, light green eyes. He was 5'10, had huge shoulders and arms, and walked with an almost imperceptible limp. He was much hairier than the Native American men. He looked like a lumberjack, and in fact had done some logging in the great Northwest until a redwood tree fell in the wrong direction and landed on his right leg. The tree practically crushed his leg, but Ernest was strong of mind, body, and spirit. He recovered quickly, and remained in the logging camp, as a cook. To his surprise, he discovered that he loved cooking. The creativity, the smells, the tastes, and the compliments his dishes consistently received.

After a few years, the cold and dampness of Washington State had taken its toll on him, and his leg. Ernest took the money he made as a cook, bought a sturdy horse, wagon, and provisions, and headed as far away from the

Olympic Peninsula as possible. He came to Miami and found the perfect place to open a restaurant. Then he heard about this bewitchingly beautiful maiden whose cooking rivaled all others.

Ernest hitched up his horse and wagon, and drove to the Everglades, sleeping on the edge of the camp every night. He waited in the long lines and ordered a plate of every dish Wekiwa made for a solid month. He loved talking to her about her recipes, and Wekiwa enjoyed having someone new to speak with about her cooking ideas, and theirs. Some nights, Wekiwa would meet Ernest for walks in the woods, and although she had the body of a Vegas Hooker, she was still a virgin. She loved the power this held over men, and had not wanted to surrender that, until she met Ernest. There was something about him, how he looked at her, how he spoke to her. It was like for the first time in her life, someone got her.

Ernest was polite, and never pushed himself on Wekiwa. While he found her beauty and sex appeal extremely alluring, he was equally as interested in her cooking. One evening, Wekiwa came to Ernest's camp to try out a new recipe. It was for fried cakes made of Coontie flour, Pond Apples, herbs from her garden, ground passionflower, and to top them off, a sauce of Florida Red Maple syrup and Cocoplum preserves.

Ernest told Wekiwa if she came with him to Miami, he would set her up as the chef for his restaurant. He found the perfect spot, right on the Miami River. He even brought some of the water from the mouth of the River for Wekiwa to taste. The camp water always tasted like sulfur, and Wekiwa enjoyed the River water so much, she used it in her fried cake recipe. The cakes were delicious, and the Red Maple cocoplum sauce was a big hit. This sold the deal for Ernest Thirst. He told Wekiwa that between her looks, cooking, and her panther sidekick, they would be famous in no time. She was tempted by this offer but objected because she thought the camp and her Mother needed her. She was, after all, the future of the tribe.

Ernest told Wekiwa she would make so much money that she could send it home each month to help develop the camp-running water, electricity, and everything they could ever want or need. Wekiwa was excited by the idea, and the great power it summoned in her soul. She became so excited that for the first time in her young life, she felt lust in her heart and loins. She patted Rainbow on the head and told her to wait for her as she climbed into Ernest's wagon. Wekiwa took her dress off one shoulder, and then the other. As her dress fell to the floor of the Wagon, she winked and called down to Ernest, "Well, get up here already!" Ernest had never seen a more voluptuous creature as Wekiwa standing nude and fully tanned before him. Her pert bronze nipples pointed upwards, reflecting the light of the full moon onto Ernest's face, beckoning him skyward.

Ernest looked longingly at Wekiwa and then at Rainbow who was giving him a menacing look. "What about Rainbow?"

"There's only one pussy you have to worry about around here Ernest," Wekiwa said as she motioned for him to come to her with her index finger.

22

nna seemed tough as nails, but the long-ago accident still haunted her. She was driving the Chevy on Interstate 95. Tina was with her. They were heading to the Ft. Lauderdale Airport to pick up Anna's sister. They just entered the highway at the 125th Street entrance and despite the lateness of the hour, there was a lot of traffic for a Saturday night at 10:00 PM. Spring breakers in town always clogged the roads, and even the dollars the tourists brought to the local economy wasn't worth the hundreds of cars whizzing by like racecar drivers.

"Geez, Mom. I can't believe how many cars are on the road this late."

"Spring breakers!" Anna had barely finished her sentence when she felt a huge thud.

"What was that, Ma?"

"That truck just smashed us!"

A white Ford truck one lane over on their left side couldn't brake in time to avoid crashing into the car ahead of it, and instead of just rear-ending it, the truck driver decided to make a sharp right into Anna's lane. The truck impacted just behind Anna's seat; the force of the heavy truck crashing into the equally stout Chevy sent it spinning across four lanes of highway into the far-left lane, heading directly into oncoming traffic. Anna gripped the steering wheel as she looked into the headlights of cars flying at her at sixty-five miles per hour, trying her best to steer around them. "Fuck,

Fuck, Fuck!" Anna yelled, as three sets of oncoming headlights approached, and she miraculously missed each one. Pretty impressive feat driving on just two wheels. From there, the Chevy flipped over and over and over, until at last, it landed in the same far right lane it had started in. When the car was back on all four wheels, Tina opened her eyes, and Anna was starring directly at her.

"Ma, you okay?"

Anna remembered the look on Tina's face. Anna tried to speak, but nothing came out. For the first time since the truck sent them on their wild ride into traffic, Anna felt scared. What really threw her was how calm, cool, and collected Tina looked. She had that same expression on her face when she napped as a small child. Tina looked Zen-like. Anna thought, *'How could she be so calm during this, and why the hell can't I speak? And what's that all over me? Blood? Why am I shaking like this? I hope that blood is mine and not Tina's.'*

"Ma! Ma! Are you okay? Tina yelled louder and louder. Anna was having some type of seizure and convulsing uncontrollably. Just then, a small Hispanic man opened Tina's crushed passenger side door. He held a knife in his hand.

"I'm here in the name of Jesus! I can cut you out of your seatbelt."

"Am I dead?" Tina asked.

"No. I told you, lady, Jesus sent me."

"Yeah, yeah," Tina said, "where the fuck was Jesus two minutes ago?"

"Ay, dios mio," the small man said as he crossed himself and walked away, shaking his head.

Besides a small cut on her knee and a scratch on her back, Tina walked away physically unscathed. Anna broke her collarbone, both legs, and three ribs. She had numerous internal injuries that the surgeons deemed inoperable. How she hung onto life for a year was a mystery to everyone, especially her doctors.

During her year asleep, Anna had visions into the other world. The World of the Dearly Departed. But, the beings she saw hadn't departed yet. They were spirits, trapped between life and the afterlife. It was Anna's eyes, her mismatched, turquoise and copper eyes, that allowed her to see into both worlds, and the place in between.

The spirits would have talked to her 24/7 if she let them, but she didn't.

She enjoyed hearing about their lives, but there were so many of them, with so, so many tales to tell. After a while, the constant drone of kvetching spirits was like an overwhelming trip to a noisy beauty parlor. So, she set limits. Anna told the spirits they would have to make appointments to speak with her, and no more than three at a time.

Meanwhile, in the real world, except for the multitude of penises she enjoyed, Tina was impenetrable. However, the shock of the accident, and the extent of her Mother's injuries softened her. While she hadn't found true love in a mate, she truly loved her family. Her mother and Gina meant everything to her.

Tina always felt like her childhood was charmed. While she remembered the magical feelings of her life before Gina was born, they became even stronger once Gina was around. Gina was adorable from the start. She was like a little clone of her Mother, mismatched eyes and all. She was a tiny baby, and the cutest thing Tina ever saw. It was love at first sight.

They slept in the same room, and every morning, Tina was first on the scene when Gina woke up. Gina would babble on in baby language, and Tina would speak to her in full sentences; just like she spoke with everyone else. Tina loved watching her little sister grow and learn. It was amazing to her that this little human could learn so much on a daily basis. One morning, Gina blew a kiss to Tina through her crib bars. She decided there and then that Gina was her baby too. They spent their childhood years in an idyllic, blissful state.

Once they moved to North Miami, Tina used to tell her friends she was raised on a magic Indian mound in an Enchanted Forest. They spent their early days playing on the Creek bank, swimming, canoeing, picnicking under the Oaks, dressing up and pretending to be Indians, singing around their firepit at night, and lazily spinning in the woven hammock swings, looking up at the sun, moon, and stars. Tina had strong memories of all of these things, especially the feelings of love, total acceptance, and freedom that came with them. Thankfully, Anna recognized the delicious bond between her girls, and reveled in it. On more than one occasion, Anna told Tina that if anything ever happened to her, that she should take care of her father and little sister.

After Frank's death, Tina stepped up her game of keeping her eye on her little sister, and even her mother. Then came the accident. The car was totaled, which was not an easy thing to do to a Chevy Fleetline. Tina carried the emotional wreckage that comes after a rollover car crash. It took her a few weeks to feel comfortable behind the wheel of her VW Bug, although she never again drove on I95. Beyond that emotional distress, Tina carried a huge amount of survivor's guilt. Her Mother was comatose, nearly dead, and Tina walked away as healthy as a horse.

To complicate things, Anna remained in Tina's workplace, St. Francis hospital on Miami Beach, for three months following the accident. Every night on her way into the excitement and trauma of being an emergency room nurse, Tina went into her room to visit her Mother. Tina would sit by Anna's bed and recollect over their early days playing in and along Arch Creek. Sometimes she would talk to the unconscious Anna about the accident because she really couldn't talk to anyone else about her experience. No one would believe her anyway.

"I don't know if you saw it too, Ma? I'm still not sure I saw it, or dreamed it? When we were crossing the highway and those headlights were coming at us, I saw it, right on the windshield at first, and then over the front of the car. It was a giant hand. It picked us up, Ma. It threaded us between those other cars. Then when we flipped, the hand... the hand, Ma. It shoved us out of the way of all of those other cars and flipped us back on our wheels. Then, when it let go. I saw it, Ma. Clear as I see you now. The hand, Ma. It was wearing a pinky ring. You saw it right, Ma?" Tina was waiting for her Mother to respond in any manner. A blink, a twitch of a finger or toe. "Tell me you saw it, Ma? Tell me you saw Dad's gold pinky ring. The one with the gray star of sapphire birthstone. Tell me you saw it, Ma!" Tina sobbed. Anna did not move a muscle.

On her fourth month of care, the Hospital transferred Anna to the Arch Creek nursing home, right down the block from her house, where Tina, Gina, and George would visit daily. Anna continued to be visited by the beings from the Other World. She was getting pretty tired of the whole thing, when she heard a voice speak to her.

"It's time to go home now, Anna."

Anna listened carefully to the voice and struggled to recognize it.

"Frank? Frank, is that you?" Anna saw a hand on her arm. For a moment she thought she saw it. Frank's pinky ring on the little finger. Then she heard a voice call again.

"Anna? Anna? Are you back amongst the living?"

Anna opened her eyes, looked into the kind eyes of George Washington, and smiled.

23

*H*erman's Nanny was no fool and accompanied Herman to the Financial District to check out the food carts for herself. She looked down at Herman, patted his head, grabbed his cheek, and kissed him. "You know, your Uncle Warren has a pushcart he hasn't used since before he hurt his back. It's sitting under a blanket in his living room. If we clean that up, you know, this just might work."

Herman looked up at his Grandmother who seemed lost in thought. Then a big smile appeared on her face. Nanny stuck out her hand, "Partners?" Herman hugged her with all his might. Two weeks later, the brisket sandwich cart was set up on Wall Street, between Water and Pearl. The first three days, people mostly passed by the brisket sandwich cart, with only a few sales. Herman had keen observation skills. People walked out of their offices, seemed to have a lunch cart destination in mind, got their lunch, maybe talked to someone on the street, or even the vendor for a moment, and then headed back to work.

On the third day, with hardly a sandwich sold, Herman had a lot of hope, and a lot of brisket, which would soon go bad. He decided to try a new strategy, which he hadn't cleared with his Nanny. These people love money. Making money and probably saving money, too. What would people who love money, love the best? Free stuff! Herman took ten sandwiches from the cart and cut them into small pieces. Then, at the top of his twelve-year-old lungs, shouted, "Free Brisket. Free Brisket!!!" Within moments, much to the dismay of his neighboring vendor, Vito's Pizza, people rushed the brisket stand. They stood around chewing for a bit, long enough for Herman's very first customer to ask, "How much, kid?"

Herman promised Nanny to sell the sandwiches for ten cents, but he couldn't resist his instinct.

"Nine cents, sir."

The man looked at Herman and smiled.

"Smart kid. Beat the competition. I'll take two." The man handed Herman two dimes, Herman thanked the man, who didn't leave, and instead stuck out his hand.

"My change?"

Perhaps Herman hadn't thought this through. He only had a handful of coins. The man, seeing the flustered look on Herman's face, patted him on the head.

"It's okay, kid, but if you want to make it on Wall Street, always do what you say, and say what you do." The man walked away, eating one sandwich, and holding the other. Herman ran to the front of the cart, and tapped the man on the back, his outstretched hand holding two pennies.

"I'm sorry, mister. I should have thought that through."

The man was immediately impressed with how Herman handled the situation.

"You seem like a good kid," said the man taking the two pennies, and putting them in his pocket. "As they say in the Boy Scouts, always be prepared." The man reached into his briefcase and took out two rolls of pennies.

"I like your thinking kid. Here's a hundred pennies. That should get you through your first batch of sandwiches."

"Thank you, mister. I don't know what to say. You're the greatest."

"Greatest, smaytish. You owe me a dollar, but I'll take nine dimes, and another sandwich instead."

Herman ran back to his cart with his penny rolls, grabbed another sandwich, nine dimes, and a penny, and handed it to the man, who smiled.

"Good, you are catching on. Us Wall Street types need to feel like we are making a deal, even if it's a penny back. Capisce? You're going to make a killing, kid. I'm telling all of my friends."

The man did tell his friends and the next day, armed with 250 brisket sandwiches, and five rolls of pennies, Herman, did in fact make a killing. He sold every sandwich by 1:35 PM, much to the continued depression of the owner of Vito's Pizza cart. Herman continued to sell out every day.

By his fourteenth birthday, Herman bought two more carts, and hired his cousins to run them. He loved his spot on Wall Street; the pace of the street and the energy. It seemed like there was always a frenzied deal about to be made, and the finance guys loved Nanny's brisket. Herman soon became a fixture in the neighborhood. The stockbrokers liked Herman because he was always professional, prompt, and perky. Pretty soon, the stockbrokers were giving Herman stock tips. Herman, being only fourteen at the time, couldn't trade stocks, but his Nanny could, and she was a fast learner.

On Wall Street, there were so many opportunities to get rich, if you knew what you were doing, and more importantly, had a few bucks to spare. Thanks to the brisket sandwiches, Herman and Nanny had money, and lots of it. By the time Herman was eighteen, he and Nanny bought a three-story Brownstone, so each family could have their own floor. Nanny's floor had a professional kitchen installed. She still cooked all the brisket herself, everyday starting at 5:30 AM. Vincent Vancetti, the stockbroker who gave Herman the penny rolls that got him started, was a regular for many years.

"Hey, kid. I like the way you handle your operation. You got what, five carts now, all over town?"

"I'm up to seven carts now, Mr. Vancetti. My Nanny had to install a new kitchen just to keep up with business. Also, I can't thank you enough, sir. If you hadn't given me those penny rolls that day. Well, you know. Thanks again, Mr. Vancetti. Today's lunch is on me."

"Thanks, kid. This is the best brisket in town, but if it weren't for you, it would just be another food cart."

"Well, thanks, Mr. Vancetti. That's very kind of you to say."

"You see what I mean, kid, you got it."

"Got what?"

"Charm, charisma. You got personality!"

"Well, geez, Mr. Vancetti. That's awfully nice of you to say."

"Nice, schmice. Listen, kid, I have a deal for you."

"I'm listening?"

"Good. With your business sense and magnetism, you could make a fortune in the stock market. And, I want you to make that fortune for me... I, I mean with, me."

"Why, that's very flattering, Mr. Vancetti, but I finished night school a few weeks ago. I'm starting NYU as a business major in the Fall. I saved up enough to cover my tuition, and my Nanny is very proud. I'm only the second one in the family to go to college."

"College, schmollege, kid. I know, I know, it sounds good, but what a waste. You remember what I told you the first time we met?"

"Yes, sir, every word."

Vancetti smiled. "That's nice, kid. Remember what I said about deals?"

"Yes, sir. Us Wall Street types need to feel like we are making a deal, even if it's a penny back. Capisce?"

"You see what I mean, kid, what a brain. You don't want to waste that on business school. So, here's the deal. You come work for me on Wall Street as a stockbroker, get your license. I'll teach you the ropes. Give it one year. If you haven't earned your entire college tuition by then, I'll write you a check for the full amount, and you go to school. If you have, I'll still write you that check as a bonus. You give me one more year and then you go to college. How's that sound?"

Herman sat in silence for several moments, while Vancetti waited, eating his brisket. A good salesman always knows, when there is silence, the first one to speak is caving in.

"You have a deal, Mr. Vancetti. And, thank you, sir."

"You won't regret it, kid. We're, I mean, *you're*, going to make a killing. Just one more thing, kid. How long have we known each other?"

"Five years, ten months, and two weeks. That's over two thousand days"

Vancetti chuckled, again amazed by the sharpness of Herman's mind. "Enough of this Mr. Vancetti crap. From now on, you call me Vincent."

"Yes. Mr. Van..., I mean, Vincent," said Herman as they shook hands. By the time Herman was twenty, he made himself, and Vincent, a small fortune. They opened their own firm, N.B. Financial Services, Inc. Only Vincent, Herman, and Herman's grandmother knew what the N.B stood for: Nanny's Brisket.

24

en drove by the Pet Store but didn't see Gina's car. *'Great,'* he thought, *'she was confounded as much by last night as I was.'* Ben drove home, but her car wasn't there either. Ben parked and walked inside, and the dogs greeted him in the driveway. He thought to himself, *'At least the dogs are happy to see me.'* He entered the house, calling for Gina, just in case. There was no response. Ben walked past the living room, strewn with kid's clothes, magazines, and pillows, and stepped into the kitchen.

Even when he knew she wasn't home, Ben always expected to see Gina there smiling at him, like he was her favorite person in the world. This had always been his favorite room in the house. He didn't know for sure if that was due to all of the fun-filled family dinners, the hours and hours he and Gina spent drinking and eating there, or if it was because the kitchen was the first place they made love. Probably all those things.

Looking out the window, Ben knew the other reason. The view and closeness of the backyard. Being in the kitchen was like being immersed in nature. The first night they made love here, Ben couldn't see the yard or the Creek. The morning after, he saw the backyard and fell in love with it, as he did with Gina. The Regal Oaks forever sentient. The Creek emitted a dark glow, covered with early morning fog that seemed to eerily drift in the opposite direction of the sluggishly moving creek. As he looked at the flow of the late morning vapor on the Creek, his mind drifted back to his life years ago, before he started this life with Gina, in this house.

As much as he loved fishing, Ben wanted to be a writer. Herman wanted his son to pursue a professional career. "A writer? A writer? Are you kidding me? Listen, Hemingway, just because I'm rich, doesn't mean you are. Sure, one day you'll get all of my money, but you need to do something with your life besides help me catch bait, fish, and *write*. A *writer*? With a mind like yours, you should be a lawyer. Write some legal briefs. Become a judge. The Supreme Court, even."

"I love you, Dad, but a lawyer? I would rather catch bait during a hot afternoon thunderstorm in August. I'm going to write, Dad. I know I have a message to share that will resonate with young people of today. Something to make them think about what they can do to save this world. The Planet."

"The Planet? Ben, it's the 50's', for God's sake. We discovered plastic is great for everything. You know, soon, they will be making cars out of plastic? Think about that! No more rust coating in Florida. A car that never rusts!! And think about this, pretty soon there will be Nuclear Energy Plants supplying clean, safe power for all of South Florida. Do you know, when I moved here and married your Mother, all of the sewer lines in Miami, dumped right into the Miami River; twenty-nine of them. Now the wastewater treatment plant in Key Biscayne removes all of our sewage, cleans it, and pumps it right into the ocean just offshore. The world has never been better."

"All of those things are exactly what I want to write books about, Dad. We are destroying the environment, and your generation just doesn't get it."

"Listen, boychik, a nice, handsome Jewish boy like you doesn't need to write books about this. We all think our parents are schmucks when we are young and idealistic. We think we know more than they do, that we are going to change the world, until we grow up, get jobs and have ungrateful kids, who do the same thing to us. That's evolution for you. If you think the environment is so bad, become a lawyer and sue the hell out of everybody. That will teach them!"

"That's just not what I want for my life, Dad."

"Oy vey. Just like your grandfather."

"Papa wrote?"

"No, he spent his life sweating, covered in paint in the boatyards, but in his heart, he was a writer."

"Did he ever write anything?"

"He did. I found an envelope after he died. It was stuffed with crumbled up papers, full of mostly unconnected thoughts, and one page with three sentences.

"That's really cool, Dad. What were the three sentences?

"Do you know how many writers it takes to change a lightbulb? None. Screw you, writers don't want to change anything."

"That was a good one, Papa."

"I thought so too. Listen, boychik, go to school, become a writer. Follow your dreams. Do what you love. What else is the point of me being rich I guess, except for you to mooch off of me. Do you think you could do one thing for me?"

"What's that, Dad?"

"Use Papa's joke in your book."

"Thanks, Dad. I love you."

"Me too, kiddo. Your Mom would love to have been here to see this. I'll tell you one thing, though."

"What's that?"

"If she were still with us, you would be going to Law School!"

25

*E*rnest Thirst felt such desire, he clumsily leapt into the wagon, banging his bad knee on the floorboards, shouting. "Fuck!"

"Exactly!" Wekiwa said as she manhandled Ernest's face while kissing him deeply. She had seen the sex act many times—animals, insects, reptiles, even alligators, but she never experienced it before. In the distance, from the camp, she heard an unfamiliar drumming and chanting. *Ommapapo! Ommapapo!* The deep, soul-shaking rhythm of the sound seemed to be informing her movements.

Ommapapo! Ommapapo! Wekiwa felt like an animal, pouncing on top of Ernest as if he were her prey. As soon as Ernest was inside her, something snapped in Wekiwa's head. She grinded on top of Ernest, facing him, facing away, trying every imaginable position that felt delicious to her. She only let Ernest get on top of her when it was almost morning. As the sun came in the sky, so did Wekiwa. Rainbow let out her loudest *Grrrahrrrrrr* to date, which stopped the distant *Ommapapo Ommapapo* drumming.

It was only at that point, in the silence, that Wekiwa realized that she wasn't in control. She hadn't been all night. It was the sound that had been moving her, and she only stopped when it did. She had never orgasmed before, and it felt heavenly. But at the same time, she knew she had been absent for some of the experience. The sounds had taken over. Wekiwa called out in the morning midst. "Great Spirits! Great Spirits! Is this your doing? Speak to me of this sound?" There was no response. Wekiwa looked at Ernest. She had momentarily forgotten he was there or had even been part of this. He was staring straight into her eyes, and Wekiwa was startled at what she saw, blinking rapidly as she didn't believe it to be true. Rainbow let out a warning growl at the sight.

When Wekiwa saw Ernest's eyes, she knew she had transported him to another dimension. She just wasn't sure where? His eyes. His green eyes were now as turquoise as hers. He was transfixed.

"Ernest?" Wekiwa said, uncertain if he would respond.

"Yes, Wekiwa," Ernest replied. "Whatever you wish of me, you only have to ask."

Wekiwa didn't know if it was her food, the Miami River Water, the act of sex with her, or all of them, but Ernest Thirst seemed to be under a spell. The question was, did she control this magic. She tried a simple test.

"Do you know what Wekiwa means?"

"Sorry, I don't speak Indian."

"You will learn, and it's Native American."

"Anything you ask of me, I will comply."

"Time for your first lesson. Do you know Wekiwa means spring?"

"That's beautiful," Ernest replied, unblinking in his gaze.

"You may call me that from now on."

"Yes, My Spring," replied Ernest

Wekiwa saw that it wasn't merely sexual desire. Rather, she knew if she simply asked, Ernest Thirst would slog through the sawgrass barefoot and naked, with Rainbow, claws bared, holding onto his back, all the way to Miami. All she had to do was ask. Wekiwa needed to explore this great power more to learn it's secrets and potential, and when she did, she would be the greatest medicine woman her tribe ever knew. Was it her cooking, the water, the sex, the sounds? All of these things? Just then a plan emerged in Wekiwa's mind. She would open her Restaurant with Ernest. She even had a name for it—Flowing Springs. She would learn what magic was at work and infuse her food with this aphrodisiac mind control—Miami River water, plants from her garden, native Coontie, and if needed, she would use sex. Besides, the sex felt really good.

Wekiwa looked toward the Heavens, then at Rainbow, who ran around the wagon three times, then let out another growl. Wekiwa felt a new awakening within her; like a rattlesnake shedding its skin. She lifted Ernest's head to see his turquoise eyes still glazed over. He was still spellbound. Wekiwa was excited. Not in a sexual way, although God knows she enjoyed the orgasm beyond any previous physical feelings of her young life. It was more than that, though. In the past, she could control the boys and men in the camp merely by asking a favor of them, but they were still present, on the earthly realm. Wekiwa knew when she discovered the right combination of plants, herbs, sex, and water, she could control the world, well at least for now, Miami.

Wekiwa retrieved some small bowls from her bag of cooking utensils, Coontie flour, herbs, plants, and seeds, bid farewell to her mother and grandfather, climbed into the front of the wagon, and pointed it east, in the direction of Miami. She motioned for Rainbow to jump in back as she commanded Ernest to come forward. The mesmerized Ernest crawled from the back of the wagon to the floorboards in front of the wagon's seat. He looked up at Wekiwa, his eyes glazed over in a turquoise haze, and spoke.

"Your pleasure is my pleasure, My Spring." She pulled back on the horse's reigns, and quickly released.

"Yahhhh!" Wekiwa yelled to the horse as Rainbow let out a piercing growl. The horse took off quickly, pushing Wekiwa against the backboard of the seat and propelling the kneeling Ernest to a place at her feet. Wekiwa reached down and held Ernest's face in her hands, then spread her legs and pushed his face into her crotch.

"You really want to make me happy?"

"Yes, my Spring."

Wekiwa let out a playful moan, leaned back against the wagon seat, pulling Ernest's head in even closer, and thought to herself, *'Now I know why Mother called this coming of age.'*

26

*G*us LaCroix found himself driving east on I10 and saw a sign for Mama's Down Home Kitchen, near the exit sign for Live Oak, Florida. He didn't recall leaving Ponchatoula, Louisiana, or getting on the highway, but he suddenly found himself in need of food and rest. Gus typically would have waited for the next fast-food joint; however, the fifteen-foot-tall picture of a steak sandwich on the restaurant's billboard called out to his stomach, which had a bad habit of interrupting him when he least expected it.

Gus took the Live Oak exit, followed the arrow toward Mama's Down Home Kitchen, and pulled into the parking lot. He turned off the key in the ignition, got out of the truck and stretched. Entering the restaurant, he went to the bathroom, took a pee that didn't want to end, and looked in the mirror. His eyes were bloodshot, and his face was covered with a mixture of five-day beard, dirt, and something that resembled dried ketchup. At least, Gus hoped it was ketchup. The last few years had been a blur of PBR and crappy moonshine, from his homemade still.

Thinking back, this might be the first time Gus found himself close to sober since he fled Haulover Marina after the incident. He always knew he had a terrible mean streak, which got him into plenty of trouble, but never thought that he would actually kill someone. Gus washed his face, slicked down his greying, strawberry blonde hair with sink water, walked to a corner stall, and sat down. A waitress slowly walked over with a menu.

"Hey, Red. What can I get you?" asked the red-haired, gum-chewing waitress, in a slow southern drawl.

Gus looked at her name tag. He always called wait staff by their names. In his own way, Gus could be charming—for about five minutes.

"Hey, Jane. Looks like we match," said Gus, pointing at his hair with a flirty smile. "I'll have a coffee, and that steak sandwich. I hope it's as good as it looks on that billboard."

"Oh, sorry, hon. We don't make that anymore. Mama died three years ago, and she was the only one who knew the exact recipe. The owner's just too cheap to change the sign."

"You gotta be kidding me! That's the only reason I stopped."

"Nope. Not kidding. Our chili is pretty good, though; extra cheese is on me for disappointing you."

"Maybe after I eat, we can visit a bit, Jane," said Gus with a well-practiced wink.

"See that cook behind the counter? The one with the scar on his cheek?"

Gus looked at the extremely large cook, wearing a white t-shirt and stained apron, and gingerly waved to him. The cook looked down, smashing his spatula harder than necessary on whatever was cooking on the grill.

"Yep."

"That's my husband. They call him Tiny, but he ain't. Get it? Tiny cos he's so big."

"He does look like a rather large fella."

"Oh, that ain't the half of it, if you know what I mean. So, you better stick to what's on the menu, before I tell him you was hitting on me."

"No offense, Jane, I mean Mrs. Tiny. Chili and coffee will do just fine."

"Coming right up, Red."

Jane brought Gus a coffee and a glass of ice water. The coffee was too hot to drink, so he sat there stirring his spoon, lost in his own memories. As many times as he relived those two days, it was still veiled in a hazy shadow in his mind. He knew for sure it was raining that morning. Gus had tried time and time again to convince Herman Fox to raise his prices, but Herman just wouldn't budge. By the time Gus got his drunk ass out of bed and to the docks that morning, it was 9 AM. Herman was always the first boat out and had already caught most of the pilchards and herrings in the area, and sold them all at $1 a dozen to his regular customers. It took Gus an hour, over fifteen throws of his cast net, and three PBRs, to catch about three dozen baits. He was tired, hung over, and pissed off.

Herman passed by, waved, and shouted as he pulled into the dock, tying up his boat. "The early bird catches the fish, Gus."

In that rare, nearly sober moment, watching Herman tie his lines, Gus' dark, devious, PBR infused brain, hatched a plan. Gus would wake early tomorrow, 3 AM, take his boat out, and string #15 piano wire in the channel near Herman's boat. The wire, used to catch big fish, was strong enough to catch huge sharks. In Gus' mind, he thought when Herman came through the channel markers, the wire would knock Herman off his boat, and cause enough damage to Herman and the boat to keep him away from the dock for a while. At least long enough for Gus to make rent money before he got evicted from his apartment.

Gus decided the best way to stay awake until 3 AM was to keep drinking, but at a slower pace. He stopped at the Quickie Mart on 135 Street and bought a twelve-pack of PBR. Then he walked two more blocks to Woody's, spent the last of his money on a steak sandwich, and went back to his apartment.

At 2:30 AM, Gus started riding his bike to the marina. He broke into the dock box of the Go Hard charter boat, stole two coils of #15 piano wire, fishing pliers, and a pair of Raybans, because who doesn't need a new pair of shades. He got into his skiff, opened the cooler, and took out his emergency rations: a half bottle of Wild Turkey with a rusty cap. He was thirsty and downed most of the whiskey in a few gulps.

Gus was clear-headed enough to forego starting his noisy, gas spewing motor, so as not to attract any attention. He knew it needed a tune up, but he didn't have the time, money, or motivation to have it serviced. Gus connected his electric trolling motor to the battery, and quietly pulled away from the dock. He made his way to the channel markers with their red and green signs and flashing lights. Pulling up to one of the pilings, he grabbed hold, and tied a loop of wire around it. Gus carefully pulled his boat away, threading out trolling wire as he navigated to the other piling. He grabbed hold of the piling and looped the other end of the wire around it.

Gus sat down and took a hard pull from the Wild Turkey bottle, until all he felt was air passing his lips. He looked back up at the wire, and it seemed to be the perfect height to him. It would surely catch under

Herman's boat as it came up on plane entering the channel. The wire would pass under the boat and wrap itself around the propeller, damaging the prop, and tossing Herman into the water. *'That would fix his ass good'*, Gus thought to himself.

He pathetically sucked any last drops of whiskey from the bottle and tossed it into the water. Driving his boat back to the dock, he tied up it up and planned to head back home to sleep. He wanted to distance himself from the scene of the crime. Instead, Gus fell asleep in the bottom of his boat. He woke up at dawn, just in time for Herman to shout a hearty good morning to him. Gus was too drunk to respond and momentarily forgot about the wire. He looked up in time to see Herman take off toward the channel, jarring Gus' memory, and he thought to himself, *'Bon Voyage Motherfucker'*.

Gus got up and took off running toward the channel. He wanted to watch the boat get trashed, and also wanted a good place to hide out. Quickly, he found a stand of mangrove trees and slogged his way to the furthest edge for the best view. He found himself exhilarated by the chance for revenge against this guy who took away his business. As Gus looked out at the channel in the just rising sun, he saw a smiling Herman gunning the engine on his skiff. Herman looked like he did every morning. Like he didn't have a care in the world. *'That would end in a second,'* Gus thought.

Just then, Gus heard a twang, like a banjo string breaking, and looked out to see Herman's decapitated head flying through the air, into the inlet. Gus felt the blood drain from his own head as he stumbled backward into the Mangroves. He ran, as fast and straight as his drunken feet could carry him, toward his skiff. Along the way, Gus' mind cleared enough to know he needed gas. He grabbed the two portable gas tanks from his boat, ran back to the Go Hard, and inserted a rubber hose into the boat's fuel tank. Gus couldn't remember the last time he had enough money for gas since he had been siphoning from the charter boats for months now. He figured those guys were rich and wouldn't miss a few gallons. Hell, he could run all week on the fuel they burn in an hour. Gus filled his tanks, spit out the gas that leaked into his mouth, and connected one tank to his skiff's motor. He turned on his trolling motor and headed out the channel.

As he passed the port marker, he saw a coconut in the water. On second look, it wasn't a coconut. It was Herman's head bobbing up and down in the skiff's wake. Herman's eyes were wide open looking straight at Gus as the boat was running in circles about twenty yards out. Herman's decapitated body was standing in place on the boat's stern, his hand still holding the motor's tiller. Instead of remorse, Gus thought to himself, *'Well like my Daddy told me, always keep your head on straight.'* Gus scooped Herman's head up in a fish net, gunned his skiff's motor, and headed north.

27

*G*ina pulled up to her usual parking spot in front of the Pet Store. Two doors down was Ms. Alice—People and Pet Psychic. Gina opened the door to Ms. Alice's, and Vlad barged ahead of her, pulling his leash out of Gina's hands.

"Vlad. Bad Boy!" Gina yelled as a barking Vlad ran through the red and black curtains.

"Vlad. Get back here or no more tummy rubs," Tina yelled.

The barking ceased as the curtains opened, and out popped Ms. Alice, with Vlad in tow, licking her ankles as if they were covered in cream cheese.

"Hello, neighbors! What brings you here?"

"This is Vlad. So sorry for his behavior, Ms. Alice. He's not been himself lately, which is actually why we're here."

"I see," replied Ms. Alice as she reached down, held Vlad's head in her hands, and gazed into the Doberman's eyes. Vlad licked Ms. Alice's face like a popsicle on a hot summer day. "I see," said Ms. Alice again, still holding Vlad's transfixed head in her hands.

"For the last couple of days, he's been acting strangely."

"I see," replied Ms. Alice without any change of expression.

"Yes, well it's like this…" Gina said as Ms. Alice interrupted with a raised hand, flipping it upward.

"No need to say anything. Vlad has told me the entire story."

"He has? Wow. We need to get him, or you, a good agent. I hear The Tonight Show is looking for good animal acts," Tina replied.

"You always struck me as a bit cocky, Tina, but you've seen my work."

"Oh, you know I love me some cocky," Tina said as her attempt to high five Ms. Alice went unanswered. "Sorry, Ms. Alice. You know I'm a big fan. I'm the one who told Gina to bring Vlad in."

While Ms. Alice's psychic reading and botanical business had been next to Goldfish & More since the girls were young, Gina had never seen Ms. Alice work, so she was something of a mystery to her. Tina on the other hand, had.

Two years prior, Tina's friends, Elena and Paul brought their dachshund to Ms. Alice for a reading, and Tina tagged along. She was very impressed. The dog had been withdrawn as of late and was constantly licking its paws. Paul had taken him to the vet, who had prescribed a cream to help, which didn't work. Ms. Alice sat with the dachshund on her lap for a few minutes and then told Elena and Paul that their dog was full of anxiety about their upcoming move to Chicago. They both sat amused and dumbfounded at this revelation.

They told Ms. Alice that they had been considering the Chicago move for some time but hadn't taken any formal steps toward leaving. Ms. Alice then asked the dachshund if he wanted to move to Chicago. He told her he would be fine, as long as he could stay with his family. Also, he heard it was cold in Chicago and wanted a sweater. Elena and Paul had neglected discussing the dachshund in the move, so he felt like he might be left behind. Being a rescue dog, this created great anxiety in the tiny pooch. When Elena heard this, she picked up her little dog, hugged him close, and told him that wherever they lived, he would always have a home with them. The dog immediately licked Elena and Paul all over their faces, then jumped to the ground and licked Ms. Alice's ankles. Elena went home and knit the dachshund a sweater that evening.

"Tina! Please, behave!" Gina said.

"That's quite enough, ladies. Most people think what I do is a joke, until the Spirit World reaches into theirs, then after that, they never leave me alone. So, do you want to know what's gotten into Vlad?" Ms. Alice turned to Gina, let go of Vlad's head, and reached toward Gina's. "May I?" asked Ms. Alice as her outstretched hands found their way to Gina's cheeks.

"You may," Gina replied.

"I've wanted to do this since you were a little girl. Since I saw those eyes!" Ms. Alice held Gina's face in her hands and looked deeply into her mismatched eyes. Just a moment later, Ms. Alice's hands began trembling. She removed one hand from Gina's face and motioned for Tina to come closer. "This involves you too, Tina."

Tina moved closer, and said, "Okay, just promise you won't turn me into a frog or anything."

"If only I could," Ms. Alice replied as she touched Tina's face. Except for Vlad's faint panting, the room was silent. The deeper Ms. Alice explored Gina's eyes, the more stressed she became. Tina on the other hand, found the entire situation humorous.

"I can't wait to tell the other nurses about this."

"When you do, Tina, make sure to tell them how you saw your Father's hand that night," Ms. Alice said.

Tina froze, her mouth agape.

"Yes, I see the pinky ring too. That's your Father's ring, all right. I always loved that ring. Very mafioso. You know, my Great Grandfather was Italian. I have been in this spot for twenty years. Your Father was always respectful to me, although he never knew I saw him cross himself every morning after he greeted me in the parking lot."

Tina remained entranced. "Tina. Tina!" Gina called out, but Tina was uncharacteristically uncommunicative.

"She will talk soon enough, Gina. As for you, my dear, you are a horse of another color. Literally. It's those eyes of yours. Just like your Mother's."

"Yes. It's just science. It's called Heterochromia," Gina replied defensively, then pulled away from Ms. Alice and headed for the door.

"You can't outrun your gifts, or your destiny, Gina."

"I don't know what you're talking about. We should go. Tina. Tina!!! Let's get out of here." Tina remained wordless, her unblinking eyes transfixed on Ms. Alice. "What have you done to her? I've seen those programs about LSD. Is that what you did to us, touch us with acid on your hands?"

"Did you take any acid last night? By the way, how did you like the clown mask?" Ms. Alice responded.

Now Gina froze in place.

Just then, Tina spoke, "He was there that night, Sis."

"Who was there? What night?" Gina asked.

"Dad. The night of the accident."

"Oh, Tina, not you too. Are you both in on a joke or something? Well, it's not funny. Let's go, Tina."

"The accident, Gina. I saw Dad's hand. He reached down and cradled me when the car flipped. He guided us through the traffic. He tried to help Mom too, but she pushed his hand over to me."

"Tina, stop. You're scaring me."

"Don't be afraid, Gina," said voices coming out of Vlad's snout, but it wasn't Tina's voice.

"Who is that?" Gina asked.

"It's us, Gina. We've been waiting for you," said the voices wafting out of Vlad's mouth. Gina felt like she couldn't breathe. She reached back for a chair and sat down.

"The Spirits are all around us, Gina. You of all people should see that," Ms. Alice said.

"All people? See what?"

"The Supernatural. The other World," Ms. Alice replied, "Oh, dear, those eyes of yours. What I could do with those eyes," said Ms. Alice as she playfully reached for Gina's eyes. Gina jumped up. "You see, Gina, you have the sight, but it's been disconnected. The Spirits in Vlad are trying to connect you. Your eyes, my dear. They give you the power to see into other worlds. The world between the living and the dead, and the World of the Spirits. Vlad has already connected with that world. In fact, some of the Spirits speak through him now." Vlad looked up and barked.

"This is craziness. Let's go, Tina. Vlad, come, boy," Gina said, as she leapt from the chair, but nobody else moved.

"The Spirits, they are inhabiting your house. You feel it, don't you?" Ms. Alice inquired.

Gina sat back down.

"I have felt a presence there lately. Like the house is alive," Gina numbly stated.

"There. I told you. You have the gift."

"Sounds more like a curse to me."

"Oh, it can be, but not in your case, or your Mother's."

"Not that again. I think we better go. I've had enough excitement for the last twenty-four hours."

"Sorry to tell you, Gina, but your journey has only just begun."

"Oh, and where's my journey end?"

"It ends, where it all began. At the Creek!"

28

Ben sat looking out the kitchen window, still adrift in the past. His mind floated back to the time when he finished high school and backpacked through Europe. When he got to Italy, he was torn between his romantic desire to visit Venice, and the logic that informed him it would only bring painful memories of the last place he saw his Mother alive. Two days later, Ben found himself wandering the wonderous, mazelike streets around Venice's Grand Canal. He walked for hours and passed over a bridge near Piazza San Marco where two different Gondoliers were trying to woo a couple into a Gondola ride. The losing Gondolier got upset and used his oar to send a friendly splash of water in the direction of the winner. Instead, the water sprang off the oar onto the bridge, drenching Ben. The losing Gondolier shouted up to Ben on the bridge.

"Hey, mister. I'm really sorry. I'm just getting off work, let me take you to my Uncle's Trattoria for dinner."

Ben had been traveling all alone for months, ever since that cute blonde from Indiana left him for a Frenchman in Brussels. While he was a bit wary of the splashing Gondolier, the fifties were a more trusting time, and Ben was hungry, tired, and a bit lost.

"Hey, mister! What do you say?"

"Thanks. I'm Ben."

"I'm Maximo. Be right up.

"Thanks. I know I shouldn't say this in Italy, but it's been a while since I had a good meal."

"Il nonsenso! My Uncle is the best chef in Venice. His place is right around the corner."

Maximo and Ben walked down the winding road. They stopped at a Trattoria on a winding street with a wood burning stove you could see from the window. It started raining.

"This place looks groovy."

Maximo opened the door and ushered Ben in. "Uncle Tony. This is my new friend, Ben. I owe him dinner, and a change of clothes."

"Buena sera, Ben. Any friend of Max's is family here. Come in the kitchen. I will heat up a towel in the oven for you. That will warm you right up."

Ben followed Tony and Maximo into the kitchen. He was impressed with the charm and warmth of the small place, which reminded him of home. In fact, there was something very familiar about the place. Like he had been there in a dream.

"This place seems a bit magical. I feel like I have been here before."

"Maybe you have. Have you ever been to Venice?"

"Once, on a cruise."

Ben watched as Uncle Tony's entire face changed from a happy glow, to pale and sickly. Maximo put a hand on Tony's shoulder and said something to him in Italian, causing his demeanor to change again.

"Hey. You boys go get a table near the stove and warm up."

"Thank you, sir."

"Hey, it's Uncle Tony, please."

Ben smiled at Tony as he toweled his hair dry. "Did I do something to offend your Uncle?"

"It's a long story. Well, maybe not so long. You see, Tony's son, my cousin, died in a terrible accident on a cruise ship a few years ago. He never got over it. No parent should ever bury a child."

Now Maximo watched as the color drained from Ben's face.

"You okay, my friend? You look like you saw a ghost."

"Sorry. We walked in so fast, I didn't notice. What's the name of this place?"

"Geppetto's Kitchen."

"You're Murray's cousin?"

"You knew my cousin? Hey, that's great."

"I was on that cruise," Ben replied.

"Which one?"

"His last one."

"Oh no, that's tragic. Murray was the funniest guy ever, and a great chef. Did you meet him on the ship? Did you see his act?"

Ben was silent for a few minutes.

"Hey, Ben. You okay? Let me get us some vino."

Maximo returned with a carafe of Chianti. "Drink this. You look like you need it." Ben downed a glass of Chianti and looked up at Maximo. "My Mom. You see."

Ben's eyes welled up.

"Here. Have another glass, Chianti is good for the soul."

"Funny you should say that. Speaking of souls. My Mom. She was with your cousin."

"Oh, a little cruise ship romance. Your Father must have been furious. I see why you are so upset."

"No, she was with Murray in that vat of Frutti de Mare."

Maximo sat back in his booth, looking into the fire and tears welled in his eyes. He sat that way for a moment in silence, then downed the rest of his wine. Pouring another glass, he yelled back to the kitchen, "Hey, Uncle Tony! Get out here, pronto, and bring more Chianti. It's Murray. He found a way home."

Uncle Tony brought out every house specialty on and off the menu and kept the vino flowing freely. They talked for hours about their loved ones, and how fate brought Ben into this restaurant. At 5 AM, long after the customers and rain left, they said their goodbyes.

"You didn't show up here by accident, Ben. You promise me to write your book. I want to be able to tell everyone I know a famous author."

"Thanks, Uncle Tony, but I haven't even written anything yet."

"I can see it in your eyes. You have that charisma, like my Murray. You will be famous one day. Can I ask you a favor?"

"Of course."

"When you do write, find a way to keep my Murray, and your Mother alive."

"I will try my best, Uncle Tony."

"You're a good boy, Ben. Your Mother would be proud of you. Hey, wait. I have something for you. To bring you buona fortuna. That means good luck." Tony disappeared for a moment and returned with some beads in his hand.

"These were my Murray's rosary beads. He told me he couldn't pray with them, because his Mother was Jewish, but I know he just wanted to make me laugh."

"Oh, Tony, I couldn't keep those. Besides, I'm Jewish too," Ben said with a laugh. When Ben's hands touched the beads, he felt an electric charge running from the soles of his feet to his elbows, jolting his funny bones, and forcing his face into a contorted smile.

"Always joking, you Jewish boys, huh?" Tony said as he placed his hand on Ben's cheek. "You take these with you. There's a reason you found your way to Geppetto's Basement last night."

"Thanks, Uncle Tony. Maybe I'll give them a try. The whole Jewish thing doesn't really work for me anyway."

"See I knew you were a good boy, plus, you know the Pope gives us a month's vacation in Vatican City for every Jew we convert," Tony said with a chuckle.

Ben knew he wanted to write about the environment, and not some piece of fiction. In that moment, as he looked at the extinguishing embers jumping lazily around the wood burning stove, Ben could see it as clearly as the last time she kissed him goodnight. His Mother's face, shining in the fire. He shook his head a bit to focus, but there it was. Next to it was a face he didn't recognize. A handsome young man with dancing blue eyes. Ben blinked, but there it was again when he opened his eyes. The images faded after a moment, then Ben looked next to the fireplace. There was a picture on the wall, and it was of the same young man. The picture was autographed. 'Pops, always keep them eating and laughing—just not at your food. Love, Murray.'

Ben's mind slowly drifted back to the present. He looked out at the Creek and thought of his Mother. He saw a splash. He gently walked to the Creek's edge and looked into the water. It was a manatee. He hadn't seen one for at least a year; not since people started dumping trash into the Creek. Ben gazed through the water at the manatee. To his surprise, the manatee looked straight at him, seemed to form a smirk on its bristled lips, picked up one of its forelimbs, and splashed water all over Ben. He stared down at the manatee in disbelief as it kept its gaze focused on Ben then opened its mouth, as if to speak. Ben's mouth fell open as well.

"Hello, Ben. Who were you expecting, Flipper?"

29

*G*us's spoon clinked on the bottom of his nearly empty coffee cup. He looked around for Jane for a refill. Gus' mind drifted back again to that cursed day. He hadn't meant to kill Herman and had no idea what compelled him to take his head. Was it to get rid of the evidence, to have a trophy, or to keep the police guessing? He didn't really know, but it was almost as if the head had ordered him to do it. He still vividly remembered cold chills running up and down the length of his body as he lifted Herman's head out of the net and saw his eyes still open, staring Gus down. Gus tossed the head into a burlap chum bag and winced. This sobered Gus up enough to realize how stupid, or how drunk he had been.

When Gus ran that piano wire, he forgot to account for the tidal change. When he strung the wire at 3 AM, it would have passed right under the boat and caught the boat's underside and propeller, but by 6 AM, the tide had fallen enough to bring the wire neck high. The tides in Miami change approximately every six hours, but he failed to account for that. Gus never was very good at math.

Gus had a buddy with a 33-foot Chris Craft moored in Dumbfoundling Bay. His friend often talked about journeying across the state in his boat, and this would be a perfect opportunity. Gus could hitch a ride with him up the intracoastal to Stuart, where they could take the Okeechoobee Waterway through the locks on Lake Okeechobee to Fort

Myers on Florida's West Coast. Nobody would be looking for him there, if they were looking for him at all.

Gus pulled the plug on his boat, hoping it would sink within minutes, and boarded the Chris Craft. As he stepped on, he called out. "Hey, Harvey. Mon ami. It's Gus. You ready for that trip across the state, brah?"

"Gus? Gus? Is that you? Shit, yeah. Grab yourself a beer from the cooler and pull the anchor. I've been waiting for this trip for ten years. What are you going to do with your boat?"

"Damnedest thing! I was tying up, and she started going down. I'm afraid she's a goner."

Harvey looked off the stern and saw the bow of Gus' boat bobbing in the water. "Damn, boy! You know how to go out with a bang. You sure you don't want to tow her along? We could probably raise her."

"Nah. It's better this way. I'll collect big time on the insurance, and I really would like to see Lake Okeechobee."

"Aye, Captain. Let's go."

The boat's insurance had lapsed years ago, but only Gus knew that. They made their way across the state, drinking copious amounts of beer. Gus bid Harvey farewell when they docked at Fort Myers.

"Hey, Gus. You just gonna leave me here?"

"I got some problems back home, mon ami."

"How you gonna get there?"

"You know me, brah, I always land on my feet."

"Here you go, man. Don't forget your cooler. And, take this cos I know you're gonna need it." Harvey tossed Gus a PBR.

"Mersi. See ya, Harvey."

"Not if I see you first, you big dipshit," said Harvey tossing him another beer.

"Au revoir, mon ami!"

Gus hitched his way up the coast to I10 and caught a ride with a trucker who took him about fifty miles away from the parish. Gus stole a kid's bike from outside a house in Mobile, Alabama, and rode it all the way home. He had been hiding out there, in his Great Aunt's tornado shelter for years until the middle of last night, when he inexplicably felt obliged to drive back to Miami Beach. He grabbed his Aunt's truck keys and several thousand dollars Aunt Ethel had stashed in a Café Du Monde coffee can, then split. Gus' mind found its way back to the present, as Jane came back with the chili and a full pot of coffee.

"Sorry it took so long, hon. Tiny needed my help getting a lid off a jar. He looks big and strong, but I can open a jar of pickles faster than a raccoon can scoot up a tree with a hound dog on this tail. It's all in the wrist, you know."

"Yeah, sure."

"Here you go, Red. I brought you some extra cheese, chopped onions, and hot sauce. Tiny don't make his chili too spicy. He tells people I'm the only spicy thing he likes to eat. He's such a hoot."

"Lucky guy, that Tiny."

"Oh, I'm the lucky one. Like I said, he ain't Tiny. You need anything else, Red?"

"No, just the check. I need to head out."

"Where you off to, Red?"

"Heading to Miami Beach. I need to see an old friend."

"Hey, Tiny! This guy's heading to Miami Beach."

"Come here! Now!" Tiny shouted, flashing his spatula like a machete.

"Sounds like Tiny really needs you back there, Jane. Maybe another pickle jar?"

"Oh, he knows better than to yell for me like that. He's yelling for you."

"Me?"

"Oh, yeah, and you better hurry, he gets real impatient when he flashes his spatula like that."

Gus rose from the table and walked to the counter. "Can I help you, Mr. Tiny?" Tiny motioned in the direction of a shelf above the bread, toward a dusty, flowered urn.

"Take that with you."

"Excuse me, Tiny?"

"That's Mama. She always wanted to go to Miami Beach."

"What am I supposed to do with it, I mean *her*?"

"Dump her in the ocean. She'd be real happy, and I'd be much obliged."

"Well, sure, Tiny." Gus took his hat off in a respectful manner. "If it's not to bold, may I ask, was Mama, your Mama?"

"Nope. My first wife."

"Oh, sorry for your loss, Tiny. I'm glad you ain't pining for company, though."

"If you don't mind my asking, what happened to Mama?"

"Died in bed."

"Well, that's the way to go. Nice and peaceful like."

"It wasn't exactly peaceful, but she died with a smile on her lips," said Tiny with a wink, smashing his spatula down repeatedly on a helpless hamburger.

"That's not a bad way to go either, Tiny."

Tiny put the urn down on the lunch counter and told Gus lunch was on him. He even sent Gus off with a slice of homemade peach pie to go. When Gus picked the urn off the counter, he felt an electric jolt running from his fingertips to his elbow, making his arm jerk.

"Darndest thing," Jane said. That happened the to the last guy heading to Miami Beach. Poor thing was so frightened, he dropped the urn back on the counter and took off running. Good thing he was fast, cos if Tiny had caught him! I think it's that, you know? What do they call that again? Satin electricity?"

"Static electricity?" Gus queried.

"Yeah—that's it—static electricity."

Gus picked up the urn and headed outside. He was too preoccupied with how he got there to be worried about an urn and put it in the cooler. He still didn't remember getting into his Aunt's truck that morning, taking her money, or why he was heading back to the scene of the crime. He knew one thing, though. Aunt Ethel was going to be pissed!

30

*G*ina walked next door, opened the door of Goldfish & More, and turned on the lights. Tina and Vlad followed her inside. Gina took a large rawhide bone from the shelf and handed it to Vlad, who walked to the corner, sat down, and started chewing.

"What in God's name was that about?"

"I wanted to tell you I saw Dad. Well, at least his hand, the night of the accident, but I thought you would have me locked up."

"There's still time for that, Tina."

"It's all true, Gina. Dad saved our lives the night of the accident. We should have died, but he was watching over us. I swear I saw it."

"The mind can do all kinds of strange things under stress, Tina. You know that. You're a nurse."

"And how do you explain everything else Ms. Alice knew, like about the house, and the clown mask. Why was Vlad wearing that anyway?"

"I promise I'll tell you, but I need some more wine, or maybe a joint. Jemma has some good stuff hidden away, and I know just where she keeps it."

"You can get as drunk or as high as you want, it won't change anything, Gina. And, you know, Mom definitely has predicted some crazy stuff in our lives. The Native Americans say those eyes of yours are magic."

"Yeah, right. Watch me pull a rabbit out of this hat," Gina said as she lifted a white bunny from its pen and hugged it.

"Okay, fine. Let's change the subject. Tell me when you are ready."

"What's your favorite fish here, Sis?"

"Oh, I love them all, but I would have to say Spot is my soulmate of a fish."

Spot was a giant Red Oscar fish, originally from Tropical South America. Gina inherited Spot from a conscientious customer, whose tank he had outgrown. Rather than dumping the huge fish into a local canal, the responsible pet owner brought him to the store. South Florida's waterways are full of non-native tropical fish, who've grown too large or aggressive for their tanks, only to be tossed into the local ecosystem. While at first pass, this might seem like a better idea than euthanizing a pet, inserting an aggressive animal into a foreign environment disrupts the flow of nature. Oscars are fierce fish and can easily displace a largemouth bass or other native fish from their breeding grounds.

At first, a novelty, Florida's native species were fast becoming outnumbered by non-natives such as Oscars, Peacock Bass, parrots, reptiles like Iguanas, red-headed agamas, chameleons, Boa Constrictors, Burmese Pythons—some big enough to eat deer, wild pigs, even the occasional alligator. This deeply upset Gina, who offered her customers a 'no questions asked' return policy for any animal sold that outgrew their aquariums or cages. Goldfish & More soon became a well-known sanctuary for large reptiles, parrots, and a wide variety of tropical fish.

The issue of invasive species bothered Ben even more. He wrote about these mostly unnoticed, but important transformations to Florida's natural environment, in his first and only published novel, *South Florida; Treat It Like A Native*. Ben poured his heart and soul into that book. Despite that, almost nobody bought it. Sure, Ben had a small following of environmental activists and the Health Food crowd, but it hadn't had the impact Ben hoped for. Although in the future, the book would be considered pivotal work in understanding and preserving South Florida's fragile native ecology. An author friend of Ben's told him your first book is like the first time you make love. You think it's the most amazing thing you ever did, but in retrospect, you had no idea what you were doing; it was clumsy, awkward, and ill-received at best.

"See. I knew it. You have a thing for fish. You always did love this place more than us," Tina joked.

"You caught me. I'm running away to Atlantis with Spot. I wanted to talk about Ben."

"I'd rather talk about the fish."

"Ben is an amazing writer. He used to joke that when we met, I was his muse. He was devasted when his first book didn't get the reception it deserved. He wrote fifty pages of his next book, and then only eight pages since. Ben said his mojo wore off. I kidded him that it was my mojo that must have vanished, but honestly, I don't know what happened."

"Come on, Gina, it's not that much of a stretch. Rich kid, never had to work for a living, has had money dripping out of his butthole for his entire life. Now he's wasting his time working on that bait boat."

"That's not fair, Tina. Ben's not like that. He keeps the bait business going because he loves talking to the fishermen about conservation, and they appreciate him. Strong fisheries make for successful fishermen you know."

"Fish conservation. Tell that to the bait. Poor little fish."

"That's part of the problem. The fishermen need to be educated to the fact that they are destroying the turtle grass in the bay. That's where the bait fish breed and grow. When they rip up the grass with their propellers and anchor lines, it destroys the fishes breeding grounds. The turtle grass also holds the sand in place and filters the water. It's a very delicate ecosystem."

"Zzzzzzzzzz. Sorry, I was sleeping. What did you say?"

"See, this is why Ben's writing is so important. That's why he got both his Biology and English Lit degrees and hung out in all of those comedy clubs. He even tried stand-up comedy. Remember? Ben's material was pretty good, but his stage presence needed work. I think in some way he was trying to connect with his Mother since she, you know, died with that comedian, and Ben promised Murray's Uncle to keep his memory alive. Ultimately, Ben wanted to get these kind of messages across to people in a humorous way so they would pay attention."

"Ben, humorous? That guy couldn't get a funny look if he were dressed as a priest at a kid's birthday party."

"Ben is the funniest person I know."

"You sure you're talking about *Ben*? Tall guy, kind of gawky looking. What do you see in him? I know you don't like to talk about him like this, but tell me, does he have a huge one, or what?"

"Tina! That's my husband you're talking about, not one of your one-night hook ups. But, if you are asking...," Gina started blushing and giggling, "but that's not why I love him."

"So, what really happened last night, and where is Ben?"

31

"It was the weirdest thing, Tina. We were in the backyard, in the double hammock, gazing into each other's eyes, holding hands—everything was amazing. We really have, or I guess I should say, *had*, a great relationship. We actually thought about doing it right there in the hammock, but the kids were home." Just then, Spot the fish started blowing bubbles at the top of his tank, which meant, *feed me*. Gina got up, and went to Spot's tank, holding some freeze-dried krill in her hands. "Here you go, Spot. Sorry your breakfast was late."

"I knew you loved that fish more than Ben. Back to the story, it's just getting good."

"Okay, but these fish aren't going to feed themselves. Come help me, Tina"

"Only if you keep talking, and not about fish."

Gina and Tina started feeding the fish on opposite sides of the store to see who got to the middle first, a little game they started playing when they were kids.

"First one to the middle doesn't have to clean the Goldfish tanks," Tina said. She hated cleaning the Goldfish tanks—they were the messiest fish in the store.

"So, we got out of the hammock, hand in hand, heading for the house, when there is a big splash in the Creek. We turned around and walked toward the Creek, and there were only ripples, but then all of a sudden, we both let go of our hands, looked at each other, and felt nothing but hate. I could see it in his eyes, and I know he could see it in mine. That burning, passionate desire turned into a smoldering disgust that welled up from both of us and filled the space around us. You know that expression, you could cut it with a knife? It was like that. The air was thick with vial contempt, and downright disgust for each other. No matter what kind of fights we've been through over the years, this was different. We went from wanting to jump each other's bones, to wanting to bury them. If we had guns, I think we would have shot each other right there. It was terrifying."

"Geez. What the hell?"

"I know, but it got worse. We made our way inside and the kids were sleeping, so we stayed in the kitchen and started saying horrible things to each other. It was awful. My stomach felt like it was being dissolved in acid."

"Geez. That's it? A splash in the Creek, a little fight, and a stomachache?"

"You don't understand. It felt like we were both dying. The next thing I know, I pick up the banana bread in the baking dish."

"Oh, I love your banana bread. Did you use those little Cuban red bananas from your yard? Mocha frosting?"

"Yes, and no. I did cream cheese frosting this time."

"Oh, I love that too. How was it?"

"I have no idea. I grabbed Ben by the hair on the back of his head and pushed his face into the baking dish—hard."

"I would have paid good money to see that." Tina snarked as Gina started crying.

"I'm sorry, Sis. What made you do that? Waste a perfectly good banana bread, I mean?"

"That's not funny. I have no idea, and... and..."

"And, and... what"

"I hurt him. His face hit the dish with a thud. I'm sure his face is bruised. Oh, it was just horrible."

"If I were you, I would have licked that shit off, and done him right there in the kitchen. Then you could pretend it was just foreplay." Gina started crying again. "Sorry, Sis. Then what happened?"

"I don't know. He stormed out the door and didn't come home this morning. You know we haven't slept apart for one night in all these years.

Even when the kids were born. I feel awful. I still don't know what got into me."

"Maybe it was just all pent up in you all these years, Gina?"

"No! I love Ben. Sure, we fight like any couple, but never anything like this."

"I'm sure he will come home. Do you have any of that frosting left?"

"Yeah, why?"

"When he does come home, just rub that all over him and lick it off. He'll forget the whole thing." Gina started laughing and dried her tears. Just then there was a big splash. Gina looked over and saw Spot flopping on the floor.

"Spot, what's gotten into you?" asked Gina as she scooped him up in her hands. As she did, Spot looked up at her, with his mouth moving deliberately. Gina's logical mind knew he was just trying to breathe, but another part of her thought for certain he was trying to communicate. Gina guided the big fish back into his tank. As he entered the water, he looked back at her, and she could have sworn she heard him speak. Gina just stood there staring at Spot in his tank.

You okay, Sis? You look like you just saw a ghost."

"Did you hear that?"

"Hear what, Gina?"

"Oh, nothing. I think I'm losing it."

"Go ahead. I don't think anything else that happens today will shock me."

"When I was holding Spot, I swear on a stack of bibles that he spoke to me."

"Maybe you are losing it, Gina. As the fish said to the bait, *I'll bite.* What did Spot say to you?"

"He said, the Mermaid did it."

"Let's get you home, Gina. You need some rest."

"That sounds like a good idea. Oh, I almost forgot something else that happened last night, or at least *I think* it happened."

"Don't tell me, you were abducted by aliens."

"The last couple of days have been so crazy, if little green men showed up now, I would probably go with them, Tina."

"What happened?"

"I'm a bit foggy, but I think I screwed the babysitter."

"I thought you had those nice science geek girls watching the kids. Since when do you have a male babysitter?"

"I don't!"

32

Anna Phylaxis sat on the deck staring out at the morning mist on the Creek.

"More coffee, dear?"

"You know me, George, I'll never say no to anything dark and hot."

"That's why I married you," George said as he leaned over and kissed Anna softly on her lips.

"Have you noticed anything strange lately, George?"

"Why yes, you seem even more gorgeous than usual, my dear."

"Flattery will get you everywhere," Anna said, as she stood to hug George and nuzzled her cheek into his chest, "but have you noticed?"

"Something strange?"

"With the Creek? Look at it."

"You're right, as usual. I never saw the Creek so clear before. Why, it's almost the color of the ocean in St. Thomas."

"Yes. I was thinking it looked like that spot we went on our honeymoon."

"Ahhhhh, Sapphire Beach. The things we did there that first night. Still makes me tingle just thinking of them. And you, wearing that special honeymoon outfit I got you."

"You didn't get me any outfit?"

"Exactly. Thank God nobody caught us. I'm not sure what we did was legal in the Virgin Islands. And, it certainly wasn't anything a virgin would have dreamt of."

Anna kissed George's neck and said, "You are a bad influence on me. I still can't believe we were lucky enough to wind up together."

Anna thought back to many years ago, when she awoke from the car accident hearing voices, and saw George sitting in a chair next to her bed. There were yellow roses on her nightstand. The room was cold; *hospital room* cold, but George Washington's smile warmed her like sunlight.

George, Anna, and Frank had been friends since they moved into the house next door on Enchanted Place. Actually, Anna had a crush on George from the moment he showed her the house. George had kind, deep brown eyes, stood 5'10, had a medium build, and perfectly formed biceps. However, what truly impressed Anna, was George's intellect and kindness. Also, he could tell a story about the most mundane subject in a way that left her absolutely mesmerized. When George first told her about the Native Americans who lived on the land, Anna thought she could evaporate into his very words, and arms.

George was born in Nassau, had a crisp, British Island accent, and Anna thought he spoke like he had been educated at Cambridge. It turned out he was. Even as a small child, George loved reading and history. He excelled in school and was provided an all-expense paid scholarship to Cambridge University. His Mother was beaming with pride when he got on the ship for the crossing to England. His Father told him he should get a business degree, but George had other plans. George loved history, especially about indigenous people. He wrote his dissertation about the earliest European's, the Sami, who were fishermen and reindeer herders. He graduated with a doctorate in History, then applied for various teaching posts and was offered a position at the University of Miami.

He moved to Miami and developed the first curriculum for coursework in Native American studies at UM. University faculty are not well paid, and people were flocking to Miami like baby chicks to a warm light, so George saw an opportunity. He opened his real estate business to pull in some extra money, and it turned out to be very lucrative. While he enjoyed the company of women, and had many tumultuous relationships over the years, he never found true love. That is, until he met Anna. From the moment he saw her with her parasol and gloves, he hoped he found a kindred spirit with the same appreciation for history as him—and he had. He would have been so disappointed if she just dressed like that to make a fashion statement.

While Anna and George were always attracted to each other, they never acted on it. Until after Frank died. George made sure he offered Anna the support of a friend and neighbor and helped with 'heavy lifting chores' around the house. Gina and Tina loved George, and Tina was the first one to tell her Mother, "She should jump his bones."

Exactly one year after Frank's death, George showed up at the door with yellow roses and an invitation to dinner for all of the Phylaxis girls at Cap's Place in Lighthouse Point. Cap's is only accessible by boat. The girl's loved the boat ride as much as the restaurant. When they arrived at the dock, George gave the girls a history lesson. Cap's had quite the history. In the 20's it had been a rum-running casino, and then a respectable restaurant. Its patrons, to name a few, included Franklin D. Roosevelt, Winston Churchill, and Al Capone.

Fresh Hearts of Palms salad was a specialty, as was their seafood. By the time the girls finished their Key Lime Pie and boat ride back to the parking lot, Gina and Tina were satiated, happy, and wet from splashing water on each other on the boat, and Anna from the rising wetness in her loins.

It had been a year since Frank died. Frank was the only man Anna had ever slept with, but George was the only man she ever fantasized about. When they returned home, George bid the ladies goodnight, kissed Anna on the hand, and walked across the grass to his home. Anna hurriedly kissed the girls goodnight and waited for them to fall asleep. A minute later, she found herself running across the moist grass in her bare feet toward George's front door. George was sitting on his back porch reading in a rocker. Artie Shaw's version of Stardust was playing on the radio. George looked up and smiled as he saw Anna approaching.

"Took you long enough!" George said as he wrapped his strong arms around Anna and felt her dissolve into him. Anna looked into George's eyes and felt herself quivering with the decade-old feelings she had kept hidden deep inside her for this man. She put her hands on the back of his neck and pulled his face to hers. Looking into his kind, loving eyes, she felt excitement and joy. At fifty-one, Anna had never felt so young.

They kissed. It was a long and passionate kiss. She reached for his pants and felt a bulge that exceeded even her wildest fantasies about George over these many years, and there were many. It had been a year since she even hugged a man. Anna felt herself orgasming before they made it in the door. Once inside, she slipped off her violet and white lace dress, and it crumpled to the floor. She held George's manhood in her hand and realized she needed both hands, and maybe even a third just to hold it. Anna was fascinated. She didn't even know if she could handle it inside her. They kissed their way to the bedroom. "I have been fantasizing about this for years, but you know in my fantasies, it was even bigger," Anna teased as she nipped at George's neck.

"Sorry to disappoint," said George as he playfully recoiled.

Anna pulled him back to her. "I was kidding. I don't even think that thing will fit in me." Anna took a deep breath and slowly pushed George's fullness inside of her. She let out a deep, piercing *'Yessssss'* moan that let George know that she could in fact handle it. Anna couldn't believe that after all of these years, she was finally with him in this way. The man of her dreams—the naughty ones. Anna had never experienced such bliss and knew she was going to come again. She pulled George's ear to her lips. "Now. Now!" George happily complied, as did Anna. In chorus, they both said, "I Love You," and dissolved into each other like warm bread dough.

George and Anna married a few years later in their backyards. All of the residents of Enchanted Place were in attendance. Anna moved into George's house and left her house for the girls to live in. Tina moved into an apartment on South Beach soon after. That was long ago. Anna snapped out of her trip down memory lane, pulled away from George's neck, and sipped her coffee. "Now, what were we talking about again? Oh yes, The creek."

33

His friends called him Al. His full name, given to him in the 1800's by Billy Bob Sawgrass himself, was Ulwe Alatcha, the Seminole words for tall tree. Al was over five hundred years old. The Spanish Moss hanging from his lower branches gave Al an ancient appearance, like a long gray beard adorning the face of an old man. When he awoke that morning, he looked up to feel those damn squirrels chewing off his acorns again. Al shook a branch at them.

"Hey, Rocky and Bullwinkle. How would you like it if I chewed your nuts off? Knock it off! There're enough acorns on the ground to get you through next December. Leave some alone to grow up into more trees. More trees equal more acorns. Think about it. Plan ahead, squirrels. Geez!"

The squirrels chattered loudly at Al and scampered down his main trunk.

"And, you have three nests in me already, so stop your damn branch chewing. It really hurts, you know."

The carefree squirrels shook their tails at Al and hopped to the ground. Squirrels always reminded Al of humans who came to rest under his shade after they drank too much coffee. They could never keep still and were always yacking. Al dropped a dead branch, just a few inches from the squirrels, causing a great commotion.

"That was just a warning. Next time, it's on your heads."

"Sorry, Al," the squirrels chattered in harmony.

"And no more running around up there before sunup. I need my beauty rest, you know. Those screech owls were hooting it up until 2 AM."

"Sorry, Al," the squirrels said, this time in an insincere manner.

"I'm getting too old for this shit."

With that, Al stretched his mighty branches, and flexed his roots. Being five hundred years old does come with its benefits. Al was the oldest tree in Biscayne Park. His roots stretched out far enough to touch the roots of the 4 other Oaks in the yard. The homeowners loved and cared for Al. They never cut away his inner branches, not even before hurricane season, like some of the other homeowners in the Village. Just the thought of tree trimmers made Al's leaves cringe. Some of these uneducated and greedy tree trimmers talked homeowners into mutilating their trees by cutting out all of the inner branches. These dubious tree trimers told the ill-informed homeowners that these inner branches trapped the wind, causing trees to topple in storms.

The truth was, these inner branches provided essential nutrients to the trees, keeping their branches strong, supple, and able to survive a storm. A good arborist would never cut these inner branches. It would be like removing a human's stomach, leaving them to die, and telling them how trim they looked. Yes, Al was lucky indeed. In addition to his entourage of four smaller Oak trees, there were trees and plants of all kinds: Macadamia, Black Sapote, Orange, Key Lime, Pink Grapefruit, Pomegranate, Allspice, Palm Trees, Bamboos, Orchids, Cactus, Succulents, and a wide variety of ferns and flowering plants, attracting butterflies and birds of all kinds to the yard. It was indeed a very natural oasis.

Al was so huge, his roots reached under the street and across the median, touching the surrounding Oaks. These trees had an underground root network reaching south through Miami Shores and El Portal, and north to North Miami; especially into Arch Creek Park, where some of Al's contemporaries lived. Al refused to allow his root network to speak with the City of Miami trees. That area was overrun by Banana Trees, and Al just didn't like the Banana Tree Republic atmosphere.

Through this root-network, the trees were able to communicate. They frequently communicated about the weather conditions. Miami had two seasons: 1). rainy, hot humid season, and 2). not as rainy, not as hot and humid season. The trees exchanged information to help them survive. The larger trees, with Al in the lead, knew for example when not-so-rainy season was at its peak. The big trees would let the little trees know they should drop their leaves to form a blanket of moisture retaining insulation over the sandy soil. Communication like this was essential to insure the survival of their species, and the planet itself. Without the life sustaining oxygen, the trees provided to mammals, life on Earth would cease to a halt.

The trees also liked to communicate about other things, especially gossip. Al's tallest branches reached over eighty feet high and stretched just as wide. His horizontal branches touched those of the other Oaks in the yard, and theirs touched the branches of the Oaks and Banyans in the median. The dense foliage provided a microclimate in Al's yard. Like Arch Creek, it was cooler than the rest of the neighborhood, thus a welcome sanctuary for a wide variety of hawks, screech owls, songbirds, bees, racoons, foxes, the occasional coyote, and of course, the ubiquitous and ever chattering, tail-shaking squirrels.

On this particular morning, it was a Tuesday, Al's tallest branches saw a splash in the water in Arch Creek. His roots felt a strange vibration he hadn't felt for centuries. It was both haunting and familiar. The sound vibrations passed through the water that covered his roots. In South Florida, you only have to dig down about twenty feet to hit the Florida aquifer; the water that flowed from the Everglades to Miami under a bed of limestone rock. Al could feel the vibrations, and his leaves started shaking to the rhythm. *Ommapapo! Ommapapo!* It was the sound of beating drums and chanting. It was the language of the people that left long ago. The Tequestas. Within seconds, Al's entourage was shaking their leaves too, followed by all of the other trees in the neighborhood.

Al remembered the Tequestas, who were peaceful, quiet, beautiful people. They respected all of the life forms—trees, animals, the soil, the water, and the air. They walked and rode horses. They lit small, well-tended fires, didn't wear many body coverings, and made love under Al's branches, on his fallen leaves. Their children were happy and learned to hunt, fish, gather shellfish, and grind Coontie flour. They built dugout canoes from Cypress Trees and followed Arch Creek into Biscayne Bay, to catch fish, sharks, turtles, and even manatees for food. Some traveled from the Bay down the Miami River into the Everglades.

The Tequestas had veneration for all life forms and only killed what they needed to eat. Before they ate an animal's meat, they thanked the creature for sacrificing its life to sustain them. Al always felt at ease when the Tequestas lived under his branches. He liked the humans who lived in his yard now, but several of the people in the neighborhood, used noisy, spewing machines for everything from moving from place to place, to cutting the grass beneath Al's friend's branches. The people ran from their noisy machines and hid from the sunshine and rain inside their sealed homes. They came outside mostly in the mornings and late afternoons, when the Earth rotates away from the sun, or on chilly days. Being Miami, it never really got that cold.

Thankfully, Al's humans, the Lawrence's, were a bit different. They carefully hung hammock swings from two of Al's horizontal branches. The couple picnicked in the yard, cooked food over well-tended fires, and wore little in the way of clothing. They made love under Al's branches, and smoked pungent leaves in a pipe, just like the Tequestas and later, the Seminoles.

Ommapapo! Ommapapo! Al tried to stop his leaves from shaking to the sound, as it was not-so-rainy season, and he had already released thousands of leaves on the ground. He concentrated, and the shaking stopped. After his success, Al communicated through his roots to the younger trees. They could all read each other's tree minds, and many had not heard of the Tequestas. The smaller trees, who had years ago sprouted from Al's acorns, spoke to Al through their branches.

"We hear the sound, Father. We feel it. We're scared. What does it mean?"

"It means, children, she's back!"

34

George and Anna sat sipping their morning coffee. "Well, George, what could be causing that color change? And… something else... Oh, you'll think I'm going crazy."

"You? Crazy? You are the sanest person I know, my dear. Maybe some of the old, dead branches and leaves moved out in the storm we had a couple of weeks ago, and the old Creek water was flushed out with Bay water?"

"First of all, the water couldn't clear up like that overnight. So, promise you won't lock me up."

"Promise. And, if they lock you up, I'm coming with you."

"You know I always come with you, George; that's why I married you!"

George kissed Anna tenderly on the forehead. "Now go on and tell me all about you being crazy."

"Last night, I heard a splash in the water."

"I hear splashes all the time; tarpon, snook, mullet, they all jump around out here at night."

"No, this was different. It was a big splash. When I came out, I saw a huge tail disappear under the water."

"Tail. Maybe it was a gator. They get in here sometimes, you know. Even crocodiles."

"No. This was big and flat. Like a manatee's tail."

"So, it was a manatee, that doesn't sound so crazy."

"There's something I didn't tell you."

"Go ahead. So far no loony bin for you."

"After I saw the tail disappear, I heard a noise."

"What kind of noise?"

"It was a voice. I swear."

"A voice. Maybe Gina or the kids were calling you from their yard."

"No. It was after 11. All of their lights were off. Besides, I know what their voices sound like. This was a voice I've never heard, and I heard music too. Well, some very deliberate sound in the distance."

"Now you are getting closer to cuckoo. What did this voice sound like? And, the music? Maybe some dueling banjos? We did see Deliverance last week."

"George. You promised. I'm being serious now."

"Sorry, my dear. What was the music?"

"It was chanting, and drumming. It was very rhythmic. I could feel it through the ground. Even the tree leaves seemed to be shaking to it. And the voice... it was as if it was speaking to me."

George saw Anna trembling, so he gathered her in his arms. "I believe you, Anna. What did the voice say?"

"Oh, you already think I'm nuts."

"No. I believe you. What did the voice say?"

"I'm back."

35

*E*rnest Thirst drove his wagon east on what is now known as Flagler Street. His eyes were still ablaze with turquoise. "My Spring. We are almost there."

Wekiwa slowly rose from the back of the wagon where she had been resting. She put on her deerskin dress, ran her boneskin comb through her hair, and sat on the front seat of the wagon next to Ernest.

"So, this is Mayaimi?"

"Yes, My Spring. Do you like it?"

Wekiwa looked at the streets lined with shops of all kinds. Although she ventured up and down the Miami River in a dugout canoe, she had never been far from the tourist camp she grew up in, and this was her first visit to Miami, or any town. There were many horses and wagons tied up all along the street, and many more making their way through downtown Miami. The road was dirty, dusty, and made Wekiwa cough.

"This place is disgusting!"

"Forgive me for disappointing you, My Spring."

"Are you kidding. I love it already. There's greed, I mean, *money* everywhere. I can smell it."

"Yes, My Spring. We are very close to your restaurant now."

"Good," said Wekiwa as she placed a cloth around her mouth and nose to keep the dust out, then stood up and got a better look around.

"The place is right at the mouth of the Miami River," Ernest said.

Wekiwa had learned from her Grandfather that their ancestors, the Tequestas, lived along the mouth of the Mayaimi River for many centuries until they had all died, or had been killed off. "The Mayaimi River travels from the Everglades where my people live, all the way to Biscayne Bay, and all of the river travelers shall pass by my restaurant—Flowing Springs. My people lived here long before your people, Ernest. Time to reclaim some of what was taken from us. Do you even know what Mayaimi means, Ernest?"

"No, My Spring. Tell me. Whatever it means will sound beautiful flowing from your mouth."

"Mayaimi is an Indian word. Your people didn't even spell it right. It's MAYAIMI! It means, *Big Water*. It was my ancestor's name for this River, and this place. You know you can paddle here in a canoe from my home."

"That is beautiful, My Spring." Ernest pulled back on the reigns and stopped his horse in front of a building. "This is it, My Spring. Have I pleased you?"

Wekiwa considered the structure in front of her for some time. It was fifty times the size of her house, made of unpainted brown wood, with a tin roof. There were large windows, most with broken glass. Wekiwa climbed off the wagon and walked inside as Rainbow stretched in the wagon, jumped down, and followed her.

The place smelled so strongly of must, it made Rainbow sneeze. There were tables made of cypress wood with many wooden chairs. There was a large high table in the back with shelves over it and dark wooden stools in front of it. As Wekiwa walked farther in, rats, mice, and bugs scattered under the debris on the floor. Rainbow swatted with her big claws, caught three rats and a mouse in one paw, and popped them into her mouth. Wekiwa scratched Rainbow behind the ear and laughed. "Good work Rainbow. You're in charge of pest control." Rainbow purred like an overgrown housecat at her praise.

They made their way through the space to what Wekiwa was really looking for—the kitchen. It was so overwhelming that Wekiwa almost shed a tear. At her camp, Wekiwa cooked over an open fire and salted her meat and fish to keep them fresh. This place had all kinds of things Wekiwa knew nothing about. She called to Ernest.

"Yes, My Spring?"

"Explain these things."

Ernest walked up to the stoves. "These are stoves for cooking, My Spring. It brings the fire inside, and you can control the heat without adding more wood or dousing the flame." Ernest took a box of matches from his pocket, turned on the front burners of both stoves, and lit them all. Rainbow hissed loudly when the flames erupted from the stove, and Wekiwa stood in disbelief.

"How long will those flames burn?"

"For as long as we pay the gas bill, My Spring. Do they please you?"

"Yes. Very much so. Show me more."

Ernest went down the row of burners and turned the flames down on two burners and up on the other two.

"How is this, My Spring?"

"Very good. What are those?"

"These are ovens, My Spring. They work like the burners, only they heat up these big metal boxes for cooking."

"And what of this?"

"It's an ice box. You fill the bottom with ice and keep your food in it."

"Why would one do such a thing?"

"To keep it fresh, My Spring."

"Don't you salt your meats?"

"No. We don't have to when we have one of these," Ernest responded as he opened the refrigerator door.

"Good. We can catch more game and store it in there."

"Oh, we don't have to hunt or fish, My Spring."

"Then how will we feed everyone."

"Men come in wagons with meat, and boats come right to the dock out back with fish. The fruits and vegetables are just up the block. They even get some of their produce from other countries. It comes on big boats from all over the world and gets delivered right over there," Ernest explained while pointing east toward the Atlantic Ocean.

"Excellent, Ernest."

"There's something else to show you, My Spring."

Ernest walked back to the high table with many chairs. "This is a bar. It's where my people come to forget all of their troubles, or start new ones."

"Why here?"

"Those rusty shelves over the bar, they used to be full of liquor, and those taps, they were full of beer. You should try it."

"Ah, alcoholic beverages. Some of the tourists that stopped at our camp had whiskey bottles. Grandfather and Mother said to stay away from them, as it would bring sadness to the person consuming them, and to the Great Spirits."

"I did not mean to offend you, My Spring! I mean, it might give you great pleasure, My Spring." With that, Ernest reached into his vest pocket, removed a flask, unscrewed the top, and handed it to Wekiwa, who held the flask to her nose and drew back as the burning scent of whiskey wafted into her sinuses. Wekiwa sat on one of the barstools and spun around with the flask hovering before her lips. Rainbow hissed as Wekiwa held her breath and took a slug. She coughed and sneezed when the sting of the alcohol hit the back of her throat, not speaking for several minutes as Ernest and Rainbow watched on. Then, she smiled a very bewitching smile, held the flask up to salute Ernest, and drank down the flask's entire contents. She felt a warmth all over, and her head became lighter than air.

"I think I am going to like Mayaimi."

36

"Which babysitter, Gina? The blonde or that cute little brunette? It was the blonde, wasn't it? You always did like them tall."

"The brunette. I think… it's all such a blur, Tina. I remember being on the kitchen table, and, and… I was wearing that clown mask."

"You and Vlad have the same taste in facewear, I see. This place really is going to the dogs!"

"I'm still not sure it wasn't a dream or hallucination."

'Tell me the details, you little slut you."

"Whatever I did, would pale in comparison to just one of your nights out."

"I don't know, this sounds pretty good, or pretty bad, depending on how you look at it. What kind of clown mask was it?"

"I wanna say Bozo. Give me a minute to think. Yep, Bozo."

"Nice. I might have gone with Ronald McDonald. He has those really big feet, and you know what they say about big feet."

"Is that even true?"

"From experience, yes. Besides, what size are Ben's shoes?"

"Twelve."

"And his equipment?"

Gina said giggling, "Let's just say if it were a candy, it would be Good & Plenty."

"So then why did you do the babysitter?"

"I have no idea. Ben left with his face covered in cake and frosting, then I went outside to clear my head and heard another splash in the water. I went inside, and there was Margo, the brunette. She asked if I could pay her because she wanted to go get ice cream at Carvel."

"Oooh, did she bring that back for your little party?"

"Very funny, but I do love their ice cream. So, we walked out back because I left my purse on the patio table. We hear a splash again. I get another really weird feeling, but that time, it was sexual."

"Like I said, you little slut you!"

"I gotta tell you, I've never felt anything like that before, and when I looked at Margo, I could see the passion in her eyes too. We started kissing and touching each other; all over, if you know what I mean," Gina said as a blush spread over her cheeks.

"You're the slut in this story, not me. Go on."

"We made our way into the house, kissing and groping all the way to the kitchen."

"The only time we separated was when she reached into her backpack, took out a Clown mask, and put it over my head."

"Kinky. I had a guy once who used to make me wear a bunny mask. I kind of liked it. You know that expression, screwing like rabbits? Let me tell you, those rab—"

Gina cut Tina off, "Please, this is hard enough!"

"That's what she said!"

"Tina, please! If anyone heard this conversation! Geez!"

"You know, I learned in biology that a mated pair of cockroaches chew off each other's wings to make the other stay monogamous."

"Ewwwww. Why would you even tell me that?"

"Because I don't think us animals are monogamous by nature. The cockroaches know the only way to keep their mates faithful is to stop them from flying away. Ben should have chewed off your wings a long time ago. So, how was it with a girl?"

"I never even kissed a girl before. And she's so young, only eighteen. Her lips were soft, and she was incredibly gentle. Everything she did felt like, well, like a woman was touching me. I mean I love Ben, and the sex is great, but this was so, so... what word am I looking for?"

"Hot as Hell!"

"Seriously, Tina, the thing I remember the most was how soft and sensual it was. It was sensuous, but it was also scary because somewhere inside of me, I knew it was wrong."

"Details, baby. Details!"

"Oh, after that, it's all a blur, but I wasn't in control. It was like someone else had taken over my body. I could see what I was doing, through my own eyes, but I also saw something else. Oh, I can't explain."

"Take a deep breath, Sis. I'm here for you," Tina said, as she reached out and hugged Gina, who fell weeping into Tina's arms.

"I saw another dimension, Tina." Gina held her head in her hands and ashamedly looked away.

"Hey! I'm your Sister. You can tell me anything. I won't chew off your little wings," Tina said with a straight face, causing Gina to break into laughter. "It's really too bad Dad isn't here. He would be so proud. And, in his house!"

"That's just it, Tina."

"What?"

"I think Dad is here, and he's not alone!"

37

Ben shook his head in disbelief. He went into the house and called his best friend Michael Lawrence. Ben asked Mike to come over right away and bring his diving gear.

Ben and Mike had been friends since they were kids, when they met at Camp Beth David. Mike was nine at that time and twelve-year-old Ben was a junior counselor. Despite their age differences, they had a common love of all things related to fishing and became fast friends.

Mike grew up to be a marine biologist. He lived in Biscayne Park, just down the road from Ben and Gina's house. Biscayne Park is a tiny village of just over 1,000 homes, and 3,000 residents. Those numbers don't account for the kaleidoscope of butterflies, bees, various pollinators, mosquitoes—and bats to eat them—owls, hawks, parrots, painted buntings, orioles, ibis, blue jays, cardinals, Florida's state bird—the mockingbird, foxes, coyotes, raccoons, opossum, hundreds of squirrels, thousands of mature native trees, exotic trees, such as black sapotes, lychees, and macadamias.

Speaking of nuts, it has been said that while other communities keep their nuts hidden away, Biscayne Park keeps their nuts right out there on their front lawns. The residents of Biscayne Park are a mix of some of the most creative, nature-loving, outspoken, artists, musicians, writers, spiritualists, atheists, scientists, and some of the nuttiest people anywhere, but in a good way.

The village was originally a landscape area and nursery for Miami Beach and was carefully planted with and around native and non-native trees. Some of the Oaks are hundreds of years old. The people in the village have a reverence for their trees. It was rumored that in the 50's, a woman with a visual impairment who mistakenly broke a branch off one of the village's sacred two-hundred-year-old Oaks, was sentenced to plant a hundred flowering trees around the village as her penance. A seeing-eye dog was provided to offer assistance; and dig the holes. This type of rumor made the village even more attractive to people with an element of funkiness in their souls; that, and you could make it to the beach in ten minutes, downtown Miami in fifteen, and Lauderdale in thirty.

Mike worked at the University of Miami. He spent most of his days on a boat in Biscayne Bay or the ocean, transplanting laboratory-grown turtle grass and coral polyps onto the bay floor in order to replenish the species.

He was one of the first scientists in Miami to identify and chart the destruction of the natural ecosystem in South Florida. Even in the early 70's, years of people boating, diving, and fishing started to impact the environment. Corals were dying off from the Florida Keys to Ft. Lauderdale. Turtle grass in the bay was destroyed by thoughtless boaters. These actions caused erosion of the seabed and diminished the breeding grounds of thousands of fish, Stone Crabs, lobsters, and other economically and environmentally important species.

When Mike first had proof of the environmental impact, he shouted it from the rooftops. He published his work in every journal possible and went to the local media. Ben cited Mike's research in his book. While this caused Mike to gain acclaim in the scientific and hippie communities, he was, let's just say, less than popular with recreational and commercial fishermen and boaters. Mike had, in fact, gained such infamy with the fishermen, he used to kid that when he out, he had to wear Groucho Marx glasses and mustache disguise. The fact that Mike already had a mustache, wore glasses, and bore a cursory resemblance to Groucho, did not escape his friends.

While the mainstream media wrote Mike off as a kook, Danny Gomez, solitary reporter, and owner of the Miami Guardian, did not. The Guardian was regarded as a rag paper, available for free on Newsstands, in local Health Food Stores, Pita Restaurants, and the odd convenience store. It's counter-culture advertisers were mostly the same environmentally and health-conscious customers who frequented the stores where the Guardian was distributed. This caused an almost incestuous relationship between the paper, its readers, and its advertisers. Danny's reporting over the last year had come down to the latest health food craze. Last month's feature story was: Tofu Recipes for your Vegetarian Dog.

Danny thought Mike's story, and Ben's book, which was relentlessly and freely advertised in the Guardian, might give him some credibility as a journalist. Two years prior, Danny's story about reducing the beach lighting to save the sea turtles brought him just a hint of respectability. Danny reported that upon digging out of their beach nests in the wee morning hours, turtle hatchlings mistook the bright street and condo lights for the reflection of the moon and stars off the ocean, causing them to follow the lights and head directly across the busy streets, to their deaths. While Danny was the first reporter to cover this, he was not the last, nor the prettiest.

The night Danny's story in the Guardian hit the free Newsstands, Jasmine Rice, model turned weatherperson, turned WJOK anchorperson, glommed onto Danny's research, just in time for the 6 PM news. Of course, Jasmine was credited with the coverage, but Danny did receive a miniscule amount of on-air recognition for breaking the story. Thanks to Danny's work, people actually stopped the installation of bright lights on new condos on A1A, the road nearest the oceanfront.

Danny saw Mike's research as his ticket to becoming a respected journalist. Self-interest aside, he also really liked Mike. He was a humorous man, a good scientist, an outdoorsman, a thinker, and overall, someone just trying to do the right thing; not for himself, but to make the world a better place. Mike liked Danny as well. While he knew The Guardian was not exactly The New York Times, he appreciated the need for a paper for the people, by the people. Mike enjoyed Danny's writing style as well. It was colorful, poetic, often inflammatory, and honest to a fault. Plus, Mike appreciated that The Guardian provided some good stir fry recipes, and buy one, get one free restaurant dinner coupons.

At thirty-five, Mike already felt like a relic. He was hoping Danny's coverage of his environmental work would serve to add legitimacy to his career. For the time being, all he was doing was pissing off the boaters and fishermen and was glad to have someone besides Ben to take his concerns seriously.

Mike's wife, Hazel was half Seminole Indian and had a unique spiritual relationship with planet earth, but after a while, even her saintly eyes glazed over when he spent four hours talking about the changing sand density in the Northern part of Biscayne Bay. Mike got in his orange and white VW Van and took the short drive to Ben's house.

38

*G*us LaCroix pulled Aunt Ethel's truck onto a dirt road in Homestead, a farming district between Miami and the Florida Keys. Years ago, Gus stayed there in a trailer with his drinking buddy, Larry Fine. Larry was born with two thick shocks of curly red hair on both sides of his head. Even as an infant, he looked remarkably like Larry from the Three Stooges. His Father, Notso Fine, was a big Three Stooges fan, hence naming him Larry, as their family had a fondness for odd names. Larry's grandfather, Parking Fine, bought the farmland years ago and grew tomatoes, strawberries, and corn. At ninety-three, Parking still smoked fish he caught in the nearby Florida Keys and sold it from a very popular roadside stand, purposely built right next to a No Parking Sign.

Larry was supposed to take over the family business, but the only thing he was interested in growing was marijuana. As such, Larry spent most of his time, stoned, drunk, or incarcerated. He was a great disappointment to his family. Larry's family had strong Christian values, and rather than throwing him out on the streets, they let him live in an old airstream trailer in the very back of the farm. Gus hadn't seen Larry since he fled to Ponchatoula, Louisiana.

Larry and Gus met in jail in Florida City. Gus was on his way back from a drunken fishing weekend in the Keys and got pulled over for a DUI. Larry was on his way to the Keys, but started drinking early that morning, and his swerving 1965 Mustang never made it past a cement light pole on US1 in Florida City. After four days, nobody showed to bail either of them out, so they were credited with time served and released on their own recognizance.

"Hey, what was your name again?"

"Gus, Gus LaCroix."

"Oh, yeah. I'm still going to call you Red, okay?"

"Go ahead, everyone else does. But, I gotta say, you are even redder than me, man! Larry Fine. Did your parents think that name through?"

"Hell yeah. It's a tradition in our Fine family."

"Fine family. I get it. Fine family. Is your Dad a comedian?"

"Nah, just a farmer. His Daddy named him Notso."

"Notso Fine. That's funny dude!"

"Yeah. Well, see ya. I'm heading home, man."

"Where's that?"

"Oh, just down the road a piece," Larry replied.

"You wouldn't happen to have a couch I could sleep on for a couple days, mon ami?"

"Mon ami? Are you a furinnure?"

"No, brah. I'm Cajun, from Louisiana."

"Do you party, Red?"

"Hell, how do you think I wound up in this place?"

"Well, follow me, Red. I got the finest dope around."

Gus spent what turned into an eight-day weekend at Larry Fine's trailer, which was adorned with Three Stooges posters. Gus used to head down to Larry's anytime he wanted to score some pot, drink, and hang with the only person who could keep up with his binging. Plus, he liked sleeping it off in the airstream, waking up in the morning, picking fresh buds to smoke from the farm, and starting all over again. Sometimes, if he wasn't too hungover, Gus would wander into the tomato field, and bring back a few for breakfast. There was nothing like a fresh tomato with salt to cure a hangover, especially with a few shots of cheap vodka.

Gus pulled up to the trailer, turned off the truck, and knocked on the door. Nobody answered. He sat in his truck, hoping that Larry Fine would wake up soon. Before he knew it, Gus fell asleep and awoke to something cold and hard wedged into his cheek.

"Is that a gun, Larry Fine, or are you just happy to see me?"

"Who's that anyhow?"

"Hey, Larry! It's me, Gus, Gus LaCroix."

"Who?"

"Red"

"Red!!! Why the hell didn't you say so! I could have shot that red right off your damned head," Larry said as he put his gun in his pocket.

"Where the hell you been, Red?"

"Back home in Louisiana, mon ami."

"You want to try my new strain of Maui Wowie? This shit will mess you up real good."

"That's exactly what I need. Thanks, brah." Gus took a big hit of the joint Larry Fine offered, and then another, before handing it back to him.

"Damn, boy. This shit is sweet. Can I crash here for a while? I got some bidness to take care of."

"Any money in it, Red?"

"Nah. Just trying to right a wrong."

"Hell, Red. Count me in. Revenge is like sex or weed. Ain't really no bad kind."

"It's not like that, Larry. I'm the one that needs to make it right."

"Well, count me out of that boring shit, but yeah, you can crash here."

"Thanks, I appreciate you, Larry Fine. You're bout the only friend I got left, mon ami."

"Don't get sappy, Red. You want to show me some love, just keep the mini fridge stocked with PBR."

"Deal! I just got to get my stuff."

Gus went out to the truck and got a soiled, brown duffle bag out of the passenger side. He reached into the bed of the truck and pulled out a medium-sized cooler. Gus opened it, took out a can of PBR, and picked up a large plastic bag, containing an object the size of a coconut. Sitting on the truck bed, he guzzled half the PBR, and held the bag up to his face. Inside was a human head. "Well, Herman, I think it's time we reunite you with your body, right?"

As Gus lowered the bag back into the cooler, the eyes opened, just for a second, just enough for Gus to see them. He dropped the bag into the cooler and shuddered. "Sheeshh! That spooks me out every time." Gus bent down to close the cooler lid, and as he did, he heard laughter. Gus looked over and saw Larry Fine laughing and slapping his thigh.

"Damn, Red. Looks like maybe you got a little ahead of yourself. Whatever you're up to, definitely count me back in."

39

Wekiwa loved her restaurant as if it were part of her body and soul. Like many of the structures in Miami in the early 1900's, it was built of termite resistant, Dade County Pine. While covered with grunge when Wekiwa first saw them, the dark brown wood walls glistened by the time Wekiwa and Ernest finished scrubbing them down.

Rainbow ate her fill of rats and mice, and the floors were swept and mopped until they showed their beautiful grain. Once cleaned, the building smelled like freshly cut pine on a fall day, and Wekiwa's vision of the Restaurant's decor became crystal clear.

Wekiwa sowed beautiful lace curtains with turquoise and teal embroidery. She shopped on Flagler Street and purchased brass lighting fixtures from the Middle East, with stones and lights that twinkled like diamonds, casting a warm, mystical feel all around the renewed space. The bar stools were upholstered with red velvet fabric and glass bar shelves replaced the rusty steel to hold the liquor.

The kitchen received a deep cleaning as well, after which the stove glistened in the light coming through the windows that had all been replaced with fresh glass. Wekiwa bought the finest copper pots, pans, and utensils of all kinds to outfit her upgraded cooking station. She also took her time to cultivate a collection of fine china, silverware, tablecloths, linen, and an assortment of glasses for table placements. The space was transformed from darkness and grime, into a sparkling oasis fit for a Sultan.

Wekiwa fixed up the back room for her living space and slept there with Rainbow every night during the first year. Ernest slept in his wagon. She decorated her bedroom in subtle gold tones that glimmered like sawgrass, with Indian fabrics hung on the wall to remind her of home.

Ernest saved hundreds of dollars to buy the place, but he signed the deed over to Wekiwa that first night. While most restaurants in the 20's developed their menus based on locally sourced foods, Wekiwa's vision of local ingredients were meats, fish, plants and herbs from the Everglades.

She loved cooking frog legs, gator, snook fillets, rattlesnake, deer, armadillo, and other meats. And while Sofke was a basic food for Indians, all but a handful of Miamian's had ever tasted the dish. As such, there were no potatoes or rice on the menu, and Wekiwa developed all kinds of twists on Sofke—garlic mashed Sofke, Sofke with vegetables, Sofke with key lime cream sauce. She used Coontie to bake fresh cakes, biscuits, and other epicurean delights. Her vegetable dishes were flavorful and unique, as Wekiwa used pond apples, and hearts of palm cooked with Indian spices from Catori's garden. For all of these things, Wekiwa sent Ernest to the camp to load up on supplies and to send money home to her Mother.

People had never tasted such food, and to top it off, a live panther walking the floor of the restaurant nightly. In just a few weeks, Flowing Springs had such rave reviews, that Wekiwa became one of America's first celebrity chefs. Diners would come from all over the world to sample her cuisine and eat with a panther.

Wekiwa was a shrewd businesswoman. She purchased several adjacent parcels of valuable land and tripled the size of her Restaurant. She opened a gift shop which sold Rainbow panther dolls that were handsewn by members of her tribe. Wekiwa also bought a small, shallow draft steamboat for Ernest to travel the Mayaimi River to replenish supplies from her mother's camp each week. All profits went right back to the people who made them. It was through actions like this that Wekiwa became a hero amongst her tribe. The women who sewed the dolls were forever grateful. In fact, they made so much money, that even some of the men in the camp started sowing Rainbow panther dolls.

Wekiwa tried to enlist a photographer for restaurant patrons to have their picture taken with a panther. However, Rainbow did not take kindly to flash photography and pounced on the photographer. The man got the perfect shot of Rainbow leaping on top of him in mid-air. It was the best picture of his career, and the photographer vowed to come again as often as needed; however, with no more flash photography. The picture of Rainbow in flight appeared in the Miami Cryer under a headline that read: Prodigious Pussy Pounds Photographer into Prostration—Photographer Vows To Come Again! The next night, Flowing Springs reservations were sold out for six months in advance.

40

Mike parked his VW Van in Ben's driveway. He brought plastic sample bags, gloves, a mask, snorkel, submersible camera, as well as an underwater microphone and tape recorder he used for recording dolphin clicks when he was in grad school.

"Hey, Ben."

"Hey, Mike. Thanks for coming."

"You think I would pass up a chance at a talking manatee?"

"So you believe me, Mike?"

"Hey, you believed all of my crazy stories over the years. Remember when I told everyone Mrs. Mendlebaum was blowing the Rabbi on the camp bus, and you were the only one who followed me to the bus?"

"Followed you? Hell, I even brought my polaroid camera?" Ben joked.

"Yeah. That picture got us out of Hebrew school homework for life. Surprisingly, Mrs. Mendlebaum had a really great rack for an old lady."

"Old? What? Wasn't she thirty-five?" Ben asked.

"Yeah, but when we were kids, she seemed ancient. Hey. Whatever happened to that picture?"

"I still have it."

"So, a talking manatee? Where did you last see it?"

Ben walked Mike to the edge of the Creek. When the manatee disappeared under the surface, Ben marked the spot with two large limestone rocks from the yard. "Exactly here."

"And when did it last appear?"

"About an hour ago."

"And did it by any chance do this?" Mike took a squirt pistol from his pocket and sprayed it in Ben's face.

"Jackass," Ben laughed as he wiped the water from his cheeks.

"Just trying to lighten the mood. What the hell happened to your eye, anyway?"

Ben told Mike the story of the previous evening. How Gina shoved his face into the banana bread. How upset she was. How upset they both were.

"I didn't link any of it to the splash we heard in the Creek until the manatee showed up today. And there's something else?"

"Oh, did Flipper show up too?"

"That's what she said."

"What?"

"Never mind. It's all so strange."

"Nothing strange about a talking manatee. Nope. Did you get a polaroid?" Mike asked.

"Of what?"

"The manatee."

"Very funny?" Ben said.

"In ancient times, manatees were thought to be mermaids, you know. Sailors even fell in love with them."

"I didn't get a close look at this one, Mike, but let's just say it was no mermaid."

"You know, even Christopher Columbus mistook a manatee for a mermaid. The very first record of a manatee in North America came from Columbus' ship log. Really!" Mike stated in a very excited manner.

"Always the scientist."

"True, except when it came to Mrs. Mendlebaum. I don't think I was ever the same after that."

"Neither was the Rabbi. I'll bet he still thinks you're going to tell his wife. I wonder what she looks like now?" Ben asked.

"The Rabbi's wife?"

"Nah, Mrs. Mendlebaum," Mike said nostalgically.

"Keep it in your pants there, Jacques Cousteau. Why don't you don that fancy equipment and see what the hell is going on down in this Creek. I have my mask and snorkel too."

"Give me a minute to set up this microphone. It's been a while since I turned it on."

"That's what she said!" Ben joked again.

"Yeah, very funny. I'm coming now."

"That's what she said too."

"No wonder Gina clocked you! Sorry. Too soon?"

Ben looked truly hurt.

"Hey, sorry, buddy. Just kidding," Mike said in a conciliatory tone.

"Yeah, whatever. Let's go look for this mermaid."

"You first. I'll be right on your tail."

"That's just what the Rabbi said to Mrs. Mendlebaum."

"Smartass!"

As Ben and Mike entered the Creek, the water temperature suddenly dropped ten degrees, and all of the fish swam off. They submerged and looked at each other through foggy masks. The Creek water wasn't its usual tea-brown tannin color, produced by the decomposition of leaves and branches in the water; instead, it was colored light blue like a Florida spring, and just as cold. It was so clear; they could both see all the way to the Arch Creek Bridge to the South.

Ben swam in that Creek thousands of times over the years and could barely see past his hand every time. Today, it looked magical. Just as Mike gave Ben the thumbs up signal to surface so they could talk about the clarity and color of the water, he felt a nudge against his back. It was forceful, but playful all at once. At first, Mike thought it was a floating branch, but then he saw Ben's eyes frozen in shock, and as wide as flying saucers. Mike turned around slowly and saw it. The manatee, only, only it changed before his eyes. It looked just like a woman, and a beautiful, naked one at that.

Could it be? Mrs. Mendlebaum. Mike blinked his eyes and dropped his microphone. The creature picked up the microphone and spoke into it.

"You two certainly were naughty boys. Mrs. Mendlebaum, indeed."

41

Murray Ferrari was leaning over a pot when he felt a playful tug at his apron. Without turning around, he reached behind him and softly grabbed Betty's wrist.

"Amore mia. Open wide."

"Oh no, Murray. I'm not falling for that again. My mouth is still numb from this morning."

Murray kissed Betty passionately before responding, "And you were wonderful, as always, amore mia, but I wanted you to taste my aioli sauce."

"Okay, but no funny business. I'm not closing my eyes this time. Go ahead, put it in."

"That's what she said," Murray said, laughing as he dipped the wooden spoon in the saucepan and filled it halfway with sauce. "Now wait until I blow on it."

"That's what she said," Betty teased as she grabbed Murray's ass and winked.

"Try this, amore mia."

"It's almost perfect, but you know what I think it needs?"

"Almost? Almost?"

"Murray! Don't be so sensitive. Just a little more nutmeg and maybe a bit of white pepper."

Murray picked up his grinder and added some fresh nutmeg and a pinch of white pepper, then tasted it. "Ah, you're right, as usual. Here, try it now."

"Now that really pops in my mouth, Murray."

"Now that's what you said this morning!" Murray said, as he playfully licked a bit of spilled sauce off of Betty's cheek.

"And, why do you still wear that apron, when we don't even have clothes anymore?"

"It's sexy, no?"

"No! Hopefully we won't age, because if your boys start dangling under that thing, I'm going to insist you tuck them in."

"Tuck them in? Tuck them in? Don't break my balls! Funny, right?"

"Almost, my love."

"Almost, Alm..."

Betty interrupted, grabbed Murray's butt, and pulled him in for a kiss, "All right, it was funny. You know I can't resist you. I honestly don't know how I do it, considering you got me boiled alive."

"More like a quick poaching, amore mia. And that sauce, it was to die for, *right*? Too soon?"

"It's been over twenty years, and that joke still gives me heartburn. Thank God you're better in bed than you are at comedy."

"Ouch! Don't you worry, I'm working on a new act. You and the gang are going to love it."

"Well, at least you have a captive audience, even the dog." Betty looked over at the Doberman who was peaking under the house's crawl space and drooling. "Why do you think that dog can see us?"

"Amore mia, I tell you every time, it's my food. It drives him wild."

"I'm so proud. My lover, the dog food chef."

"Hey! That's no way to talk to Murray. He's an amazing cook, even though his food goes right through me," said a voice floating in to join them. "If only he could get my Nanny's Brisket recipe just right. I keep telling you, Murray, more booze. That's the secret," Herman's head said.

"I'll add more bourbon next time, but try not to get ahead of yourself, Herman. Ahead of yourself, get it?"

"This guy still almost cracks me up. If only I had hands, I would clap, or punch you."

"Oh, Herman, I wish they would have sent you here with your body too. I miss that big soft belly of yours," Betty said coyly.

"Me too. If I ever get my hands, I mean, my teeth on that Gus Lacroix, I'll rip his head off!"

"Don't you worry, my friend, we will haunt that son of a bitch *areal agood*. Cutting off a man's head with wire, in his own boat. You would think he grew up with my Uncle Paolo."

"Now, boys, let's not lose our heads! Sorry, Herman. Too soon?"

"Good thing I kept my sense of humor, Betty. It's bad enough I have to go through the afterlife as a disembodied head, but then to be stuck here with my dead wife and her young lover. Geez. You would think I was being punished. Good thing I like to watch," said Herman's head, chuckling.

"Oh, Herman, let's be fair. There are plenty of times you do more than watch. Thankfully, Gus didn't cut that talented tongue out of your mouth."

"Tongue. Oh, what I wouldn't give for one of my Nanny's tongue sandwiches."

"Tongue. Please, Herman. You know I never like to eat something that's been in someone else's mouth," said Murray.

"That's not what you said last night," Betty replied, winking at Murray and gently squeezing Herman's ears. "We could almost be a throuple, if only you had all of your accessories."

"Speaking of accessories, that was some wild shit happening in the kitchen last night. A clown mask. Now, that's funny," Murray said.

"I wonder what got into that babysitter?"

"I think Gina got into her," Murray quipped. "Funny, no?"

"No!" Betty and Herman replied.

"I never thought Gina would cheat on Ben. He was always such a good boy. A bit naïve, but good, and faithful as the day is long. And to shove his face in that banana bread. Why would she do that to him?" Herman queried.

"Well, we know one thing for sure. She isn't Jewish. No self-respecting Jew would waste cake like that. It's an insult to cooks everywhere. If it weren't for my rosary beads being here, and our course, Betty, mia amore, I would just make like a banana and split. Funny, no?" Murray joked.

"No! It's that damn manatee. I told you she was trouble the minute she showed up. She has some kind of strong magic. Ben is such a good boy. I see how he worships Gina and how she loves him. That manatee, she cast a spell on those girls," Betty said.

"This is why I love her, Herman. You picked a smart one here. Too bad you couldn't hold onto her. Get it? Hold on, because you have no arms," Murray wisecracked.

"It's a good thing you can cook because I think some of your jokes died with you, my love," Betty said.

"Ouch!" said Murray, clutching his chest.

"No, this is serious. What do you think that manatee is up to?"

As Betty spoke, the ground under the house started shaking. She looked out of the crawl space grate to see the leaves on the trees shaking violently. She flew out into the yard, and there wasn't a hint of breeze. The air was dead still. The leaves, however, were moving at warp speed, and the ground was shaking. Betty looked into the Creek and saw the color. Light blue and crystal clear. It was always a sort of yucky brown, with some cups, beer cans, and other trash stuck to its delicate surface. Today, it looked pristine. Betty saw a splash in the water and two figures standing by the Creek bank. She flew over for a closer look, followed by Herman's head and Murray.

"Hey, wait for us!" yelled Herman and Murray.

All of them were floating just under the Spanish Moss hanging from an Oak Tree, just inches away from Ben and Mike.

"That Mike. He was always such a good boy too. Very smart," Herman said.

"He was, but you know he always had a crush on me," Betty replied.

"Oh, Betty. You can't blame him, especially when you wore those little halter tops when you picked the boys up from camp."

"Yes. Mike was always walking behind me, hoping for a side-boob glance. Still, he was a good kid. What do you think they are doing with that big equipment?"

"Hey, That's*a* what she said!" Murray joked as he flew under water. "Amore mia, Herman, look, it's the manatee. She's talking to them."

"Talking? Maybe you were right, Betty. What is she saying?"

"I'm not exactly sure, but who the hell is Mrs. Mendlebaum?" Betty asked.

42

*W*ekiwa loved cooking and the creativity it unleashed within her. Whenever Wekiwa considered a dish, in her mind, she saw the finished product, plated and being consumed by her customers. Her imagery was so strong, that her tongue tasted it, and her mouth watered at the very thought of each new dish. This process informed her ingredients and presentation.

Flowing Spring's house specialty was Alligator Tail with a cocoplum glaze, Sofke garlic mash, and fresh Everglades pumpkin. The ingredients were all sourced from her tribe, who made a substantial profit off of each order. Catori's garden plot grew hundredfold, and she had several young bucks cultivating her crops. This pleased Catori to no end, because after all, what middle-aged single woman isn't happy having a few young men hanging around.

Wekiwa's passions did not end with cooking and eating, although she delighted in both. Wekiwa and Rainbow's favorite activity was scoping out new prey. Rainbow always led the way, and at around 10 PM, every Saturday evening, she began her prowl. She would methodically patrol each table, rubbing her ears on the table legs, inconspicuously sniffing each guest from a slight distance. When she sensed a male with a high testosterone level, or a female with a high estrogen level, she would lift her tail, and let out a friendly purr. This typically resulted in the guest petting Rainbow's head, back, or sometimes, her happy spot on her back, where her tail joined her body.

When Wekiwa heard Rainbow's purring, she would pick up a pot lid to view her reflection and fix her hair, then leave the kitchen to come into the dining room. Every single time Wekiwa entered the dining room, she received a standing ovation, which she dismissed with a casual flick of her hand. Wekiwa would then make her way to Rainbow's newest friend, ask how they were enjoying their meal, and offer a special dessert on the house.

Wekiwa's desserts were as highly praised as her entrees and side dishes, but the extraordinary ones she made for her Saturday night's specially selected diners, were magical. Wekiwa discovered the recipe for Ernest's attraction and undying attachment to her. It was a combination of processed Coontie, herbs from her mother's garden, and ground passionflower, all made into a tart, that Wekiwa named Passioncakes. Then to top it off, Wekiwa needed to touch her prey, flash them one of her trademark smiles, and finally, gaze into their eyes. Her turquoise eyes. And later, a kiss to seal the deal.

If the guest was dining alone, it was a fairly simple transaction. Wekiwa would deliver the expressly prepared treat, and upon dropping the plate on the table, touch her intended's hand while smiling and looking them in the eye. Once the diner consumed the food, they found themselves in a passion-seeking, blissful state, which could only be quenched by Wekiwa. The diners who found themselves in this state could not move from their tables until once again touched by Wekiwa, who they would then blindly follow to the ends of the earth.

Wekiwa remained in the kitchen until closing time, usually around midnight. After the last diners left, with only her prey remaining, Wekiwa returned to the dining room, touched the forearm of her prey, and led them to her room behind the kitchen. Rainbow followed closely behind. Wekiwa disrobed and instructed the guest to do the same. She then kissed the person, or persons on the mouth and watched their eyes for the transformation. Sometimes the conversion took place immediately; sometimes it took up to two minutes.

Once their eyes turned turquoise, Wekiwa knew they were hers to do with as she pleased. If the person had a dinner companion, the process became trickier. If Rainbow found both of their hormone levels satisfactory, she would purr twice, as opposed to once for a single diner. With that signal, Wekiwa prepared and delivered, two special desserts. If the person had a companion who did not meet with Rainbow's approval, they would receive a similar looking dish, which contained a combination of Coontie, morning glory petals, and herbs Wekiwa discovered would put them into a sleepwalking state. She would also lead this diner to her room at the end of the night; however, that person was placed into a comfortable chaise lounge to sleep it off. Even amongst the noise of Wekiwa's lovemaking, they remained fast asleep until morning.

Wekiwa delighted in the variety of lovemaking and learned much about sexual pleasuring from her trysts. There was only one problem. At the end of her first month in business, there were four men and one woman, all with turquoise eyes, sleeping in Ernest's wagon parked beside Flowing Springs. Wekiwa tired of feeding them, and once used for her pleasure, she bored of them.

The complication was, she didn't know how to turn off the power of her incantation. The next Saturday night, Wekiwa found herself walking into her bedroom with a Texas oilman, her latest conquest, when the turquoise mysteriously faded from his eyes. She kissed the oilman, and his eyes flickered back to turquoise. She inspected the oilman from the tips of his boots to the hairs on his head. The only thing that looked slightly unusual was a bit of white dust on his hands. Wekiwa lifted the oilman's hand to her face and sniffed the dust. The smell was as familiar to her as her own scent, but just to make sure, she stuck out the tip of her tongue and dabbed it into the dust. It was sharp. It was bitter. It was Coontie! Unprocessed Coontie flour. She retraced the oilman's path with her keen eyesight. His boot prints left a barely perceptible trail that passed through the kitchen and past the small round table Wekiwa used to process Coontie.

She filled a ceramic cup with the unprocessed Coontie and returned to the still-standing man. Lifting a pinch, she placed it on the oilman's hand. He blinked five times, opened his eyes wide, and was startled by his surroundings.

"Oh, pardon me, ma'am. How on earth did I wind up here? The last thing I remember was that Passioncake dessert. Why, you're the Chef!" The oilman tipped his hat. "It was delicious, by the way, but where am I? And where is my wife?"

Rainbow let out a loud, *Grrrrairrrrrrr*, which caused the oilman to turn around. As he did, Wekiwa kissed him on the lips, and he resisted for only a microsecond. Wekiwa did not enjoy kissing for any length of time, but kept her lips locked on the oilman until he succumbed. When she released him, his eyes were turquoise, and he was once again at Wekiwa's beck and call. Wekiwa found this compelling. She told the oilman to wait and went out to the wagon. She dabbed a pinch of unprocessed Coontie onto the hand of a previous conquest, the owner of a large orange grove. Thinking back, Wekiwa really enjoyed this one, as although he looked to be large and lazy, as a lover, he was surprisingly sensitive and spry. The orange grove owner blinked his eyes five times with a dazed look on his face, and the turquoise instantly vanished. Wekiwa quickly grabbed the orange grower and kissed him. He slumped into her, opened his restored turquoise eyes, and spoke, "How may I serve you, My Spring?"

"Go back to sleep," Wekiwa quietly ordered. The orange grower closed his eyes and slumped to the wagon floor in a heap. She was utterly fascinated by her discovery. She didn't know how long her enchantments would last once she released her prey, or if her kiss would once again return them to do her bidding after their absence from her. She did know one thing, though. There was no more room in the wagon.

Wekiwa had a particularly calculating mind. She quickly developed an experiment, and through the process, in addition to being the first Celebrity Chef, she also invented the first restaurant gift certificate. Wekiwa used her finest stationary and wrote out, *Complimentary Dinner for one at the Chef's table of Flowing Springs, on the Miami River- Valid only the first Saturday of this month*. She placed the certificate into an envelope and put it in the orange grower's pocket. Wekiwa told him to go to Ernest's wagon and go to sleep. Climbing up into the wagon herself, she commanded Ernest to take them up the River to the Royal Palm Hotel.

Once there, Wekiwa dabbed some unprocessed Coontie on the orange grower's hand and deposited him there. The Royal Palm was a grand structure built on the Miami River in the late 1,800's. It featured electricity, elevators, and a swimming pool. The hotel was, in fact, built on the site of a Tequesta Indian Village. As such, Wekiwa thought it only fitting that she begin her experiment on this sacred site.

The next Saturday, the orange grove owner appeared at Flowing

Springs and presented the certificate. He was led to a table in the kitchen where Wekiwa materialized.

"Ma'am, haven't we met?" The orange grove owner asked as he tipped his hat.

"Yes. I brought your dessert out when you last ate my food."

"Yes, yes. Why you're the chef. How stupid of me, ma'am."

Rainbow passed the orange grove owner, raised her tail, and let out a *Grrraarrrrr!* The man jumped a bit and turned. Wekiwa held the stunned man's face in her hands and kissed him. He did not resist at all this time. She ceased her kiss quickly and looked into the man's eyes. They were turquoise. Wekiwa repeated her experiment with the oilman, giving him three weeks to return. Her kiss swiftly brought him back under her spell as well.

Wekiwa felt as if there was nothing she couldn't do with her charms. She could place people under her control, release them, and now retrieve them with ease. And, more importantly, she could control and manipulate people of great wealth and power. Flowing Springs was so prosperous that she didn't need to put spells on people to gain more wealth, but Wekiwa felt a rush every time she gained favor through her sorcerous deeds.

She continued with her sorcery for one year. Then suddenly one day, it came. The feeling was dark and relentless. It was wicked. It welled up from deep inside her like drumming around a campfire, traveling from her feet to her head. She heard it in her ears. *Ommapapo! Ommapapo!* She felt it coursing through every fiber of her being. She felt a growing heat within her that she knew would consume her if she didn't put an end to it. She stood paralyzed in her restaurant's kitchen. Her feet felt like leaden sandals. Rainbow growled. There was a war going on between Wekiwa's will to move and her body's desire to remain in place. She battled her own feet to the dock and with one last thrust of her legs, dove into the Miami River.

43

Hazel Lawrence loved her husband, Mike. They met as children at Sabal Palm Elementary School in simpler times, before the Vietnam War, before nuclear power, moonwalks, and certainly before the tightknit Jewish community of North Miami Beach was ready to welcome a mixed-race child with a Jewish Mother and a Native American Father.

Having a Jewish Mother automatically made Hazel a member of the tribe—the *Jewish* tribe that is. Her schizophrenic, bipolar, Native American, environmental attorney Father, Joseph Clearwater, was not welcome in any tribe.

The children in Sabal Palm were carefree, happy white children, predominantly Jewish. Hazel had been home schooled until she was eight and was academically way ahead of the other kids at school, except Mike. Hazel was, however, way behind the other kids emotionally. As a result, she was quiet, never raised her hand in class, sat alone at lunch, and kept to herself. Mike on the other hand always shot his arm way up in the air to be the first to answer the teacher's questions. He had a quiet confidence, yet he also kept to himself, mostly reading during recess.

When Mike first saw Hazel sitting in Mrs. Hoolihan's 3rd grade class, his little heart was smitten. Hazel had darker skin than the other kids, long, shiny, black hair, and eyes the color of her name. Mike held his books, and his breath, as he passed her seat in his row. He didn't know what got into him, but as he walked past Hazel, he mindlessly reached out to caress her hair. It was like silk. He felt like he was touching the head of an angel. He felt immobilized. In fact, he couldn't move. His ring caught onto Hazel's beautiful black hair, and he dared not budge an inch. Hazel, feeling the tug on her scalp, looked up at him mercifully and smiled. Mike smiled with all of his heart as Hazel casually removed his ring from her hair.

Nobody else had witnessed this exchange. It was their little secret. At lunch, Mike walked over to Hazel, sat down, smiled, and offered her one of his Twinkies. She took it, smiled back, and they ate in silence. Hazel and Mike sat together for lunch every day after and quickly discovered that they had so much in common. They both loved reading, liked playing quiet inside games, like Monopoly and cards, and they both liked math, but above all, they enjoyed nature. Mostly, though, they relished each other's company. Hazel had a dry sense of humor, like a Monty Python character, and was quick with one liners. Mike was logical, but a bit hotheaded. He would get worked up about all kinds of things, and rant on and on, mainly about the environment. When they were twelve, walking in the woods around their North Miami Beach neighborhood, Mike grabbed Hazel's hand and pointed at the strawberry-filled lot next to her house.

"Well, look at that," said Mike, pointing to a real estate sign.

"Don't you know what that means, Hazel?"

"We'll have new neighbors soon?" Hazel said, laughing.

"Seriously, they just sold the two lots next to our house too."

"You mean the tomato patch?"

"Yes. Pretty soon, there will be no U-pick strawberry, corn, or tomato fields around here, and it's not just happening near our homes. It's all over. If we don't do something soon, our neighborhood will be nothing but concrete. People need to realize how sensitive these ecosystems are. We are destroying our homes, and the planet! They better start paying attention before it's too late."

"Oh God, you sound just like my Father. I can get you some of his meds, you know."

"Very funny. Now I know, Hazel, I know my life's calling."

"You going to be a farmer? My Mom has some old suspenders you could use. You might look cute in those."

"You are a joke a minute. I'm serious. I'm going to be an environmental scientist."

"So, I guess that means I'll have to get a real job when were married."

Mike gulped, swallowed, and queried, "*Married?*"

"Do you know how many years I have invested in you already, Michael Lawrence?"

"So, was that a proposal?"

"I… I… I guess so."

Mike leaned over and gave Hazel a pop kiss before exclaiming, "I accept!"

Hazel and Mike have been together every day since.

44

The principal, Mrs. Feldman, was in her office preparing for a PTA meeting. She stepped out for a stretch and saw Gracie sleeping on two chairs. Gracie was always such a delight. She was smart, playful, and a good sharer—all the qualities of a wonderful kindergartener. Mrs. Feldman couldn't for the life of her imagine what had gotten into Gracie. She went back in her office to get a sweater and covered the sleeping girl, who was softly snoring like a little mouse. She called to one of the front office secretaries, "What happened here?"

"Nobody answered the phone at home, Mrs. Feldman. Gracie didn't seem to be able to control her laughter and asked for lunch. We gave her some cheese and crackers, and an apple, which she devoured, then she just conked out like she hadn't slept for a week."

"Sounds like my oldest kid, Debbie—or as my husband likes to call her—the bad one. She gets like that after a concert at the Hollywood Sportatorium. Too much wacky weed."

"You know I thought of that, but she's only five, Mrs. Feldman."

"Of course. It was just a passing thought. Try her parents again. Do you have a number for her Mom's Pet Store?"

"We tried there earlier. Nobody picked up."

"Try again. Maybe she's running late."

"Yes, ma'am."

The secretary called the Pet Store again. "Hello, Mrs. Fox?"

"Speaking."

"Oh, good. Hold please for Mrs. Feldman."

"Mrs. Feldman? Is everything all right with the kids?"

"Hold just a second, Mrs. Fox, I'll put Mrs. Feldman on the line."

Tina was making funny faces at Gina, trying to make her laugh.

"Oh, hush!" Gina said to Tina.

"Excuse me?" Mrs. Feldman inquired.

"Sorry, I was talking to my annoying sister. Is everything okay?"

"We're not really sure, Mrs. Fox. Gracie is sleeping now."

"Sleeping?"

"I think she's fine, but you better come pick her up. I'll tell you everything when you get here."

"Thank you, Mrs. Feldman. I'm leaving the shop right now."

"I knew your boys might be trouble one day, Sis, but little Gracie?" Tina said.

"I don't know what the heck has been going on, Tina? First, this thing with Ben, then the babysitter, now Gracie. As they say in those mysteries, something is afoot. Feed the rest of the fish for me, will ya?"

"Only if you say pretty please."

"Will a, *go screw yourself*, suffice?"

"That will do. Now go, pick up your kid. I'll feed the rest of your little buddies here and make sure Spot stays put. I'll meet you back at your house."

"Love you, Tina."

"Love you too, Sis."

Gina got in her car and drove to Gracie's school. It was only a three-minute drive, but it seemed to take forever. Gina stopped at a red light on 16th Avenue and tried to link the events of the last twenty-four hours together. She wondered what the hell was going on. She missed Ben. The light changed green, so she stepped on the gas. A car ran the red light and almost crashed into her, but it swerved at the last moment: it happened a lot at that intersection. Gina leaned on her horn and yelled, "A-hole!" out the window. A couple of moments later, Gina found herself walking into the Natural Bridge Elementary School office, not remembering exactly how she got there. Gracie was lying on two chairs, looking so peaceful when Mrs.

Feldman stepped out of her office. Mrs. Feldman was a jovial women who stood all of 5'1 with a beautiful face, and a tummy the size of Santa's. In fact, now that her hair turned gray, and with her little round glasses, she looked exactly like Mrs. Claus.

"Hello, Gina. I'm so glad we were finally able to get ahold of you."

"Oh, I'm terribly sorry. Had you tried earlier?"

"Why, yes, several times. The front office staff called your house and the Pet Shop."

"Apologies, Mrs. Feldman. It's been a very strange couple of days, to say the least. Is Gracie ill?" Gina asked as she gently brushed her fingers through little Gracie's hair.

"Step into my office, Gina. Would you like some coffee or tea?"

"Well, if I'm getting sent to the principal's office, I think I will have some tea."

Mrs. Feldman called out to her office staff, "Can one of you nice ladies please bring Mrs. Fox and I some tea. Come in, dear. Remember the last time you were in here, Gina?"

"5th grade. You were so nice to me, but then again, I put this place on the map when I won the County Spelling Bee."

"I was so proud of you, Gina, and still am. And you had just moved here from New Jersey. Most kids take years just to acclimate to a new school, but not you, and not every principal is lucky enough to have two generations of a family come through their school."

"Yes, ma'am. What is going on with Gracie, and why is she sleeping out there?"

"Well, dear, her teacher said she started off the morning fine, but then she became hysterical, laughing at just about anything. Her teacher brought her here. She got hungry, ate, then fell asleep. We called your house and the Pet Store, but nobody answered the phone."

"So sorry. Like I said, it's been a crazy couple of days. I can't for the life of me figure out what would cause such behavior."

"About that, Gina... I hate to ask, but because of how she was acting, did you, or your husband have any marijuana in the house?"

"Us? No!!! Now I know what getting called to the principal's office was like for the bad kids."

"Sorry, Gina. It's just that my daughter, Debbie—my husband calls her the bad one. She has gotten high a few times and acted exactly like that—the little shit."

Gina broke into laughter. "Why, Mrs. Feldman, I never thought I would hear you curse."

"Oh, you should hear me driving home after a PTA meeting. Now the mothers are trying to buy an air conditioning system for the entire school through bake sales. Do you have any idea how many chocolate chip cookies it will take to air condition this school? Those ladies mean well, but they drive me nuts. Then they expect special treatment for their kids because they are helping out. I could just… Sorry, back to Gracie. If it wasn't you or your husband, is there any chance someone else may have brought some pot into the house?"

"Well, there's Jemma, but she would never give her sister drugs."

"Oh, Jemma. She's a beauty, and so smart. How is she doing in college? Does she know her major?"

"Oh, she loves college. Not the studying part, of course. I think she is majoring in psychology and the psychology of boys right now." Both women giggled.

"Oh, I remember those days. There was this one boy, Hank. He was so… Oh, sorry, there I go again."

"Oh, that's okay. This is the most fun I've had all week. I just can't imagine Jemma doing something like giving drugs to her five-year-old sister. But then again, we have these two teenage babysitters. One of them, well… I don't even want to go there."

Gina thought back to the night before with Margo. *'Maybe Margo was high. That would explain a lot, but I wasn't high? Maybe she drugged me? But I've smoked before, and I never hurt Ben, or slutted around.'*

"Gina. Gina, dear, are you okay? You seem lost in thought."

"Oh, sorry, Mrs. Feldman. I was just thinking about who might have left drugs around the house. But Gracie is only five, she would never inhale smoke, and nobody I know would give a five-year-old pot."

"You know, people cook it into food these days. Just the other day, a fifth grader was caught with pot brownies."

"Oh My God! A fifth grader? How is he?"

"He's fine. His pothead uncle, however, is in jail for distribution of cannabis. In terms of the student, turns out he doesn't like chocolate and was trading them for Twinkies when one of the lunchroom monitors caught him."

"That's terrible. I'm glad he's fine. Did Gracie cause any trouble?"

"Oh no, dear, she was fine, just laughing, eating, and sleeping."

"May I take her home now?"

"Of course, dear, but you said it's a been crazy couple of days, and you know I'm a good listener."

Gina looked into the kind eyes of Mrs. Feldman, held her head in her hands, and started crying. Mrs. Feldman came over and gave her a big hug, then handed her a tissue box from her desk.

"Oh, you poor thing. Turns out principals are a lot like therapists. What's wrong, dear"

"I wouldn't even know where to begin. Did you ever have one of those days when you wished you could go back to sleep and push restart?"

"Only every other day, dear," Mrs. Feldman said with a grin. "I've been an elementary school principal for thirty-two years." Both women laughed again.

"Oh, you always could make me laugh. I better get Gracie home and search the house."

"I know I just seem like this old Jewish Mother type, but you know some of my ancestors were Kalut. They lived in Russia, on the Chinese border, actually. They were shamanistic reindeer herders."

"Kalut, huh? That's a new one on me, Mrs. Feldman."

"My grandfather told me some of their legends. One of them has to do with people with different colored eyes."

"Oh, what's that?"

"They say that a person with two different colored eyes can see into the afterlife. And, your Mom has the same exact eyes, as you, right?"

"Yes, ma'am, she does."

Gina had just heard this from Ms. Alice, and long ago from Ben. He told her it was a Native American legend. Over the years, Gina had gotten used to the occasional odd look, or comment about her eyes, but she never really thought it gave her special powers. She would have been much happier to have Tina's eyes. They were so pretty, and normal looking. Not that she felt like a freak, but now. Well, now she didn't know what to think. Her life was starting to feel like a fairy tale—a haunted one!

"You sound just like Ms. Alice."

"Ms. Alice, near your Pet Store?"

"You know she's my niece?"

"Your niece? I thought she was from Romania."

"Alice Feldman was born in the Bronx. She came here as a baby with my sister. She pawns herself off as a gypsy fortune teller because who would go to Ms. Alice Feldman for a psychic reading. All that said, like me, some of her ancestors were shamans, and she definitely has shared some spooky stuff with me over the years. She even predicted Debbie would become a pothead."

"Wow! Now I don't know what to think?"

"Sure you don't want to talk, Gina?"

"Maybe one day, but thank you for the offer."

"I'm here every day. Don't forget your kid on the way out."

"Thanks again, Mrs. Feldman. You are one of a kind."

"Thanks, kiddo. And, if you do find any of those brownies, stop on by for a visit one Friday afternoon. I've got some stories to tell."

Gina stood up, gave Mrs. Feldman a big hug and kiss, lifted her sleeping child into her arms, and left. 'Pot brownies', Gina thought to herself, 'What the hell is happening in our kitchen?'

Gracie opened one eye and looked up at her Mother as she placed her in the back seat of her car.

"Hey, my little sleepy head. How are you feeling?"

"Mama?"

"Yes, honey?"

"I'm hungry."

"I'm taking you home now. I'll make you whatever you want," Gina said as she kissed Gracie's forehead and tousled her hair.

"Thanks, Mama."

"Gracie, what did you eat for breakfast today?"

"The dogs ate my Cheerios."

"No wonder you are hungry. Did you eat anything else?"

"Just a tiny brownie I found in the bench cushion."

"A Brownie, huh?"

"How was it?"

"Not as good as yours, Mama. It tasted kind of bad after a few bites."

"Can you tell me what happened at school today?"

"Billy painted a parrot. It was purple." Gracie started laughing but stopped quickly. "Why was that funnier this morning, Mama?"

"I don't know," Gina said, fighting the combination of laugher and anger arising within her. "Do you remember anything else, Gracie?"

"No, Mama. I was sleeping. Am I in trouble?"

"No, baby. Everything is fine."

"Mama?"

"Yes."

"I promise, no more brownies for breakfast. They make me feel funny."

45

*H*azel and Mike married when they turned 18. Their parents chipped in for a deposit on a house on the Biscayne Canal in nearby Biscayne Park. Mike enrolled at Florida International University's school of environmental studies. He applied for student loans but had no other source of income. Their parents helped at first. Hazel got a job selling advertising specialties. When she first started, it was just easy money, but after a couple of months, Hazel really liked the job. The company, Ad One, had a salesroom that was nothing more than open office space full of forward-facing desks, with one desk in front facing all the others. At first glance, the setup looked like an elementary classroom; however, the ashtrays, telephones, stacks of telephone books, and heavy cigarette smoke wafting through the air let one know that this was far from a classroom.

Every morning at 6:45 AM, Hazel would walk to her office just off 135 Street. There were boxes of fresh, hot Krispy. Kreme donuts and a not so fresh, not-so-hot, pot of black coffee. Before the internet, many small businesses advertised with things like bumper stickers, key chains, baseball caps, pens, and other items. Most of their customers were small and family-owned businesses. Places like garages, plumbers, electricians, bakeries, and the best time to reach a live person was first thing in the morning, before they sent their work crews out. Each day, the Ad One salespeople picked up a telephone book from a U.S. City of their choice, called a business, and gave them their version of a scripted sales pitch.

"Gooddddd morning, may I speak to the owner please?

"Yes, I'm the owner."

"Oh, this is the owner, great. I'm Hazel Lawrence from Ad One. How are you doing today?"

"I'm fine. How are you?" was the customers typical reply, if they hadn't already hung up.

"I'm great! I am very happy to inform you that your business has been selected to receive a free gold necklace valued at $25 with every order of advertising specialties. Our advertising products are all made here in the U.S. of A, with your logo or slogan, the name of your business, address, and phone number printed right on them. We have a large selection of products. Can I interest you in some bumper stickers?" Hazel replied.

"Maybe. What would I even write on there for a donut shop?"

"How about this, *our doughnuts are so fresh, you'll have to slap them?*"

"You know, I really like that idea. I'll take a thousand bumper stickers. And how about key rings? How much are those? And tell me about that necklace. My wife has a birthday coming up. *So fresh you'll have to slap them.* Did you think that one up yourself, Hazel?"

"I'm glad you like it. Why, yes, I did think that up." This was in fact one of Hazel's favorite slogans, as unlike the other slogans that came from a list on her desk, she actually did think this one up herself.

It was an upbeat atmosphere. The shift leader, Chip Lively, welcomed each person to their seat with a hearty handshake, and a "Gooooddddd Morning!" Chip was the ultimate telephone salesperson. He had a master phone line, with an extremely long cord that reached throughout the entire room and connected to the phones for all of the salespeople on the floor. He could listen to anyone's call at any time, *and he did.* He could tell just by listening to the voice on the other end of the phone if someone was going to purchase an item, was on the fence about it, or just jerking his people around. He could also tell how his salespeople were handling their potential customers, and if they were really selling, or just killing time.

Since the salespeople worked entirely on commission, there was a big incentive for them to sell. If they didn't produce after a while, they were fired, as they didn't make any money for themselves, or the company. Sometimes Chip would listen in on a call, walk over to Hazel's desk, and give her the thumbs up. Other rare times, when she was struggling with a customer, he would motion for her to cover her phone mouthpiece as he fed her a line of the perfect thing to say to close the deal. Chip liked Hazel because she always smiled while she talked on the phone, and this came across to the customers. Also, she was sincere and succinct. Sometimes when Hazel was on a roll, making lots of deals, Chip would broadcast her calls on the speakerphone to excite the staff. This would get the other salespeople revved up, motivating them to make more high-pressure sales pitches that would result in closing deals. That's why they call these places, *Boiler Rooms*.

Hazel knew this job wasn't exactly good karma, but the businesses received quality advertising specialty items and also got the free necklace, even though it was just gold-plated and worth about $7 in Woolworths. But the main thing she liked about the job were the hours and how much money she could make. Plus, she never lied to customers. They always got the advertising products, which were of good quality, fairly-priced, and made right in their North Miami warehouse, providing jobs to dozens of residents.

Hazel always was an early riser, as was Mike. She started her workday by 7 AM and ended her shift at noon. Where else was she going to make $500 a week working just five hours a day? Hazel loved her free time in the afternoon. She would come home, make herself something simple to eat, like a sandwich, change into her comfy clothes—cut off jean shorts and a halter top, go outside, sit at the picnic table under their ginormous Oak Tree, and gaze out at the Biscayne Canal that ran behind their home.

The canal was originally dug to drain farmland, but it turned out that it drained too much water, and the soil could no longer retain its moisture. After that, the land was parceled out for the development of homes. Hazel loved to sit outside, especially in the Winter when it was cool out. Starting every November, the manatees would swim up the canal to take advantage of the warm water and safe refuge. There were very few predators in the canal, and most of the boats did not have those awful propellers that sliced up the manatee's backs and tails.

The majority of the boats on the canal were canoes or rowboats. Hazel had a red canoe she would paddle up and down the canal with every day after lunch. As much as she enjoyed being with Mike, she enjoyed the solitude of her early afternoon voyages. Hazel loved when the manatees swam under her canoe. She would stare through the water in awe of the grace of these creatures. Despite that fact that manatees could weigh over a thousand pounds, they moved effortlessly through the water. Some days, Hazel would bring a head of lettuce on her canoe trip and feed it to the manatees. They would reach up with their hairy, gray snouts that looked like shrunken elephant trunks, and take the lettuce from Hazel's hands. On this particular day as she was feeding a manatee, a second manatee swam up, turned upside down, waved its tail, and seemed to wink at the first manatee; and at Hazel. At first, Hazel thought she was dreaming it. Then the second manatee surfaced, slurped down the remainder of the lettuce, and once again winked at her.

Since she was a little girl, Hazel always thought she could communicate with animals. There wasn't a dog, cat, squirrel, raccoon, or any other wild or domestic creature Hazel encountered, that she couldn't figure out. In fact, any creature Hazel got close to was instantly her friend. She knew if they had a stomachache, needed food, had a splinter in their paw, and just about anything else. Mike used to call her, *the critter whisperer.*

So, Hazel was stumped when the manatee ate her lettuce, winked at her again, and seemed to smile. She found herself unconsciously smiling back when she heard it. *Ommapapo! Ommapapo!* The manatee's tail was flapping in rhythm to the sound, and Hazel felt the vibrations through the deck of the canoe. She looked toward the canal bank at their Oak Tree, who she didn't know why, but she affectionately called Al. All of Al's branches and leaves were shaking in rhythm to the sound as well, causing thousands of leaves to fall to the ground. *Ommapapo! Ommapapo!*

Both manatees suddenly disappeared without a ripple in the water, like they were never there at all. Hazel felt a chill run down the back of her neck, migrating slowly down her spine. The air and her blood ran cold. She shivered as the air temperature rapidly dropped—like it does before a thunderstorm.

Hazel quickly paddled back to their house, remembering the legend her great grandmother told her when she was a little girl. The legend of the flapping tailed creature in the Creek.

46

*G*ina pulled up to the house and was grateful that Ben's car was there, as was Mike's van. She held Gracie's hand as they walked into the house.

"Look, Mama. Daddy and Uncle Mike are swimming in the canal."

"What the F..." Gina caught herself saying and stopped. "Let's get you something to eat, Gracie."

"That's okay, Mama. I'm sleepy again. Will you tuck me in and read me a story?"

"Mama has to go talk to Daddy. Come sit on the couch. I'll get your blanket. You can watch any TV show you want."

"Goodie!"

Gina took a throw blanket off the couch, covered Gracie, and brought her a glass of milk and some mac n' cheese.

"Here you go, baby. I just made this. Here's the remote control. I'll be right out back if you need me."

Gracie reached up and pulled Gina's neck down for a kiss. "Yummy. mac n' cheese. You are the bestest, Mama."

"No, you are the bestest!" Gina said.

Gina briskly walked out the back door and headed for the Creek. "What are you two up to?"

Ben and Mike heard Gina's voice, and just like that, Mrs. Mendlebaum vanished. Gina saw the microphone equipment and snorkeling gear as she looked around. "Hi. Ben," Gina said sheepishly

Gina always did everything so confidently, especially her greetings. Usually, her *Hellos* fell just short of a politician asking for your vote. Ben never heard such a soft, apologetic tone in her voice. He took off his mask and jogged toward her. Gina saw his black eye, shuddered, and flew into Ben's arms. She stayed there for some time, softly sobbing. Ben was silent. He was so glad to have her back, he didn't care about anything else. Without taking his arms off her, he put his mouth to her ear and whispered, "I missed you so much."

"Oh, Ben. I'm so, so sorry. I don't know what happened," Gina said as she gently pulled Ben's face to hers and softly kissed him, just under his black eye. "Oh God, did I really do that?"

"It's nothing."

"Hey, Gina. What am I, chopped liver? Don't you even say hello?" Mike said.

"Oh, hi, Mike. Sorry, I would ask what you two rocket scientists are up to, but I really need to talk to Ben."

Ben was still in shock from the shapeshifting, talking manatee, but so relieved to see Gina and hear her voice, he wouldn't have cared if there was a herd of singing elephants in the canal.

"Gina. I'm so glad to see you, but why aren't you at the Pet Store? Oh, I don't even care. Mike, excuse us for a few minutes, man."

"Oh, sure, we have a talking manatee down here, and you guys want to hug. How domestic of you. Come on, man! It's a talking manatee."

"Is this like that time you said you saw the Swamp Ape in the Everglades Mike?" Gina joked.

"Well, I did. This time, I have a witness, though, and a tape recording."

"Ben?" Gina queried.

"Oh, Gina, I'll tell you all about it. I think it has something to do with last night. Let's go inside and talk. Mike, you know there's beer in the little fridge on the patio. Help yourself. Please wait for me. This day is getting crazier and crazier."

"I'll be right back. I'm going to get my underwater camera," Mike said.

"Good idea. We need to document this," Ben responded.

"Document it. Hah, I'm thinking we can make a bundle off some good pictures of Mrs. Mendlebaum. I'll bet they would fetch a fortune at Penthouse Magazine."

"Mrs. Mendlebaum? Penthouse? What is he talking about, Ben?"

"I'll explain, Gina. You try to get that picture, Mike. We'll be out soon."

"Don't worry about me. I've got beer and a Creek with a talking manatee that turns into a naked woman. What could go wrong?"

Gina wrapped her arm tightly around Ben's waist. They started walking in the house and Gina heard a splash. It wasn't close like the one the night before. In fact, it seemed very distant. "Did you hear that?"

"Hear what?" Ben said.

Gina felt the hairs on her neck vibrate and her eyelids started rapidly blinking. She saw a woman walking out of her kitchen. She was Native American, stunning, tall, had black hair, and was holding a deerskin dress. Gina grabbed Ben's arm tightly and tried to talk, but nothing came out.

As the woman walked past, she smiled the most riveting smile Gina had ever seen. Although she felt like her mind and body weren't connected, Gina smiled back. Then she saw them. Two turquoise eyes that shined like beacons, calling her to follow. A panther appeared from the edge of the Oaks. It had the same turquoise eyes. Gina knew it would not harm her. The panther purred as it walked past Gina and caught up to the naked woman. The woman walked past, and without looking back, dropped her dress to the ground, dove into the Creek and vanished, as did the panther.

"Gina, Gina. Are you okay?"

"Didn't you see her, Ben?"

"See who, Gina?"

"That woman who walked naked into the Creek."

"Mrs. Mendlebaum?" Ben asked.

"Who? Who the hell is Mrs. Mendlebaum?"

"Our old Hebrew School teacher."

"Wait, how did you see her? She vanished in the canal when you got here?"

"Your Hebrew School teacher vanished in the canal?"

"Sort of. You see, at first she was a manatee, then she turned into Mrs. Mendlebaum."

"A manatee?"

"Yes. And, well, you wouldn't even believe me if I told you."

"You just told me a manatee turned into a Hebrew School teacher, and I just saw a naked Indian dive into the Creek, with a panther by her side, so try me."

"The manatee talked."

"I think I must have given you a concussion last night, Ben," Gina said as she kissed him again.

"Well, what about Mike? He saw it. He heard it. Ask him when he gets back from his van. And you just saw a naked Indian and a panther."

"Oh God, Ben. What is happening?"

"I'm not sure, Gina, but I don't think God has anything to do with this, or maybe he has?"

47

Anna Phylaxis-Washington found herself mindfully starring out the window of her house toward the Creek, as if summoning the waters to rise with her thoughts. While she could see George on the sofa, reading the latest real estate journal, Anna felt herself lapsing into the other world. The one she was stuck in for a year after the car accident. The one where she talked to the lost souls who were trapped between the living and the dead.

The spirits visited her most days now, and she became used to the ever-present scenes playing out just for her. In fact, some days she even looked forward to it. Anna discovered that the spirits inhabited the crawl space under Gina's house. They were quite frustrated that although Gina had the gift of sight through her heterochromatic eyes, she was still blind to her inner vision. Gina seemed to just go about her business, completely ignoring the Spirit's flagrant acts to get her attention.

Just yesterday, Anna witnessed Ben's Mother, her cute Italian lover, and Ben's Father, well at least his head, engaged in a most unusual threesome. They started on the lawn behind Gina's house. Gina was outside in a hammock when the threesome stopped and waved at her, then bounced right over her head. Not only did Gina not see them, but she didn't even spill a drop of her morning coffee or flutter the newspaper in her hands.

The threesome then meandered onto Anna's lawn and rolled into the

Creek. One would imagine the Creek water would have stopped them cold, but the Spirits existed in another dimension, which was not subject to the laws of physical elements, or gravity. Neither was Anna's vision. Anna could still see them, even on the bottom of the Creek. She was kind of grossed out by the whole thing, as two of these people were her son-in-law's parents, and one was young enough to be her grandson. Still, the Spirits called to her.

"Hey, Anna. Come on in. The water is delightful," called Betty.

"That's okay. Try to have fun without me."

"Anna, you are bellissimo," called Murray Ferrari as he whistled through his fingers.

"We just want to talk to Gina and you, Anna," Betty called out, giggling while Herman's head nibbled her ear.

"I'm all ears," Anna said.

"Oh, you're a funny one, Anna. Something monumental is about to happen. We need your help, and Gina's," Betty said. "Gina has your eyes, Anna, but she can't see our world. She is somehow blocked."

"I know, but you guys have to lay off the pranks."

"Pranks! There were no pranks?" Murray said.

"That Clown Mask! And the babysitter!!! To your own daughter-in-law! How could you Betty?! Herman?" Anna admonished.

"It wasn't us, Anna. I swear. I would never do that. Ben is my son," Betty said.

"That's what we've been trying to tell you, Anna. It's not us."

"Who, then?"

"I'll give you a hint. It rhymes with Kool-Aid," Murray said, laughing as swam the backstroke along the Creek's bottom.

"Really, Murray, Kool-Aid?" Herman rolled his eyes.

"Hey, it's funny, no?"

"No, Murray!" Betty said as she slapped him on the butt.

"Okay, kids, if you don't tell me soon, I'll be over in the Spirit World myself. I give. What rhymes with Kool-Aid?"

"Mermaid!" yelled Murray.

"What Mermaid?" Anna asked.

The ground started trembling at her question. Anna heard the sound again. *Ommapapo! Ommapapo!* as Betty dramatically said, "The Mermaid of Arch Creek."

Anna closed her eyes and rubbed them for several minutes, trying to get rid of the oncoming migraine she thought might explode all of the blood vessels in her head. Anna knew the burden of her gift, and she hoped Gina would be spared. Instead, it now seemed as though she and Gina were key to this mess.

"Tell me, Betty, does it have to be her too? I'm here."

"Hey, I get it, Ben is my kid too, but Gina, and all of you, have been chosen."

"All of us? Chosen for what, Betty?"

"To save the Creek, and to send us to where we belong."

"And where the Hell do you belong?!" Anna asked in frustration.

"Hopefully not there?" Murray replied, laughing.

"Where?"

"Hell!" Betty, Herman, and Murray replied in unison.

48

The manatee looked up through the Creek into the air above. Her old life flashed before her onto the water's flowing surface like images on a drive-in movie screen rippling in the wind. She saw herself dive into the Miami River that painful day. Her body and spirit were at War. When she first hit the water, she heard and felt her skin sizzle, as if it were on fire. She knew her thoughts had betrayed her to the Great Spirits, and she was being punished, or perhaps, *tested* for trying to control humans through her magic.

The cool water of the River slowly eased her pain. Wekiwa always loved swimming, but the small Creeks and grasslands in the Everglades were too shallow for real swimming. From the first time she dipped her toes into the Miami River, she felt it's Spirit travel through her as if they were formed from the same cells.

Every morning when Wekiwa awoke, instead of washing her face, she would instead dive naked into the River and swim into Biscayne Bay. That day in 1920, was different. She swam past dolphins eating mullet, tarpon slowly rolling on the surface, Eagle Rays leaping over the small waves, and pelicans diving for pilchards. To her delight, she saw all of this, underwater, and in Biscayne Bay's sky above.

Wekiwa saw a Bull Shark swimming rapidly toward her. Her grandfather used to describe them as fast, angry alligators with shorter tails. Despite this, Wekiwa was not afraid. Wekiwa was fearless. Wekiwa opened her eyes and starred into the shark's bottomless, black eyes. The shark did not alter its course. Suddenly, she felt a great presence in the water and heard the sound. *Ommapapo! Ommapapo!* Wekiwa found herself propelled at great speeds toward and over the shark's open mouth, then she broke the surface of the water and landed in a perfect swan dive over fifty feet away. Wekiwa was swimming at a great pace, beyond any speed she could ever imagine. The burning and heaviness she experienced just moments ago on the dock had vanished. A great coolness was passing through her feet and legs into her spine. It tickled. She was moving through the water like a young brave on a fine colt. Wekiwa gazed back, and her movement stopped. She smiled and turned two underwater summersaults as she thanked the Great Spirits for saving her from the shark, and for this great miracle. She had a tail! *'Not just any tail,'* she thought. This was a perfect tail, with turquoise and purple scales that would be the envy of any peacock.

Wekiwa was exhilarated. She traveled north in the Bay with pure joy in her soul, leaping and diving in and out of the water, like a dolphin, for what seemed like days. She slowed when she saw a small Creek and swam under a beautiful limestone bridge. It reminded her of the sinkholes that were in the Everglades. But something else drew her to this, and she didn't know what.

The water temperature dropped ten degrees. She did a few laps back and forth under the bridge and stopped dead when she saw it. The carvings. The same carvings that were in the Cypress Tree were underwater on the side of the bridge. She looked carefully at each carved panel, especially at the picture of Wekiwa in the kitchen. Surely, she thought, this was her restaurant's kitchen, but upon closer inspection, it was not. This was a kitchen she hadn't seen before, and in the background, there were giant Oaks, Coonties, butterflies all around, and a body of water. Somehow, she just felt it in her new tail. The fifth carving. It was this place. This small body of water. This Creek that ran under an Arch.

Wekiwa swam a few more feet, poked her head out of the water, and unintentionally slowed as her tail stopped moving, as if it had a mind of its own. A blue Atala butterfly lighted on her nose. Wekiwa felt tingling throughout her body. Her tail mysteriously disappeared. She climbed onto the Creek bank and took in the glorious scene.

About a quarter a mile away, she saw a Stagecoach stop, thinking this would be another great place for a restaurant. Then, along the banks, she saw something else that drew her attention. Coontie! Acres and Acres of it, and surrounding the plants, an iridescent blue cloud the size of a schoolhouse. Wekiwa walked closer. It was a cloud of Atala butterflies. The kaleidoscope of butterflies rose from the Coontie and engulfed Wekiwa. The wings of hundreds of thousands of butterflies tickled her skin, making her laugh like an infant playing peekaboo. She felt a delicious coolness rushing through her body and her spirit.

The water was sweet and cool as she took a drink from the Creek. The butterflies moved to a clearing under a giant Oak Tree, and Wekiwa lay naked on the ground under the cloud of butterflies as she laughed. She gazed at the sky through the multitude of fluttering wings and saw the faces of the Great Spirits as they appeared one by one, in the clouds. She knew what this place was to become: her home. And, she could swim there from her restaurant!

Wekiwa marked the spot with two pieces of limestone rock. As she did, she heard the sound again. *Ommapapo! Ommapapo!* The branches of the giant Oaks shook, and thousands of leaves rained down on the ground. Wekiwa thanked the Great Spirits and walked barefoot around the site. She felt the majesty of the place. Her people had once dwelled there; she could sense it in her bones. This was to be her new homesite, and she knew exactly where the kitchen would be. It would be fabulous. Wekiwa swore to the Great Spirits that from this point on, she would only use her powers for good.

One by one, the blue Atala butterflies left their swarming cloud and flew skyward, disappearing into the clear blue sky. Wekiwa's spirit soared with them, and her face shone blue from their reflection. A giant white cloud appeared and formed shape of an enormous butterfly, then Wekiwa heard it once again. *Ommapapo! Ommapapo!*

Wekiwa dove into the water and looked down to see her legs once again transformed into a stunning tail. *Her* stunning tail! She swam, back past the limestone rocks marking the location of her new home, past the Arch Creek Bridge, through Biscayne Bay, and toward her restaurant. As she approached, the same Bull Shark once again took a run at Wekiwa. She fearlessly swam into the Shark, punching it in the gills. Blood flowed into the water. Wekiwa grabbed the shark by the tail and swam to the boat ramp behind Flowing Springs. She used a dock line to secure the shark to the dock.

The sound, the drumming, chanting sound returned, vibrating through the water. *Ommapapo! Ommapapo!* Wekiwa wasn't sure if the sound was controlling her, or she it, but once again, her tail vanished. She climbed up the dock, and threw her waist forward, flipping her hair back and forth to dry it. She thanked the Great Spirits and the Bull Shark for its meat. It had been a long time since she had hunted, and it felt good.

Wekiwa walked barefoot through the Restaurant, to the chalkboard in front. She picked up a piece of chalk and wrote: Tonight's special, Shark Steaks.

49

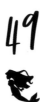

Gus Lacroix and Larry Fine awoke early. Well, early for them. It was 11:30 AM and even in February, it was humid in Homestead. The dampness permeated the air and clothes clung to your skin like wet towels. They each grabbed a beer and jumped into Aunt Ethel's truck.

The dark, black earth smelled thick like a mixture of sweet corn and manure. The lower Florida peninsula is comprised of a bed of limestone rock, covered by sand. Not dirt; *sand.* Even in South Florida's subtropical climate, the sand itself, without any supplements wouldn't grow much. As such, the largest import to all of Miami-Dade County is dirt. Good, rich farm soil. The enriched farmland, in return, supplies the state and much of the country, with delicious tomatoes, corn, and strawberries. Gus liked the smell. It reminded him of the Louisiana Bayou. Larry thought it smelled like ass.

"So, you've been toting that head around all this time?" Larry asked.

"It's been in my Aunt's freezer, brah. I shoved it way down in the bottom. Then I went hunting and filled it with gator meat. Aunt Ethel didn't even get halfway down the freezer, when I dug Ole Herman's head out of there and split."

"Nice of her to give you her truck."

"Well, she didn't xactly give it to me, mon ami."

"Now that's the Gus I remember," Larry said as he high fived Gus.

"I preciate you coming along."

"It beats sitting around watching the corn grow. So, what's the plan?"

"I'm waiting for him to tell me."

"For who to tell you, Gus?"

"First, you promise you won't call me crazy."

"Hell, I already know you're crazy."

"See it's like this, Larry. That head in the cooler," Gus stopped talking for a moment. "Oh forget it, man."

"Hell, now you gotta tell me."

"Okay, but I ain't making this shit up."

"Go on already. I'm getting bored."

"See… That head, it's Herman's, and… and…"

"And, what man?"

"And, I kilt him."

Larry took out a bag of pot and some rolling papers. "This calls for a celebratory joint, man. I always knew you was a badass but cutting off a dude's head… that's a whole new level of badass, man." Larry rolled a joint, lit it with the truck's push in cigarette lighter, and handed it to Gus. "Try this, man. I got it from my friend, Craig. It's Hawaiian. If it's any good, I'll plant the seeds. Cheers to Gus Lacroix! The executioner!"

"Hey, man, it was an accident."

"Sure, man. How xactly do you accidently cut off a dude's head?"

"I was just trying to mess up his boat. That, and scare the crap out of him."

"So, what happened, cos that head is definitely dead. Probably the rest of him too," Larry said coughing.

Gus recounted the events leading to Herman's decapitation.

"So, just one question?"

"Yeah?"

"Why did you keep his head?"

"Cos he told me to."

"Who."

"Herman."

"You mean before he died?"

"Not xactly, mon ami."

"So, when?"

"After."

"After, what?"

"After he died."

"Dude, stop bogarting that joint and give it here. You either smoked way too much, or that Craig sold me some bad weed again."

Gus pulled the truck over before they got on the highway.

"Hey, man. What? You gotta take a whiz already. We just left."

Gus walked to the back of the truck and opened the cooler. He removed the sack holding Herman's head and got back in the truck. He took the sack off of the head and placed it in Larry's lap.

"What the fuck, man! I don't need to look at that ugly thing!" Larry shrieked like an old lady upon finding a mouse in her sock drawer.

"Who you calling ugly, Larry Fine? Hell, you're the one named after the ugliest stooge," Herman's head yelled, upon which Larry took another long hit of the joint, passed out, and collapsed against the truck's seat. As he passed out, he thought to himself, *Damn, that Craig. I'll never buy that Hawaiian shit from him again.*

50

Danny Gomez looked out the window of his tiny home office in Morningside and watched the afternoon thunder clouds roll in across the Bay. Westerly breezes starting in the Gulf of Mexico made their way across the South Florida peninsula, picked up lots of water vapor passing over the River of Grass that is the Everglades, then cooled as they hit the concrete roads and buildings in Miami, releasing rain, thunder, and a phenomenal late afternoon light show as they exited over Miami Beach.

Danny dreaded returning the next call, but he had to. It was Joseph Clearwater. While Danny loved speaking with his friend, Mike Lawrence, he did not always relish speaking with Joseph, Mike's Father-in-law.

Joseph Clearwater was an extremely intelligent man. He commenced college at sixteen. That's where Joseph met Hazel's Mother, Laurie Weiner, and they fell madly in love. They were married as soon as Joseph turned eighteen. Laurie was twenty at the time and gave birth to Hazel before their first anniversary.

The tribe had gained much wealth thanks to Wekiwa and set up scholarship funds for worthy students to study anything they desired, as long as they pledged to come back and work for the tribe for five years. Joseph was the first Native American to get a law degree at the University of Miami, and he did so at the ripe old age of nineteen. He was sharp as a thorn on a rose and just as painful if you rubbed him the wrong way. Joseph spent his early legal years working for the tribe.

The first five years went very well. In fact, they went so well that Joseph felt invincible and stopped taking his meds. When Joseph showed up for a court appearance wearing nothing but a feather in his hair, claiming he could speak with the dead, the tribal elders were forced to ask Joseph to resign. Joseph did not have a bitter bone in his body. He, Laurie, and five-year-old Hazel, left the tribe peacefully, moved to North Miami Beach, and opened his own firm. During his lucid and energized periods, Joseph felt it was his obligation to fight for the rights of the land of his people. Before the Europeans came, the land belonged to the Natives. The same land the newcomers were destroying with their reckless development. The land Joseph defended with zeal.

Joseph did everything with zeal, sometimes too much zeal. He filed suit against the county, and the state of Florida to close all of their wastewater treatment plants for polluting the ocean. The officials produced studies showing that pumping treated wastewater into the ocean caused no harm. But Joseph was prepared and showed up for the first hearing with validated test results showing contaminants in the form of heavy metals and E. coli bacteria—the kind that are produced in the human digestive tract, fifty plastic bags, and for a kicker, twenty-seven water-filled condoms, which he proudly presented to the Judge to be logged in as Exhibit C.

While he did not win the case, the resulting press gained Joseph a cult following. It also brought in a lot of legal business. Many of them were crackpot cases from other environmentally conscious, and seemingly bipolar kindred spirits who saw Joseph as their environmental savior. Lawsuits ranged from significant to silly, such as declaring Bufo Toads endangered species since they were being killed off by dog owners whose pets were poisoned by licking or biting the ubiquitous amphibian.

As such, Joseph attended every state, county and municipal commission and board meeting on any and all environmental issues, big or small. He spoke at every meeting. While Joseph never let on, it was known by a few confidantes, that he was mounting the biggest environmental lawsuit in history. Joseph made it his personal mission to save South Florida. In addition to environmental causes, Joseph loved his wife, Laurie, and their daughter, Hazel with everything he had. He was also very fond of his son-in-law, Mike Lawrence. Mike was a person of good character, plus, he usually had some good weed. The weed was purely medicinal for Joseph. It provided him with some means of control during his manic up periods and helped his depression when he was down. It was actually through Mike, that Joseph met Danny Gomez. Danny usually had some good weed too.

51

*J*eannie, the babysitter, sat at a slightly sticky table in Woody's Restaurant, completing a job application. The manager walked over.

"First job? Do you need any help with that?"

"Yes, and no thank you."

"Excuse me?"

"Yes, first job, and no, I don't need any help. I just finished. Here it is, sir," said Jeannie, handing him the application. The young manager glanced at the application and looked Jeannie up and down.

"Kitchen or counter?"

"Ummm. Kitchen?"

"That's the best place to start. Once you work the kitchen line, you learn the order of the place. That's where I started, a year ago, and now I'm the assistant manager."

"Congratulations and thank you for giving me the opportunity."

"Hey, it's just Woody's, you don't need to sound so professional."

"Sorry."

"Hey, no, I was just kidding. I like how you speak. It's very mature. Can you start tomorrow at 4?"

"Yes, that would be great. Thank you, Mr. Burns."

"It's Jake. Hey, like I said, it's just Woody's."

"Thanks, Jake. I'll do my best."

"I have a good feeling about you, Jeannie. I'll train you myself."

And Jeannie had a good feeling about Jake. A really, really good feeling. He was confident, but gentle, and just her type. Blonde hair, with streaks of red highlights, blue eyes, and he was tall, taller than her, but not too tall. Plus, he smelled so good. A combination of Old Spice and French fries. He was muscular, but not jock-looking, maybe he was a swimmer, or a surfer. And his smile, it made her body tingle, right down to her feet. For a teenager, he had a real charm about him.

"Thanks again, Jake. I'll see you tomorrow. Oh, can I please get an order of fries-large-to go?"

"You know you can eat what you want while you're on your shift."

"Thanks, but they are for a friend of mine."

"Must be a good friend. Let me get that for you."

"He is. Thank you."

"He? Boyfriend?"

"He's eleven, but really cute."

Jake laughed. "You know, Jeannie, girls like you don't usually work at Woody's."

"What do you mean girls like me?"

"I don't know. You seem like you could be a doctor or anything you wanted to be."

Jeannie looked into Jake's eyes, as he looked into hers, both knowing they understood the other. "Hey, I have to run home. Family emergency. I saw on your application that you only live a few blocks from me. Can I give you a ride home? You don't want your cute friend's fries getting cold."

"Sure, that would be great," Jeannie said as she wiped her perspiring hands on her jean's back pockets. Just being close to Jake made her nervous, but in a good way, "Everything okay, Jake?"

"It's my Mom. Sometimes she gets strung out. Sorry, I just met you. I shouldn't have told you that."

"I understand. My Mom is wasted most of the time. That's one of the reasons I need this job. Sorry, I shouldn't have told you that either. My house is kind of nuts these days, but you can take me to Nick's house. He lives right down the block from me."

"Nick?"

"Remember, the fries?"

189

"Yeah, yeah, the eleven-year-old. Cool. We will make him a whole bag full of fresh ones before we leave. I'll even throw in a steak sandwich."

"Thanks. You will love Nick's kitchen. It's like a dream, except for two things."

"What's that?"

"No deep fryer or birch beer machine," Jeannie said with a wink.

Jake grabbed the bag of food and led Jeannie out to his car. It was a brand new, 1973 Plymouth Duster, red, with white racing stripes, white vinyl top, matching white seats, and a surfboard on the roof rack.

"This is the coolest car ever."

"Thanks. I just switched out the carburetor. She really moves now. Want to hear it?"

"Sure."

Jake lifted the car hood, got in, pumped the accelerator three times, and started the engine, which fired up with a loud *Vvvrrroooommm!*

"Nice. You better adjust the air fuel mixture. You have way too much gas going in there. Use a vacuum gauge. These 225 straight six-cylinder engines need a little boost, but you don't want to flood them. I've seen one catch fire."

Jake was stunned. He leaned back against his car. Jeannie was so pretty, smart, and poised. He was already falling for her, and now this. He never met a girl who knew anything about cars. Jake broke into a huge grin. "You are just full of surprises. How do you know so much about cars?"

"My Dad. He was a mechanic. He used to take me to work with him when I was a little kid. I spent my preschool years in a garage, on a greasy creeper, rolling under cars, and handing him tools."

"That's so cool."

"Yeah, until he left us. I don't blame him, though. My Mom kept pawning his tools for drugs. She is a big car wreck of her own."

"Sorry, Jeannie. My Mom's a mess too. I never knew my Dad. Mom said he was some drunk chef, and even a bigger disaster than her. They weren't together long. The low-life split as soon as she told him she was pregnant."

"That's awful, Nick. Did you ever try to find him?"

"Nah. He's not worth my time. Let's go see Nick's fancy kitchen before his fries get cold."

Jake reached out to open the passenger door for her just as Jeannie reached for the door handle. Their hands touched and they both looked down at their feet, then at each other. Jeannie felt like she had just walked into a Beach Boys song. The energy was so intense and light, all at once. In that moment, they fell in love. At least as in love as two teenagers can be.

52

The manatee peered up again at its life's reflection swiftly flowing like an incoming tide on the water's surface, and she was transported back to 1918. The year before she left the camp. Wekiwa's latest entrée for the camp was armadillo on the half shell. Armadillo's were omnivores, with a particular fondness for ants and termites, which sometimes made them taste a bit gamey. She tested her recipes on the hoard of young boys who followed her around camp like bees on a fresh blossom. The boys were so enchanted by Wekiwa that she could have fed them mud, and they would tell her it tasted like the finest deer meat. That is, all the boys with the exception of Nighthawk.

Wekiwa wasn't used to any boy, or for that matter, *anyone* beyond her Mother, who wasn't smitten by her charms. This gave Nighthawk a privilege above all other boys in the camp. Nighthawk was born with a rare eye disorder, which left him visually impaired. Due to his blindness, he never looked upon Wekiwa's eyes, thus, he never succumbed to her powers. But the Great Spirits blessed Nighthawk in other ways and his other senses were developed to such acuity, that he was able to hear a wasp land on a flower's petal from 1,000 paces. He could distinguish the scent of a water moccasin from a rattlesnake at 3,000 paces. By touch, Nighthawk could feel the difference between two nearly identical leaves.

But it was his sense of taste where Nighthawk truly excelled. His taste buds were so discriminating, that he could sense even an additional grain of salt added to one dish compared to the other. He was unapologetic in his feedback about Wekiwa's cooking, which she came to rely on. And while Nighthawk could not see, Wekiwa could certainly see him. Nighthawk wasn't the tallest, fastest, or strongest teenage boy in the camp, but he was the funniest, and the most attractive. His face had beautiful features and a strong jawline. His ears were set close to his face, and his eyebrows naturally shaped into two beautiful, naturally curved arches, highlighting his sparkling Hazel eyes which bore no sign of disease. He was a good listener, and his drumming and chanting were divine. Wekiwa found herself more and more drawn to him.

"Nighthawk. Come here and try my latest dish."

"I could smell it halfway across the camp. I think you burned it," Nighthawk said, laughing all the way over to Wekiwa's fire. "Smells like balls. Yes, that's it. Balls of Bear," Nighthawk said, still laughing.

Wekiwa poked Nighthawk in the ribs as he sat next to her by the fire. They both laughed. She reached out and touched Nighthawk's forearm. She had a true affection for him. He was in fact her only real friend in the camp. "Open wide and tell me what you think?"

"Oh, I bet you say that to all the boys."

Wekiwa stuffed the dish into Nighthawk's mouth. "Well?"

"Still tastes like balls," Nighthawk said with a teasing smile.

Wekiwa poked Nighthawk again and laughed heartily. "Careful, or yours will be next."

"I always did like squirrel stew. This tastes like a nice fat one. Good marbling. I would have gone with a bit more ground marigold, and a little less boiled Spanish Needle, but you're the one who has to eat this." Nighthawk said smiling.

Wekiwa smiled back, even though she knew he couldn't see her. She soon became acutely aware that Nighthawk was the only one, besides her Mother, Grandfather, and of course, Rainbow, who she really could show herself to. She relished her relationship with Nighthawk, but at the age of seventeen, she had no romantic feelings toward him, or anyone for that matter. Nighthawk, however, had very different feelings indeed. At eighteen, he was truly in love with Wekiwa. Not teenage love, but a deep smoldering, unending, bottomless love. Being a person of great sensitivity and introspection, he recognized his love for Wekiwa, but guarded it as he would a hidden treasure, for he knew she did not reciprocate. By the time Wekiwa left camp, Nighthawk had tried, commented, and bettered every dish Wekiwa made. He even helped her cook the nightly meals for the camp. When she later arrived in downtown Miami, she was exhilarated by the rush of her restaurant, and her powers. Still, she thought of Nighthawk often.

It was 1921, two years after leaving the camp, when Wekiwa made her grand return. She came with three wagons loaded with an array of gifts for her people. There were the finest fabrics, handmade boots, a variety of food, herbs, salt, medicines, building materials, kerosene lanterns, a beautiful wardrobe for her Mother, a set of tools for her Grandfather, and a sharp, new buck knife for Nighthawk, who was the only person in the camp who did not come to greet her.

"Greetings, Grandfather. I hope the Great Spirits have been good to you in my absence."

"Other than a little arthritis in my knees, I am fine, my child. It seems the Great Spirits have shined buttloads on you, little one," Hatori said, clutching his belly as he broke into a laugh.

Wekiwa joined him in laughter. "Come here, my child. I haven't laughed like that since you left."

"Neither have I, Grandfather," Wekiwa said through tears of laughter. "I missed you, Grandfather."

"As I missed you. Your Mother read me your letters, little one. You have prospered in Mayaimi, and you, you, you… I can't put my finger on it," Hatori said, touching Wekiwa's nose, "but you have been up to something."

"My cooking has pleased the Great Spirits, Grandfather. That is all."

"You can't fool and old fool, but you always did try, little one."

"Yes, Grandfather," Wekiwa said with her most beguiling smile.

"You know that smiling crap doesn't work on me, my child."

"Yes Grandfather. May I ask where he…"

Hatori cut her off. "I know, I know, where is Nighthawk? Since you left, he built his own sweat lodge. It's 2,500 paces down the road, turn left at the fallen Cypress. If you land in the canal, you missed it."

"Thank you, Grandfather. I missed you too!" Wekiwa said as she gave Hatori a big hug and ran off down the road, Rainbow following close behind. When Wekiwa arrived at the sweat lodge, she saw the many, many cords of firewood and an abundance of ash on the ground, and she knew Nighthawk had spent many, many nights there. She held the buck knife in her hand as she opened the flap to enter, and Rainbow curled up outside the tent. Nighthawk was sitting on the floor, legs crossed. They were both motionless for over an hour, until at last, he stood up.

"Took you long enough," Nighthawk said.

"Miss me?" Wekiwa asked.

"You didn't say goodbye?"

"I thought about you many times, Nighthawk."

"And I could not stop thinking about you, Wekiwa. I can tell the Great Spirits have blessed you, and you have blessed the tribe. For that I am grateful."

Wekiwa walked slowly across the hot dirt floor. She stopped a few inches from Nighthawk and stood there, breathing rapidly. He took the buck knife from her hands and examined it carefully with his fingers. Despite his blindness, Nighthawk reached out with his new knife and skillfully slit the single shoulder strap from Wekiwa's scarlet silk dress, which fell to the dirt floor in a heap. Nighthawk tossed the knife onto the dress.

"Sharp knife. Thanks. I hear your breath and your heart. It is beating faster than usual, and is that orange blossom honey I smell on your breath?"

"Taste for yourself," Wekiwa said as she adoringly kissed Nighthawk on the mouth. Nighthawk kissed her back, gently, but unyieldingly, with every molecule of his love for her bursting through his tongue. She placed her arms around Nighthawk, and they held each other tenderly until Wekiwa removed her arms. It had been two years since she had first made love with Ernest, and she had many lovers since, but until this point in time, she never really understood why they called it making love. She found herself lost in Nighthawk's touch. She thought to herself, *'Of all his senses, touch was truly his most potent'*. He caressed her in a manner that made Wekiwa feel for the first time that she wasn't all alone in her own skin. It was as if someone else had crept inside of her and found every spot that gave her endless joy. And, while Wekiwa had never experienced fear, for the first time ever, she knew what it was like to feel safe. Wekiwa blissfully remained in camp for a week, Nighthawk and Rainbow, never far from her side.

"Nighthawk, I must return to Flowing Springs. Come with me."

"Why must you go, Wekiwa? You have enough money for ten lifetimes for all of your people, and we need nothing else but this land. You have made us all proud. Stay here, with me. With your people."

"The Great Spirits are not through with me yet, Nighthawk. Come with me. You will love Mayaimi, and you can taste my food every day. Nobody else will tell me when it needs salt," Wekiwa said, poking his ribs.

"Hah! A blind Indian in a busy City. It is not my place, Wekiwa, nor yours."

"I must go back, but I will return. I swear that to you."

"Something tells me you will not return to me again in this lifetime, Wekiwa."

They sat by the fire of the sweat lodge, locked in an infinite embrace that only ended at sunup, when Wekiwa kissed Nighthawk in a way she never had before.

"I swear an oath to you, Nighthawk. I will return. I, I love you."

"And I you."

Rainbow circled Nighthawk, purring, and rubbing her vibrating throat against his legs. Wekiwa walked back to her Mother's house with Rainbow, before heading to her boat.

"Goodbye, Mother! Goodbye, Grandfather! I will be back next year." Once again, she did not say goodbye to Nighthawk, realizing why she hadn't the first time. It was too agonizing.

53

Danny picked up his phone and dialed Joseph's number.

"Hello, Joseph Clearwater speaking."

"Joseph. It's Danny Gomez."

"Daniel, my friend. Que pasa, amigo?"

"Things are good, Joseph. How are you doing?"

"To tell you the truth, Danny, I'm about to lose my shit."

"What's up, Joseph?"

"Are you familiar with Arch Creek?"

"Sure. I had my fifth birthday party at the pony ranch next door. Mike and I have pulled some huge tarpon out of that Creek. Don't worry, Joseph, we released all of them."

"Yes, the waters are plentiful there. Those ponies are pretty cute too. One of them reminds me of an appaloosa I had as a kid. Mine was a lot scrawnier, though. I am glad you know the place."

"I'm sorry, Joseph. I'm pretty busy, and..."

Joseph interrupted, "Listen carefully, Danny. This is extremely important. It could be the story you've been waiting for your entire life."

"I'm listening."

"They are about to pave paradise and build a car lot."

"I don't think that's how the song goes. What are you talking about, Joseph?"

"I mean it in the literal sense, Danny. They bought it and are going to turn it into an auto showroom."

"Who bought what, Joseph?"

"Lucifer Motors. They own most of Arch Creek now. They want to bulldoze the trees, destroy the natural bridge, fill in the Creek, pave over everything, all to build a huge car showroom."

"I heard about the land deal, but nothing was mentioned about filling in the Creek and paving over the Natural Bridge. Do you have your information in writing, Joseph?"

"Yes. I have all of the ownership documents and their construction plans."

"How come the regular news outlets aren't covering this?"

"Nobody cares about this little Creek, and except for you, the reporters think I'm a nutjob. But you know the history. My people and their ancestors dwelled around Arch Creek for centuries. And, if Mike and my daughter ever give me grandchildren, their ancestors as well. Some of those trees are hundreds of years old. They are sacred. That Creek used to flow all the way from the Everglades. If they close off the Creek..." Joseph's voice faded off.

"Are you sure absolutely sure about this, Joseph? Lucifer Motors? Talk about big fish in a little pond."

"You're a smart boy, Danny. The environment is very fragile, but people take that for granted. The Creek needs the water from the bay, but not too much. The bay needs the water from the Creek, and the ocean needs the bay water. Just think of all of the plants, animals, fish and birds that rely on this system. Without the shelter of the mangroves, which grow in the Creek and Bay, there would be no nesting grounds for the waterfowl, and where do you think the small fish and crustaceans grow?"

"In the Mangroves."

"Exactly!" Joseph said as he became more agitated.

"I give, Joseph. I'll cover the story. When can we meet? I want to see all of the documents."

"You know Mike's friend Ben? Meet me at Ben's house. One hour."

"Yes, I know Ben. Good guy. Tries to educate the fishermen on conservation practices. What does Ben have to do with it?"

"It's not so much Ben as it is his house, and his family. Just meet me there. One hour."

"Okay, Joseph. What's his address?"

"Ben's house is the last one in on the left on 137 Place in North Miami. The street just behind the pony ranch. Mike will be there too."

"Oh, Mike knows about this?" Danny asked with a bit of relief in his voice.

"Not yet. But I will tell all when we get there. I need the entire family there for this."

"Hazel too?

"Yes."

"Last time I spoke with Mike, Hazel was still selling advertising specialties. What could Hazel possibly have to do with this?"

"Everything."

"Hazel?"

"Yes!"

"You sure you're still taking your meds, Joseph?"

"Yes."

"Come on, Joseph, I'm a reporter and Mike's good friend. If his wife, your daughter, is going to be part of this story, we need to let them know before you spring this on him."

"You've just nailed it on the head, Danny?" Joseph said as he broke into a big belly laugh.

"Nailed what?"

"We don't want to spring this on them. Good one. Are you psychic?" Joseph said, still laughing.

"Excuse me? I really think you need to call your doctor, Joseph."

"No, I'm fine. It's just when you said spring this on them."

"What? What do you mean?"

"You'll find out in an hour. Ben and Gina's house. Spring it on them! Good one, Danny!" Joseph said again, laughing hysterically, as he hung up the receiver.

Danny picked up the phone and called Mike. Perhaps he could shed some light on this.

"Lawrence residence. Hazel speaking."

"Hazel. I love how formal you are when you answer the phone. Remember, I've seen you reel in a fifty-pound Grouper, wearing a bikini top, and cursing like a sailor the entire time."

"Danny Gomez! How the hell are you?"

"I'm good, Hazel. How about you?"

"Great, actually. I called for Mike, but I'm really glad I got you."

"Sure you are. You and Mike probably want to set up a time to drink beer, watch football, and talk about girls."

"But, Hazel, I'm reformed. Well, at least no more football."

"A likely story. Do you want me to have him call you?"

"Well, actually, I really did want to talk with you."

"I'm not going to tell you my secret fishing spot, Danny, so forget it."

"I wouldn't even try to drag that out of you. Listen, I just got off the phone with your Father."

"Crap. Is he okay, Danny? Is he off his meds again? You know how he gets sometimes."

"I know, Hazel, but he sounded good this time."

"So, what did you want to ask me?"

"Your Father invited me to your friend Ben's house in an hour. He wanted to talk to you, me, and Mike."

"Uhhh ohhh! Don't worry, Danny. I'll talk to him and call Mom. She can always get through to him when he's acting out."

"I swear. Your Dad was fine. Very cool, calm, and collected, in fact. The only odd thing was, when he hung up, he couldn't stop laughing about something I said."

"I never thought you were that funny, Danny."

"Thanks. Thanks a lot."

"What was it that you said?"

"He told me this meeting today concerns you, and when I said something about not springing it on you, he laughed and laughed. Any idea why?"

Hazel was silent. She thought to herself, *'Could it be?'* The drumming she heard a few minutes ago, the manatee, the legend told to her by her great-grandmother.

Danny spoke into the receiver, "Hazel, Hazel, you still there?"

"Sorry, Danny. Yes, I'm here. See you at Ben's house."

"Hello! Hello!" Danny shouted as Hazel hung up the phone.

Hazel shook her head, thinking to herself, those two must have gotten high. Then she thought about the sounds she just heard, and the shaking leaves on Al, the ancient Oak. Could it be true? *'Nah,'* she said to herself.'

"The legend of Wekiwa," she found herself whispering out loud. Just then, Hazel felt the ground shake again and heard the sounds in the distance.

Ommapapo! Ommapapo!

54

The manatee was still watching her life float by her on the surface of Arch Creek's waters. Thirty-nine weeks after Wekiwa parted from Nighthawk, Ernest Thirst drove the boat to the edge of the camp. He walked to Catori's house and knocked on the wooden door. Catori opened the door and stepped outside.

"Is everything all right, Mr. Thirst?"

"Come," Ernest led Catori to the boat. She climbed inside and caressed her daughter's sleeping face. Wekiwa woke up and smiled.

"Mother," Wekiwa said with a sleepy smile.

"Wekiwa. How are you, my child?"

"The Great Spirits have blessed us beyond words, Mother. Meet your grandson."

Catori's eyes filled with tears of joy as she held the hours-old infant in her hands.

"He is beautiful, my child, and so large."

"Thank you, Mother. We must talk."

"Yes, my child."

"I cannot raise this baby in Mayaimi. It is my home now, but he belongs here, amongst his people, where you and Grandfather can teach him our traditions. I will visit often and take him to stay with me when he can understand the ways of the city."

"And what of his Father?"

Wekiwa took a deep breath and sighed. "His Father must not know. This is best for both of them.

Catori kissed Wekiwa on the forehead. "Yes. Of course, my child. Now rest."

Wekiwa fell asleep. She awoke to a thud, when Ernest Thirst carelessly bumped the boat into the dock behind Flowing Springs. Wekiwa sat in the back of the boat starring out at her restaurant, with Rainbow at her feet. She had never experienced such loss until this very moment. Her chest felt as though a great bear was sitting on it, pawing its giant claws into her heart, shredding it to pieces. For the first time in her life, Wekiwa sadly wept. Her tears flowed, and she wailed as if shot by the sharpest arrow. Rainbow let out a series of high-pitched yowls that pierced the air.

Wekiwa stumbled to her feet, still covered in the remnants of childbirth. She felt herself being propelled into a darkness blacker than any moonless night. She leapt to the front of the boat and struck Ernest in the face, hard. He did not flinch. "I didn't even get to say goodbye." She struck Ernest again and again. He did not move. "I didn't kiss my baby goodbye. I didn't kiss my baby. I didn't…"

At first, Wekiwa thought the sounds she was hearing was of her slapping Ernest's face, then she recognized it. *Ommapapo! Ommapapo!* The feelings of pain and sadness were gone, replaced by a newfound rage. Wekiwa leapt off the boat and disappeared into the Mayaimi River's dark waters. Rainbow let out a *Grrarrarrr* and dove into the River by her side without leaving a ripple on the surface.

Ernest stood up in the boat as the entire length of Flagler Street shook. The owner of the Mercantile stepped outside his store. He looked down at Ernest in the boat and asked, "I didn't know Miami had earthquakes. Hurricanes, but not earthquakes. What on heaven or earth do you think that was?"

Ernest looked up at the man and shrugged. "I ain't 100% sure, mister, but I can tell you one thing."

"Oh. what's that?"

"Whatever it is, it don't got nothing to do with heaven!"

55

Marsh had been waiting for ten minutes since the school bell rang. Gracie and Nick didn't show up for their walk home. They always walked home together from school. Marsh decided to walk the few blocks home by himself. Besides, this way, he could walk to the pony ranch to visit Blu. Marsh volunteered at the ranch on Saturdays. It was only a shortcut through the woods away from his house, and in exchange for mucking out stalls, he got an hour ride on Blu. While Marsh loved all of the ponies, Blu was his favorite.

Blu was a beautiful Shetland pony, brown and white, with a long brown mane and tail. Every Saturday when Marsh approached, Blu ran around the paddock and neighed loudly. It didn't hurt that Marsh brought her a carrot or apple when he came either. Plus, Marsh never kicked her to run faster like some of the little brats.

When Marsh got there, Blu was in her stable, but neighed and rose up and down to greet him.

"Sorry, girl, I don't have a treat for you today." Blu seemed to understand and nuzzled Marsh's neck.

"Hey, Marsh, what are you doing here today?" Annie, one of the ranch hands asked.

"I just stopped by to see Blu."

"Looks like she's happy to see you. She's been in her stable all day.

Want to take her out for some exercise. Since nobody is here today, you can practice putting on her bridle and saddle."

Marsh was so excited, he practically tripped opening the stable door. "Thank you, Annie." Marsh gently put the bridle in Blu's mouth and adjusted it so it would fit just right. He put a striped blanket on Blu's back, and then the saddle, which he hitched up perfectly.

"Great job, Marsh. I don't think you need any more practice. Go ahead, take her out for a spin."

"Oh, thank you, Annie," Marsh said as he tightly hugged Annie, then turned away in embarrassment.

"It's okay, Marsh, everyone could use a hug now and then," Annie said.

Marsh smiled at Annie, led Blu into the paddock, and mounted her. He had adjusted the saddle just right and smiled proudly as he took the reins and headed onto the trail.

56

Gus and Larry took the 135 Street exit on I95 and headed east toward Ben's house.

'What makes you think his kid is going to talk to you?" Larry asked.

"Herman's kid was okay. He always treated me like everyone else."

"Well, why wouldn't he? You being such a nice fella and all."

"I was mostly drunk those days, and not too nice to anyone. Still, his kid, Ben, he looked me right in the eye and said, *good morning,* with a smile every time I saw him."

"Nice of you to repay him by chopping off his Dad's head."

"It was an accident, mon ami!"

"Sure, I believe you."

They parked Aunt Ethel's truck down the block. Gus and Larry got out of the truck, then heard thumping in the cooler. Gus opened the cooler, took out the bag containing Herman's head, and got back into the truck, followed by Larry Fine.

"Dude, this is so cool. Wait a minute, I need a hit of a joint before you do this," Larry said.

"Fire one up!" Came a voice from the bag.

"What the fuck. Open the bag. Open it!" Larry yelled as he used the truck's cigarette lighter to light the joint.

"All right, keep your pants on," Gus said as he lifted Herman's head out of the bag.

"I'm surprised you two schmendricks even found this place. Now give me a hit of that joint," Herman's head said to Larry. Herman puckered and extended his lips. Larry Fine held the joint to Herman's mouth.

"Here you go, man. Enjoy."

Herman's head took a big hit off the joint and smoke bellowed out below his neck. Larry was so spooked he jumped sideways out of the truck door and fell onto the grass. Herman's head laughed so hard, he sneezed, which caused it to flip over twice landing upside down in Gus' hands.

"Good hands there, you doofus. Now would one of you morons bring me to the backyard? They're all back there. Damn! I hope we didn't miss her," Herman's head said to Gus.

"Miss who?"

"The Mermaid!"

57

emma woke up in Gretchen's bed. It was very bright outside, and she pulled the blanket over her head. She looked down and saw that she was wearing wiener dog pajamas. Gretchen was sitting next to her, wearing bell bottom jeans and a tube top, eating a bowl of Corn Pops and reading a magazine.

"Hey, sleepy head. Want some breakfast?" Gretchen said with an outstretched spoonful of shiny yellow cereal kernels floating on a pillow of milk. "You can really sleep!"

"What time is it?" Jemma asked as her mouth avoided the cereal spoon.

"Time for your lazy ass to get out of bed. Boy, you were really talking some fucked up shit last night. What did you smoke, anyway, and why didn't you bring me some?"

"Oh God! "Jemma replied, holding her head in her hands as memories of the night before came flooding back. "Was I really messed up? Maybe I conjured up the entire thing in my head. That's got to be it."

"Let's hope so. Jemma. Otherwise, your Mom is into some kinky shit. A clown's mask? With the babysitter?"

"Oh God! I told you?"

"You couldn't shut up about it. Then you passed out. I had to clean your feet with a washcloth and change your clothes before dragging you into bed—you're welcome by the way."

"Love the wiener dog jammies. Thanks. Oh God! I'm so embarrassed."

"You should be. You're not exactly light as a feather you know. I had to get my brother to help me. You know Monty always did have a crush on you, but don't worry, I didn't let him touch any of your good parts."

"Oh God! Not Monty."

"I'm kidding. I did let him touch something, but I'm not saying what."

"Oh God! Just kill me now. I need to get home."

"Yeah. You need to confront that slut of a Mother of yours."

"She's at the Pet Store until the kids get off school every day. I'm going home to take a shower and change, then head over to the Pet Store to tear her a new one. Then I'm taking the next bus back to college. I need to get the hell out of here."

"Are you going to tell your Dad?"

"Fuck no! He thinks the sun shines out her butthole. I'm going to tell her if she doesn't tell Dad, I will. I'll give her a chance to do the right thing. I know it's the 70's, free love, and all that, but she took vows with my Father. And a clown mask, she needs therapy or something."

"My Dad had an affair," Gretchen blurted.

"You never told me."

"My parents were too ashamed for anyone to know. He told her he was bowling every Tuesday night. I know what this is like," Gretchen said as she reached out and held Jemma's forearm. I'll walk you home."

"I'm fine, Gretch."

"Oh, I know. I just want to bum a joint from you. You owe me."

Jemma smiled and hugged Gretchen. "I don't know what I would do without you."

"I know, right? I'm the best!" Gretchen said, playfully swatting Jemma's butt. "Now, hurry up. I need to get high."

With Jemma still clad in wiener dog jammies, the girls headed down the street to Jemma's house.

"Slow down, Gretchen. I'm not wearing shoes."

"Sorry, Jemma. If your Mom's at the Pet Store, what are all those cars doing at your house."

"The van belongs to Mike. I don't know about the others."

"Hurry up, Jemma, we need to get there before they find it."

"Find what?"

"Your pot!"

58

Mike got his underwater camera, a pouch full of gear, and walked to the Creek. He waved at Ben and Gina through the kitchen window. They appeared to be locked in a never-ending embrace. They did not wave back. Mike was happy to see them reunited. He always liked Gina, but relentlessly kidded Ben that she was out of his league.

Mike looked into the clear water of the Creek and soaked it all in. This is what the Creek would have looked like a thousand years ago, even ten thousand years ago, before modern man screwed up the natural flow of things. Ben made his way to the Creek's edge and expertly slid beneath the surface of the water like a seal off a wet rock. It seemed impossible, but the water temperature seemed like it dropped another ten degrees since he exited the Creek just a few moments earlier. Mike took a thermometer out of his pouch. The Creek was fifty-eight degrees. Even natural springs in Florida typically don't fall below sixty-eight degrees.

Mike adjusted his camera and swam back to the spot where they saw the manatee. He swam to the bottom of the Creek and then slowly meandered to the Natural Bridge. Mike thought if he were a manatee, this would be the perfect spot to chill out. Besides a few lingering snook, a nicely sized largemouth bass, three red-eared slider turtles, and a duck, there wasn't anything to see there.

Mike was always fascinated by the beauty of natural limestone expanse.

He had heard many theories of how the Natural Bridge was formed. Some theorized that the Creek was initially an underground stream with the Natural Bridge being the only protrusion, until the rest of the Creek lost its cover. Others thought it was a huge solution pit which formed when acid from decaying matter eroded the ever-present limestone base. Even though Mike was a scientist through and through, the grandeur of such structures was not lost on his spiritual soul.

Mike explored both sides of the bridge from top to bottom with a childlike innocence. One area of rock looked strange, almost like someone had carved it with a chisel. Mike went up for a few good breaths of air, took something else from his pouch, and swam back down. He held a small dish brush in one hand and his camera in the other. He placed the camera on the Creek floor and swam back to where he saw the carvings. Mike used the dish brush to rub the algae and plant growth off of the carvings. As he rubbed, dislodged vegetation floated everywhere, causing a swarm of fish to form all around him, gobbling up the plant matter, any displaced shrimp, and other tasty treats. The feast was so plentiful, even the duck swam over to partake in the bounty.

Despite being a marine biologist for the past fifteen years, the little kid in Mike always loved a good swarm of fish. As Mike was otherwise occupied with the fish, he failed to notice his camera disappear off the Creek bottom. The swarm cleared out and Mike swam back to examine the carvings. There were six perfectly square frames. They had exquisite carvings in them. The first image was of a Father holding an infant. The second image was a woman holding a baby. The third image was of a tall, stunning Seminole woman, with long black hair, an hourglass figure, a beguiling smile, and there was something else... her eyes shined turquoise on the wall of the bridge. She was in a vast kitchen standing over a stove, holding a mortar and pestle, grinding a mixture of herbs and flowers. She had an odd look on her face that was neither happy nor sad, but rather conveyed great mystery, with just a hint of both good and evil.

The kitchen looked familiar to Mike as though he had stood in it a hundred times. The fourth image was of this same woman transforming into a large creature. The fifth image was of the creature in a clear blue creek, its giant tail flapping wildly, with a pained look on its deep-set turquoise eyes. Wait, Mike thought to himself, *'I must have been down too long. I'm seeing things due to lack of oxygen.'*

Mike swam to the surface, took several breaths of air, then a few more and exhaled slowly. *'You're imagining this,'* Mike told himself. *'Go back down and look again.'* Mike inhaled slowly and deeply, then returned to the carvings. They were still there. As clear as day. Mike couldn't trust his eyes and headed down to retrieve his camera.

"Big smile now," said the still-naked Mrs. Mendlebaum, who was holding Mike's camera, only now Mike noticed that she had bright turquoise eyes. Mike was so shocked he thoughtlessly inhaled, filling his lungs with water. He was gasping for air. After Mrs. Mendlebaum took Mike's picture, she grabbed him around his chest, and pulled him to the Creek bank. He wasn't breathing. Mrs. Mendlebaum acted quickly. She jumped on top of Mike and started pressing on his chest. No response. She put her mouth over his and started blowing. At that exact moment, Ben, Gina, Hazel, Joseph Clearwater, Anna, and George all converged on the Creek.

Hazel couldn't quite make out who the figure was under the naked woman, but it sure looked like Mike. Hazel thought to herself, *'It better not be.'* She dove into the water and crossed the Creek like an Olympic Swimmer, pouncing onto the opposite Creek bank, where she now knew it was Mike under this nude woman, who was undeterred by Hazel's noisy presence.

"Oh, hell No!" Hazel yelled at the woman. She rushed over and tried to push the woman off of Mike, but her hands passed right through her. Mike raised his head, vomited up at least a quart of water, along with a few aquatic plants and three minnows.

The still coughing Mike looked up to see Hazel, "Oh, Hazel, did you see her? Mrs. Mendelbaum?"

"Mrs. Mendelbaum? Is Mrs. Mendlebaum an Indian?" asked Hazel as she took another swipe at the woman, her hand passing right through the vision.

The rest of the crew made their way down to the opposite side of the Creek.

"Hazel!" yelled Joseph.

"Yes, Father?"

"I want you to meet someone."

"Who? Do you know her, and why was she kissing my husband?!?!"

"Husband? You did okay for yourself, little one," said the naked woman.

"Who the hell are you?"

"Hazel! Mind your elders."

"Elders? This slut is my age. Maybe younger."

"I may be a slut, honey, but I would kill to be your age. Good job, Joseph! You raised a feisty one."

"Father, you know this whore?"

"Hazel!! Please, don't make this worse."

"What?!"

"Hazel. This is Wekiwa—your..."

Just then Gina, overcome with figures of men and women talking and twirling inside her head, let out a loud shriek, closed her eyes, and fell backward. The last thing she saw was Ben catching her in his arms.

59

Danny Gomez pulled up to the house on Enchanted Place and was overcome with an eerie feeling of déjà vu. *Have I been here before?* Danny felt his anxiety drop as he saw Mike's VW Van. Thank God Mike was here. What could Mike have to do with Lucifer Motors? Maybe Mike has some environmental pollution dirt on them, but what role could Hazel play?

Danny got out of his car, causing Vlad and Princess to begin their typical *let's scare off the visitors* charge, when they lifted their snouts, sniffed the air in Danny's direction, and ran off into the back yard. Danny loved dogs, all animals, actually, and laughed at this unusual greeting. He walked up to the door, knocked, and looked through the window. He didn't see anyone in the home but was seized by a tingling in the back of his neck that crawled down his spine, deep into his feet. That kitchen. I know it. Certainly, I would recall being here before.

Danny knocked again and walked inside. "Hello, Ben? Mike? It's Danny Gomez. Joseph invited me. Anyone home?" He walked to the kitchen, then stopped dead in his path when he saw the hanging copper pots and the Oaks lining the Creek out back.

"Wekiwa!" Danny said quietly out loud. Wait. What is going on here? Maybe Joseph is testing out some of those Native American mushroom potions his family used to make. That's gotta be it. He must have figured out a way to aerosolize it. Crazy Joseph. He's messing with me.

Danny sat down at the table and took it all in. The stove, the spices, the hanging pots, and the smells. His taste buds were vibrating, and he could taste something so deep in his mouth, his throat tightened at the flavor. Yum! Sofke and ground passionflower. Wait, what the hell is Sofke and passionflower? I've eaten here before.

Danny stood and walked into the pantry. He saw bottles of spices, jars full of fruit, and a mason jar containing what looked like flour. He unconsciously reached for the jar and was incapacitated by the chilling of his blood as he examined the writing on the faded turquoise label that he couldn't make out. Danny's memories came back to him faster than a flowing spring. That was it! The label. *Flowing Springs.* Danny's body began shaking uncontrollably. His eyes rolled back in their sockets, and he experienced projected images onto his brainstem at an overwhelming pace. In his mind's eye, Danny found himself transported to another time, another place, yet it felt like here. It was 1926, and he was sitting across from a beautiful woman with long brown hair.

"Carmen, isn't this the most wonderful thing you ever put in your mouth?"

"Besides you, my love, I think so."

"You are a spicy one, but his food. It's unbelievable. Are you sure you don't want to try it?"

"Do you like this dress, Ricardo?"

"Yes, you look stunning in it."

"Gracias, mi amore, but I won't be able to get out of it if I eat one more bite. It's practically glued onto me now, don't you think?"

Ricardo smiled and winked at Carmen without saying a word. At that moment, a panther entered the room and rubbed its cheek on Ricardo's thigh. He loved animals. Every kind.

"Do you even believe this, Carmen? A Florida Panther. Full grown, and tame as a kitten. And this Garlic Mash Sofke? I've never tasted anything like it. You sure you don't want a bite?"

"Not of that,' Carmen said as she leaned across the table and nibbled Ricardo's ear.

"Are you enjoying your meals?" Came a voice floating out of the air, as Wekiwa approached the table.

Ricardo stood. "I was just telling my wife that this is the most delicious meal of my life. And your Panther, what a magnificent animal."

Rainbow purred and continued rubbing Ricardo's leg.

"Why, thank you. Most people call Rainbow my pet. She is no pet. We are joined Spirits," Wekiwa said as she touched Ricardo's arm. Ricardo looked into the matching turquoise eyes of Wekiwa and Rainbow and was mesmerized.

"Ricardo Gomez, at your service."

"Wekiwa Sawgrass. I am so pleased you enjoyed your meal, although, your date here hardly touched hers."

"Oh. It's not the food, chica, it's the dress."

"I see. Next time you go out for a fine meal, I suggest wearing a looser fitting dress. Or perhaps you were saving room for dessert? Please accept these sweets on the house."

"Oh, we couldn't."

"I insist. I enjoy looking out my kitchen, watching customers who relish my food as much as I do. I saw how my cooking pleased your palate. Let's just call this a little reward. Please enjoy them."

"You are too generous. It would be our honor if you would join us."

Carmen flinched at Ricardo's words, and both Wekiwa and Ricardo noticed.

"Perhaps another time. My work is not yet done. I will be back out to check on you. I would love to know what you think of my desserts."

Ricardo stood and bowed. "We await your return with great anticipation."

Wekiwa bowed halfway, turned and left. Ricardo devoured half of his dessert before turning to Carmen. "Forgive me, my dear. Would you like some?"

"Remember, the dress."

"Yes, of course. Aren't you eating your dessert?"

"I did have two small bites and had to stop myself. It's deliciouso," Carmen said, "but I am done." She pushed the plate toward him.

Ricardo finished his dessert, and Carmen's, and pushed her empty plate back to her across the table.

"Hiding the evidence?" Carmen asked.

"Well, I wouldn't want her to think you didn't like it. She was so gracious, and exotic. And what a chef. I could eat her food every night."

Wekiwa returned to the table. She saw both desserts gone, leaned over the table, and said, "I am pleased you liked my food." She touched Ricardo and Carmen's arms and watched them both melt into their chairs. Two hours later, Wekiwa led them both into the back room of Flowing Springs.

Wekiwa directed the sleep-walking Carmen onto the chaise lounge. She led Ricardo into her old bedroom, disrobed, kissed him, and observed as his eyes turned a bright turquoise. Wekiwa found Latin men to be the most adept at love, and this one was very, very good. She actually dozed off for a few moments after they finished; that never happened to her. She found she enjoyed waking up in the arms of a strong, handsome man again.

Except for Rainbow, Wekiwa had slept alone since that last evening with Nighthawk. It had been four years since Wekiwa had left her baby with Catori. She broke her promise to the Great Spirits that she would stop using her powers that night she left her baby. She tried to stay in the light, but the darkness gripped her.

Wekiwa felt down in her depths that it was wrong, but she continued enchanting men and women for her own selfish pleasures. She had quite the life; loads of lovers of both sexes, an abundance of good food and drink, travel, art, music. She had been to Paris, sailed on a yacht through the Galapagos Islands, made love in the countryside of Sienna, climbed the Rocky Mountains, and visited Nepal.

Even though she hadn't returned to the camp in human form, she had helped the tribe, so she thought it was fine for her to indulge. She had fulfilled her destiny. The camp and tribe were prosperous. They had running water, schools, a medical clinic. Every member of the camp had a new house. Why shouldn't she indulge in life's finer pleasures?

Wekiwa hadn't realized she had been incredibly lonely until that moment. She walked over to check on Carmen. She was still dozing in the chaise where she was placed a few hours ago. Wekiwa seized the opportunity and led Ricardo to Ernest's wagon. She told Ricardo to get in, and told Ernest to get out. Wekiwa climbed into the wagon beside him, and Rainbow jumped onto the seat next to her. She drove the wagon east down Flagler Street, and then north on US 1. If she had looked back on that dimly moonlit night, she would have seen Carmen following on horseback.

Carmen only had two bites of Wekiwa's dessert, so she awoke right before Wekiwa drove off. Rainbow, however, had much better night vision and spotted Carmen as they passed Lemon City. Rainbow let out her loudest *Grrraaaaarrrrr* to fend them off. Carmen's horse bucked in fear, throwing her to the ground before taking off in the opposite direction without her. Carmen lay on the ground, holding her bleeding head, watching helplessly as the wagon containing her husband, Miami's first celebrity chef, and one pissed off panther traveled away into the night. Danny watched all of this through his rolled back eyes, as if he had been there himself, and it just occurred to him that he in fact had.

60

After Danny's beloved Abuela died, his Father had told him the sad tale of his grandparents, but even at ten, the reporter in him thought Dad was full of crap and drunk at the time. Danny's Father told him that when he was six, his grandfather was killed by his grandmother in a fit of jealous rage. It left him and his brother fatherless.

Danny loved everything about Abuela Carmen. She was elegant, smart, funny, beautiful, and clinically depressed most of the time, but not when she was with Danny. Abuela Carmen always spoke of her husband in the most endearing terms, but when she did, it was as if she were wearing a blanket of sadness. Plus, she wasn't in jail, so Danny just knew this story was bullshit. But he also had a feeling that there was so much more to this. He loved his Abuela so much and always felt such an extraordinary connection to her. Since he was little, Abuela Carmen used to tell him, *'Danny, mi amor, you are in my bones,'* and he didn't know why, but he felt likewise. His face would light up anytime she spoke with him, and he loved her more than he loved his parents, or even his dog!

Now finally, at the age of thirty-five, he knew why. It was as if watching a film through fog, but he had been here before; in Wekiwa's kitchen. He had lived in this house for a short time. He had swum naked in Arch Creek, picnicked under the Grand Oaks, and slept in her bed. *He was Ricardo!* Or at least, he had been. The feelings came streaming back. He was well fed, well loved, but he wasn't happy nor free. He felt trapped, as if held in place by some great force.

In his mind, all he wanted was to return to his precious Carmen, to his sons, to his home, but he did not command his own body. Until one day, as he and Wekiwa were lounging under a Giant Oak, after a cooling swim in Arch Creek, she found him. Danny saw her face through his memory-fogged mind. She looked furious and hurt all at once. She held a pistol in her hand. It was Carmen. She yelled something at him, but he could not respond. He hadn't spoken a word since his enchantment. Carmen lifted her arm and aimed her pistol. With the exception of curling her lips into her trademark beguiling smile, Wekiwa did not move. Rainbow slinked up behind Carmen and growled her most terrible *Grrrarrarrrerrrrrr* she had ever growled, causing Carmen to drop her pistol. Wekiwa commanded Ricardo to protect her.

"Forgive me, Carmen. Forgive me, my love," Danny said as he held his face in his hands and sobbed. He remembered it all. Ricardo grabbed the gun just as Carmen did. Her grip felt like she was fighting for her very life, and his. He could still see Wekiwa's reflection in Carmen's eyes. Wekiwa was positioned behind him, smiling. He wanted to let go of the gun. He tried. As he looked into Carmen's eyes, he saw exactly where Wekiwa stood. He turned the gun on himself, took aim, and pulled the trigger. The bullet passed through Ricardo's heart, and into Wekiwa's.

As Ricardo dropped to the ground for his dying breath, he saw Rainbow pounce, grab Wekiwa by the neck, and jump into the Creek. He heard loud thrashing sounds, saw bubbles, and then a face above him. Water was dropping on his face; Carmen's tears. "I love you for a thousand lifetimes. It wasn't your fault. She's a sorceress. I love you," she said through her sobs. Those were the last words Ricardo heard. And *Ommapapo Ommapapo,* were the last sounds he heard, as the ground shook, and he left that lifetime.

Danny needed a moment to compose himself. He was here to cover a story. These memories, they must be linked to Joseph. He brought me here. Yeah, that's it. Must be some kind of mushroom mist in this place, or maybe LSD on the doorknobs. He looked around the living room and up at the pine beamed ceiling. It was all so familiar. Danny paused, feeling some kind of pull, then glanced out the kitchen window and saw her beside Arch Creek. His blood ran cold, and his jaw slowly drooped as her name spilled from his mouth. "Wekiwa!"

61

"*G*ina, Gina! Are you okay?" Ben implored.

Gina did not respond. She was looking into the sky, her eyes transfixed. She saw them. She really saw them. Three figures floating in the sky. One was Ben's Mother. She knew her from the pictures Ben kept. The other was a handsome young man, tall, with olive skin and blue eyes. He winked at Gina and waved. Finally, a floating head appeared. Remarkably, Gina was not afraid. She recognized him as well and spoke his name, "Herman!"

"Nice to see you, kid. How've you been?"

Betty interrupted, "Nice to finally meet you in person, Gina. Well, as *in person* as a spirit can get. We have important work to do, and little time left, Gina. Let me explain. Oh, wait, this will be quicker." Betty flew over, shrank herself to the size of a gnat, and glided into Gina's ear. Betty shared the plan with Gina, who nodded that she understood. Gina looked at the scene unfolding before her and spoke.

"It's okay, Mom. I see them too," said Gina, as she gave Anna a wink and a smile.

"Anna, Gina, what are you talking about?" Ben asked, pleadingly.

"There's no time to explain, Ben. You're just going to have to trust me?" Gina said.

"Of course. The legend!" Ben yelled with excitement.

"You have heard about the Legend of Wekiwa, Ben? Joseph inquired. "Geez, word gets around fast."

"Wekiwa? Who? Never mind. I was referencing the Native American legend of people with heterochromia. They have one eye in this, and one eye in the other world," Ben elucidated.

"Anna, Gina. The Spirits are here now, correct? You can communicate with them, and they you?" Joseph asked.

"Yes. I have been talking to these Spirits since the car accident. Well, maybe a moment before," Anna responded.

Tina had just parked her Jeep in the yard and walked to the edge of the Creek to see everyone. "I knew it, Ma. You saw his hand too that night, Ma!!! I thought I was going nuts, and you never told me!" Tina's words exploded from her mouth.

"I'm sorry, dear. I thought everyone would think I was nuts if I told you I was talking to Spirits, and they were talking back."

Jemma hurried into her house with Gretchen right behind.

"Hey, wait for me!" Gretchen yelled.

"Something nuts is going on here, Gretch. Hey, who the hell are you?" Jemma shouted at Danny, who was standing in the kitchen gazing at the Creek.

"Um, sorry. I'm Danny Gomez, a friend of Ben's, and Mike's."

"Hmm. Okay. Where is everyone, and why are you in here alone?"

Danny pointed out the window. Jemma saw her parents, Aunt Tina, her Grandmother, George, Mike, Hazel, and some really big guy standing on the Creek bank talking to someone. Jemma looked more closely. It looked like a naked woman, a really drop-dead gorgeous naked woman. She had some crazy eyes. Were those blue? No, turquoise.

"Well, what the hell are we all doing in here? There's some crazy shit going on around this house lately. Geez. I leave for college for a few months, and these people just fall apart," Jemma said jokingly to Gretchen.

Jemma, Gretchen, and Danny walked out the sliding glass doors to the Oak-filled backyard. Danny breathed in deeply. He remembered that sensation of the oxygen-rich, misty, cool air beside the Creek. "It's just like the last time I was here," Danny said, frozen in place at the realization.

Gina, Anna, and Wekiwa all looked at Danny, and simultaneously said, "Ricardo!"

Tina, stood staring at Danny like a starstruck movie fan, and said, "I'll be damned! He's here."

Gina shouted up to Tina, "Hopefully you and the rest of us won't be damned."

"I told you I'd find you," Danny said to Tina with a wink.

"The guy from the hospital?" Gina asked.

Tina just stood there smiling like a lovesick teenager, nodding her head.

"You finally got a keeper, Sis!" Gina said, blowing Tina a kiss.

Mike sat up, wiped his wet face with his equally wet hands, and said, "No, no, his name isn't Ricardo. This is my friend, Danny. Danny Gomez. He's a reporter. Hey, Danny!" Mike looked over to see the naked Native American woman. "Hey, thanks for saving my life. What happened to Mrs. Mendlebaum, and my camera? Can somebody please get this lady some clothes?"

Vlad sniffed the air as he pranced to the Creek. Vlad, Anna, and Gina were the only ones to see, Betty, Murray, and Herman floating over Wekiwa.

Betty spoke telepathically to Anna and Gina, "Okay, all these strong guys around, and the women have to save the day. Who is that big one anyway?"

"That's Hazel's Father." Gina replied.

"He's a looker, all right, and *so* big. Well, if this doesn't work, we can certainly use some cultural diversity around here."

"Ewww! Just what I want to hear from my dead Mother-in-Law. It is nice to meet you, by the way. You did a great job with Ben. He's such a..."

"Sorry to interrupt, but if we don't do something soon, this whole plan turns to crap, and we are stuck here for eternity. Unless you like hearing voices in your head all day long?" Betty asked.

"Not me," Gina said.

"Oh, I kind of like it. You are very entertaining, you know. We were going to buy a new color TV, but I've hardly watched any shows since you've been around," Anna remarked.

"Thanks, but we are out of time. Here goes nothing." Betty silently communicated as the wind picked up, the temperature fell, the ground shook, and they heard it. All of them heard it, even the others. *Ommapapo! Ommapapo!* Then Anna and Gina smelled it, wafting through the air like only the smell of heavy, salted, delicious meat could smell. Was that BBQ? *No.* Brisket!

Gus and Larry approached the house, and Princess started to charge, but Vlad was still at the Creek, so the beagle retreated mid-bark and ran back to join him.

Herman's detached head shouted, "Follow that dog! I would recognize that smell anywhere. It's Nanny's Brisket!" Herman's head broke out of the bag Gus was carrying and floated onto a ghostly body that arose from the crawl space under the house. Ben screamed as he saw his Father's floating head, and Betty rushed to his side. "It's okay, honey, Mama's here, and nobody is ever going to love you like your mother."

Ben did not see nor hear her, but Gina and Anna did. "Hey! Nice try, Betty, but I love him enough for the both of us." Gina replied.

"Herman. Doll! You're finally back. All in one piece!" Betty squealed in delight as she held Herman tight and kissed him all over his face.

"Murray, it's bad enough you are screwing my wife, but did you have to screw up my Nanny's recipe. The brisket needs more bourbon. You can hardly smell the bourbon. How do you think we got them all hooked on the stuff on Wall Street?" Herman asked as Murray flew down to greet him.

"Hey, Herman, I know, I know, you have a bone to pick with me," said Murray, holding up a skull he found behind George and Anna's house. "A bone, because you know, it's a skull? Funny, no?"

"No!" Herman and Betty said in unison.

"We don't have time for this. They will be here any minute," Betty said to Herman, Murray, Anna, and Gina. In that moment, Gina and Anna took action. Gina dove into Arch Creek, swam to the other side, and stood thigh-deep in the water, right behind Goldfish & More. Anna waded into the Creek and stood behind the house, facing Gina.

"Gina, Anna! Get back here. What are you doing?" Ben pleaded.

"Trust me!" Gina yelled as she blew a kiss to Ben.

Anna and Gina stood absolutely still in the Creek, the water flowing around them. They both saw into the other world. There were so many of them. Spirits who had done wrong, or been wronged, stuck in this place, traveling along this waterway waiting for the Great Spirits to end their bondage.

62

ekiwa could not see or hear any of these conversations. She was once again lost in the past. She spent the last five decades as a manatee; eating vegetation, dodging boat propellers, facing down sharks, and lately, swimming through floating trash. During her early years as a manatee, especially in rainy season, the canals in Glades were deep enough for her to visit the camp, and if she stayed in the water long enough, she would see him. Her child.

She watched him grow. She saw Catori, Hatori, and on every visit, she saw Nighthawk. Wekiwa did not understand how Nighthawk always knew she was there, or that it was her. *Perhaps her scent?* However he did it, she was pleased. She would swim as close to the land as her nine-hundred-pound body would allow and splash him with her flipper. Nighthawk would wade in and scratch her chin. It was as close to a hug as Wekiwa had in all these years.

Nighthawk would tell her all about the camp and their child. He knew it was his. He told her he could smell it on the child. Then one day, after many years, when Wekiwa tried to swim to the camp, she could not reach it. White men brought in great machines, changing the course of the Mayaimi River, and it no longer flowed close to the camp. She could not exit the water, for she was trapped as a manatee, and she could not change back.

That was until recently. Wekiwa was lost in her miserable memories. She didn't know what happened to her child, her Mother, Grandfather, or Nighthawk. Why was she was drawn to remain behind her own house? Why could she transform into anyone only when she was there, in Arch Creek? She did not understand, until… until she heard it. The ancient call. *Ommapapo! Ommapapo!*

Ommapapo! Ommapapo! The ground quaked. The sounds, vibrations, and sight of Ricardo triggered the rest of Wekiwa's memories of her own captivity in the body of this creature, and they came back like a deluge. *'I thought I was invincible. If only I hadn't fallen for that handsome Cuban. Ricardo, poor thing. He sacrificed himself to save Carmen, and kill me with that bullet too, but I did not die that day. Rainbow plunged me into the Creek waters and transferred her life force to me. The Great Spirits did not approve. They were angry at me for breaking my promise to them and for causing an innocent man to die. I was supposed to use my powers for good. When I left the baby, my baby, the Great Spirits tempted me into evil doings. I should have stayed in the camp, with my family, with Nighthawk… with my baby! Taking care of my baby. It was a test, and I failed. The Great Spirits took pity on me, and allowed me to live, in this large, nearly prehistoric body, as a manatee, under one condition. To repent and make things right with the one I hurt the most, my baby, and to open the Spirit Gate to those trapped between life and death.'*

Wekiwa snapped back to the present. She knew what she was to do. She walked into Arch Creek and stood between Anna and Gina, bowing to each of them. Gina and Anna bowed back at her, and each other. Wekiwa bobbed upright in the middle of the Creek, her arms floating beside her breasts, effortlessly on the water's surface. Anna and Gina lifted their hands to the heavens. The wind picked up.

Joseph, Danny, Tina, George, Jemma, Mike, Hazel, Ben, and Gretchen felt the wind rumbling down the train tracks next to the Creek. They gazed into the distance as a dark menacing cloud headed toward them. As the cloud got closer, they could see the shape and color. It was a giant, iridescent blue butterfly as big as a train. It was getting closer and closer with every passing second. The sound of its huge beating wings was surprisingly quiet, like the sound of a paper airplane cutting through the air in a classroom. As the giant butterfly approached, they saw it for what it really was. A swarm of millions of nearly extinct Atala butterflies. It was the most stunning display of flashing colors anyone had ever seen. Now they understood why they call a swarm of butterflies a kaleidoscope. They were all entranced by the magnificent imagery of blue, black, and orange colors surrounding them in a fluttering frenzy. It was like watching the Northern Lights, only it was washing over all of their bodies. It tickled, and everyone stood about mindlessly laughing. Everyone with the exception of George, who fought his way through the kaleidoscope to the Creek bank, then jumped in and swam across.

When Joseph spoke of the prophecy of Wekiwa, George knew it was true. He knew it because of what he had found years ago. One skull was behind Anna's house, which was now mystifyingly floating over the Creek, and the other skull, across Arch Creek, was buried in the dirt behind Goldfish & More. George found both Tequesta Indian skulls during his archeological digs at his home, and the surrounding area.

Dating back to before the time of Christ, the Tequesta Indians dwelled in this place. And those skulls, as far as George could tell, were Tequesta relics, maybe even Calusa Indians. He had never taken them back to the University for carbon dating purposes, as George was a very spiritual person. To him, while research was important, he would never willingly disturb a sacred burial ground. George had uncovered many other fossils and had seen the underwater etchings on the Arch Creek Bridge that Mike just discovered. They were the same carvings that appeared in the Cypress Tree on the day of Wekiwa's birth.

George found fossil evidence linking these skulls. The one floating over the Creek was from an adult female. The one he was frantically swimming toward was the skull of a child. He did not know how they got separated, but he knew from the artifacts he found buried with them that a reunion must take place. The adult's skull was buried with pottery that contained the first three frames of the etchings on the Creek Wall. The baby's skull was buried in the pottery etched with the last three frames; two carved, the last frame blank. When George saw the woman in the Creek, he knew it was true. The etchings. She had turquoise eyes.

63

*J*eannie and Jake pulled up to the house on Enchanted Place.

"Hey, Jake. Leave the engine running. It sounds like you might have a fuel leak. Like I said, you don't have this carburetor adjusted correctly. Ben has a lot of tools in his garage. Pop the top for me."

"You know, you are the coolest chick I ever met."

"Flattery will get you everywhere. Now let's remove this air filter and see what's going on. Phew! I smell gas."

Ben looked through the kaleidoscope of butterflies and saw Gus LaCroix standing in his yard. "Murderer! Murderer! He killed my Father," Ben yelled.

Gus and Larry weren't the brightest tools in the shed, but they knew when it was time to make an exit. They both turned and ran. Gus didn't have that many talents, but being a scumbag his entire life, he did learn how to do one thing well: *run!* Gus was in the front yard before Ben could lift one of his sneakers off the ground and headed for Aunt Ethel's truck, when he smelled it. That irresistible scent, wafting through the air, drawing him in. He changed course and headed for the Plymouth Duster.

Looking in the open front door, there on the seat, he saw it. The name on the bag: Woody's. It must be a Woody's steak sandwich, and if the grease stains on the bag were accurate, a large French fry was in there too. Gus couldn't control himself. He slid into the front seat causing his overstuffed wallet to tumble out of the rear pocket of his jeans and onto the lawn. He opened the bag, swooped up and bit the sandwich, put the car in gear and took off in reverse, swerving backward down the road.

Jake screamed, "Hey! Get back here with my car!" He stooped down and picked up Gus' wallet. It was full of hundred-dollar bills. He numbly counted them. Maybe there was enough to buy a new car. Jake looked at the license, then froze.

"Jake, quick, let's go inside and call the cops. Maybe they'll catch him. That's a lot of cash for that asshole to have. Jake? Jake? I know you're upset. What are you starring at, Jake?" Jeannie asked, touching his forearm.

Jake took the license out of the wallet and held it up to Jeannie's face. "I'm pretty sure that was my Father! And, you're right. What an asshole!"

Gus stopped the car when he reached the intersection. He got out and slammed the hood with one hand. In the other hand hung a half-eaten Woody's steak sandwich. Gus jumped back in the car, took another bite of the steak sandwich, dropped the rest of it into the Woody's bag, turned the Duster around, and headed south on 16th Avenue. He depressed the car's lighter. As he approached 135, the Street the light was red. Gus lit a cigarette, floored the engine, ran the light, and made a sharp left turn, sideswiping a Chevy Nova in the right lane.

Gus cursed, floored the accelerator, and looked down for a second into the greasy Woody's bag to retrieve what was left of his sandwich, and some fries. He suddenly felt an eerie presence with him in the car. "Herman, is that you buddy? Hey, I brought you home like you asked." Gus heard a guttural sound and realized he had company in the passenger seat, and it wasn't Herman. It was a menacing Doberman. *Vlad!* That dog just couldn't resist the smell of cheese. The Doberman grabbed the Woody's bag in its mouth, swallowed it whole, and leapt out of the car's window and into the Creek. As Vlad hit the surface of the water, he thought to himself, *'Provolone. Definitely provolone on that sandwich.'* He burped, and a mist flew out. It formed the shape of a hand. Vlad swam to shore, thinking, *'I hate swimming. What was I even doing in that Creek? Yep, definitely provolone. Yum, cheese!'*

Gus watched what was to be the remainder of his last meal disappear into the Creek, and yelled, "My Samwich!" It only took that long. Gus looked up and saw the upcoming railroad tracks. The Duster flew twelve feet in the air and crashed down with a thud onto the Arch Creek Bridge. He heard a painful sounding crack and wasn't sure if it was from his head smashing on the shattered windshield, or from the broken front axle. Gus didn't have much time to contemplate this. The impact of the crash caused his cigarette to fly out of his hands and under the hood of the car, igniting the gas pouring out of the open carburetor. He watched in horror as the car's hood burst into flames, then frantically tried to open the burning car's door with his grease covered hands. The engine exploded before he could get out.

Herman flew over as the car exploded and yelled down, "I told you those greasy steak sandwiches would kill you one day, Gus. What a moron! You should have had the brisket."

64

Ommapapo! Ommapapo! A huge shockwave traveled through the air, all the way north to Hallandale, and south to Miami Shores. Al felt it rising from his roots. The ground shook. Through his tallest branches, he saw the fire, the explosion, the kaleidoscope of butterflies, the limestone bridge vibrating and crumbling into the Creek. He saw it all, and he was ready. It was the prophecy Billy Bob Sawgrass chanted under his branches over a century ago. *Ommapapo! Ommapapo!*

At that moment, George held up the child's skull from the opposite side of the Creek bank and shouted, "Here! Here it is Spirit! Your baby! It waits for you in the other world. Come be reunited."

Wekiwa looked toward the child's skull and wept for the first time since she left her baby at the camp in the Everglades. Gina and Anna remained in place, their hands in the air. The kaleidoscope lifted from the space above them and sailed in a burst of colors toward the crumbling Arch Creek Bridge. As it did, Joseph Clearwater dove headfirst into the shallow water and swam even faster toward the bridge.

"Dad!" Hazel yelled as Joseph swam to the shivering structure. All six-foot-seven inches of Joseph Clearwater stood neck-high in the water, bracing a giant Oak Limb under one side of the ancient Limestone Bridge, watching impotently as the other side began cracking. Joseph reached for another Oak

Limb, when a boulder of limestone broke loose and hung precariously over his head.

Wekiwa shouted, "My baby!" Instead of turning toward George holding the infant skull on the Creek bank, she dove underwater toward the bridge, not noticing that her beautiful peacock tail had grown back, speeding her along at an unbelievable pace. Wekiwa jetted to the bridge like Flipper on a tail walk, her wake pushing Joseph out the other side to safety. As she did, the hanging limestone boulder dropped, pinning Wekiwa against the bottom of the Creek. The burning car shifted and shook the ground above, propelling more limestone on top of her.

"Mother!" Joseph let out a pitiful cry as he dove underwater and swam to Wekiwa.

"Father!" Hazel yelled as she dove into the Creek. Mike followed. George and Ben were close behind.

The explosion propelled Nick's floating canoe toward the bridge at a rapid pace. As the canoe came close to the collapsing bridge, Gina saw it, and yelled, "Nick! No!!! Go back!"

The sound of the explosion also frightened and disoriented Blu, who took off through the woods at a gallop. Marsh was particularly agile and thankfully managed to hang on for dear life.

"Marsh, turn back!" Gina yelled in desperation.

A giant hand rose from the Creek, and with its thumb and index finger grabbed Blu's reigns and stopped the bolting horse, its giant pinky covered Nick's canoe and flicked it away from the bridge. The pinky was wearing a ring. Everyone saw it.

Tina yelled, "Now you show up, Dad!"

The giant hand formed into the shape of a peace sign and remained floating over the Creek. A sleepy-eyed Gracie wandered out the kitchen doors and sat down in a hammock, then shouted to Gina in the Creek.

"Hi, Mama. What's everyone doing here? What a weird day. I promise, I'm never eating brownies again," Gracie stated.

"I told you there was some crazy shit happening at my house!" Jemma said to Gretchen.

Murray, Herman, and Betty all flew down to the bottom of the Creek. Anna and Gina watched through their Spirit World eyes. Hazel was the first swimmer on site and saw the scene as well. Wekiwa was trapped at the bottom of the Creek, her tail flapping wildly, causing more and more limestone to pile on top of her.

Joseph swam down to try to free his Mother, frantically pulling rock after rock off of her. Wekiwa looked at Joseph and smiled her most sincere smile she had ever smiled. Her eyes glowed a fading turquoise. She used sign language to tell Joseph she loved him and was sorry she abandoned him. He signed, *I forgive you. I love you Mother*, while his tears were washed away by the flow of the Creek.

Hazel swam down to grab her Father's shirt collar and attempted to lift him from the bottom. Joseph stood fast and pointed at a sheet of rock on the Creek bed. It was what was left of the side wall of the Arch Creek Bridge. Ben, George, Mike, Jemma, Gretchen, and Tina and Danny, who were holding hands, were treading water next to them under the few remnants of the fallen bridge. They all swam down and held their breaths. There were now six panels fully carved into the rock. The first five panels of carvings were exactly as Wekiwa, George, and Mike remembered them.

The sixth panel, unfolded before their eyes, as if they were being carved at this moment in time. It was of a beautiful Native American woman with turquoise eyes. She was pregnant, with one hand on her belly. She looked remarkably familiar. In the distance, was a Giant Oak. Mike recognized the tree as it stood in his yard. *Al!* The Oak was surrounded by smaller Oaks, and many, many Coontie plants. In the background stood a peaceful Native American Village, a Creek running through it. A panther was roaming on the far bank of the Creek.

Everyone came up for air, except Joseph and Hazel, who watched as Wekiwa's life force left her body. She smiled sincerely at both of them and winked at Hazel. Hazel smiled back, her bright hazel eyes reflecting colors everywhere in the clear Creek waters. Bubbles rose from Wekiwa's smiling mouth, as she closed her turquoise eyes for the last time.

Bubbles! There were bubbles everywhere as Wekiwa disappeared into her own exhalations. As the bubbles frothed in the water, Herman, Betty, Murray, a woman in a waitress uniform with a *Mama* name tag on her chest, Ricardo, Carmen, Nighthawk, Vincent Vancetti, with a brisket sandwich in each hand, and a myriad of others neither Gina nor Anna recognized, soared into the bubbles and vanished. As the bubbles slowed, Frank's hand flew into the water and waved goodbye. Anna, Gina, and Tina wept.

Ben treaded water thinking, *'It was right in front of me the entire time. My next book will be about Natives: The Native Americans of Arch Creek!'*

Joseph remained frozen on the Creek bottom, adding his tears to the Creek waters. Hazel grabbed his shirt collar and pulled her gigantic Father to the surface. As they rose, butterflies flew all around them, fluttering on Hazel's head. It tickled. Hazel giggled as butterfly after butterfly disappeared into her mouth. She laughed and blinked her eyes thousands of times as she involuntarily swallowed one butterfly after another.

"Hazel! Hazel, what happened to the butterflies? You know those blue Atalas are almost extinct?" Mike asked frantically.

"Whoops! I swallowed them," Hazel responded.

Mike held Hazel close. "And you always told me you didn't swallow," Mike whispered into her ear as she playfully bit his neck and stepped away.

"Something you want to tell me, Father?" Hazel asked Joseph Clearwater.

"It's a long, long story, Hazel."

"So that was Grandmother? She was even more beautiful than in the legend, but talk about a dysfunctional family!" Hazel said as everyone broke into laughter.

"Something you want to tell us, Hazel?" Joseph said patting Hazel's belly.

Hazel placed her hand on her barely visible baby bump. A large, fawn-colored cat exited the woods, pranced over, and rubbed its head on Hazel's leg. For such a small thing, the cat let out a surprisingly loud *Grraarrerrr!*

Ommapapo! Ommapapo! Al felt the vibrations down to his root tips. This was the moment Billy Bob Sawgrass predicted. Al sent out a message to the other Oaks, and to all of the other trees too. It was time. Al shook his mighty branches like he had never done before. The trees all around Arch Creek shook in rhythm with Al. Branches and leaves descended to the ground and into the Creek, landing all around, like a blizzard. Some of these trees had their roots buried under the Arch Creek Bridge since the time of the Calusa Indians. It was part of them. It had to be saved. If only the trees could vibrate the ground at the same frequency the bridge had vibrated, they could counteract the effects. It was the prophecy.

Mike was oblivious to the shaking trees, falling leaves, or trembling ground. "A baby! A baby!! Really! Finally! I love you so much, Hazel. A baby!" Mike said as he swept Hazel up in his arms.

Hazel flashed Mike a beguiling smile and held his hands. He blinked five times, and when he opened his eyes, he found they were all in a Native American Village; the Arch Creek Natural Bridge still intact. Hazel kissed him, and Mike melted into her bright turquoise eyes.

About the Author

David Raymond is a Miami native, and Best Selling Author. David spent his public service career directing large governmental social service systems, including the Florida Department of Children & Families, and the Miami-Dade County Homeless Trust. David holds a Bachelor of Arts degree in Psychology, with a minor in Biology from Florida International University, a Master of Science degree in Mental Health Counseling from Barry University, and completed the Harvard University, John F. Kennedy School of Government, Executive Education Program. Prior to working in the social service field, David taught middle school marine biology, and was an environmental laboratory technician testing Miami's Ocean waters.

Following a distinguished career, David successfully wrote over $1 Billion in grant applications, and two novels to date. David's hobbies include reading, watching, and writing humorous science and supernatural fiction, cycling, experiencing the wonders of nature, playing his guitar, and learning the banjo. David's books are set in South Florida, with locations in Miami and the Everglades popping to life.

David lives in Biscayne Park, Florida with his amazing and spiritually evolved wife Amy, and their forever goofy Aussiedoodle, Starry. David and Amy are blessed by their amazing children, Mia, a gifted psychotherapist, Abraham, a legendary native fishing guide, their wonderful daughter-in-law, Yudith, a teacher and mother, and their delicious grandson, Ryder.

Acknowledgements

Grateful acknowledgement is made to Mackenzie Lyn Graveline, my talented and transformative editor, whose intelligent, thoughtful, and respectful work make me a better writer. Hopefully, she won't edit this part out, but if you are looking for an amazing editor, check out Mackenzie's website at www.nicegirlnaughtyedits.com

I am grateful as well to have lived within biking distance of the Arch Creek Natural Bridge all of my life. It was there that I first heard the rich history of the area, rode the ponies, played in the Enchanted Forest, and caught and released fish under the Arch Creek Natural Bridge. I am fortunate to have passed on the magic of this place to our children, and now our grandson. May future generations always have an Enchanted Place in which to play, grow, learn, and imagine. Who knows, you may even see a Mermaid.

Books By David Raymond

It's Like Having Sex With God

The Mermaid of Arch Creek

www.davidraymondbooks.com

Made in United States
Orlando, FL
27 April 2022

17248941R00148